"Some men would like nothing better than to hear you beg and scream and cry. But me, I favor an eye for an eye. A man punches me, I punch him. A man knifes me, I knife him," Sharkey said. He extended his hand to Lonnie, who gave him the Remington pocket pistol. "A man shoots me, I shoot him."

Ash stabbed his hand for his revolver. He had it halfway out when the pocket pistol boomed and his right leg exploded with pain. He fell to his knee and tried to draw. Another boom, and his shoulder felt as if he'd been kicked by a mule. He was dimly aware that Lonnie was laughing, and of the acrid odor of gun smoke. Then Sharkey stepped up to him and pressed the muzzle to his sternum.

"Time to die, you son of a bitch."

Ash had started to jerk aside when it felt as if a red-hot poker were being thrust through his chest and his world faded to black. . . .

Ralph Compton

Fatal
Justice

A Ralph Compton Novel
by David Robbins

A SIGNET BOOK

SIGNET
Published by New American Library, a division of
Penguin Group (USA) Inc., 375 Hudson Street,
New York, New York 10014, USA
Penguin Group (Canada), 90 Eglinton Avenue East, Suite 700, Toronto,
Ontario M4P 2Y3, Canada (a division of Pearson Penguin Canada Inc.)
Penguin Books Ltd., 80 Strand, London WC2R 0RL, England
Penguin Ireland, 25 St. Stephen's Green, Dublin 2,
Ireland (a division of Penguin Books Ltd.)
Penguin Group (Australia), 250 Camberwell Road, Camberwell, Victoria 3124,
Australia (a division of Pearson Australia Group Pty. Ltd.)
Penguin Books India Pvt. Ltd., 11 Community Centre, Panchsheel Park,
New Delhi - 110 017, India
Penguin Group (NZ), 67 Apollo Drive, Rosedale, North Shore 0632,
New Zealand (a division of Pearson New Zealand Ltd.)
Penguin Books (South Africa) (Pty.) Ltd., 24 Sturdee Avenue,
Rosebank, Johannesburg 2196, South Africa

Penguin Books Ltd., Registered Offices:
80 Strand, London WC2R 0RL, England

First published by Signet, an imprint of New American Library,
a division of Penguin Group (USA) Inc.

First Printing, December 2009
10 9 8 7 6 5 4 3 2 1

Copyright © The Estate of Ralph Compton, 2009
All rights reserved

Ⓢ REGISTERED TRADEMARK—MARCA REGISTRADA

Printed in the United States of America

PUBLISHER'S NOTE
This is a work of fiction. Names, characters, places, and incidents either are the
product of the author's imagination or are used fictitiously, and any resem-
blance to actual persons, living or dead, business establishments, events, or
locales is entirely coincidental.

   The publisher does not have any control over and does not assume any re-
sponsibility for author or third-party Web sites or their content.

THE IMMORTAL COWBOY

This is respectfully dedicated to the "American Cowboy." His was the saga sparked by the turmoil that followed the Civil War, and the passing of more than a century has by no means diminished the flame.

True, the old days and the old ways are but treasured memories, and the old trails have grown dim with the ravages of time, but the spirit of the cowboy lives on.

In my travels—to Texas, Oklahoma, Kansas, Nebraska, Colorado, Wyoming, New Mexico, and Arizona—I always find something that reminds me of the Old West. While I am walking these plains and mountains for the first time, there is this feeling that a part of me is eternal, that I have known these old trails before. I believe it is the undying spirit of the frontier calling, allowing me, through the mind's eye, to step back into time. What is the appeal of the Old West of the American frontier?

It has been epitomized by some as the dark and bloody period in American history. Its heroes—Crockett, Bowie, Hickok, Earp—have been reviled and criticized. Yet the Old West lives on, larger than life.

It has become a symbol of freedom, when there was always another mountain to climb and another river to cross; when a dispute between two men was settled not with expensive lawyers, but with fists, knives, or guns. Barbaric? Maybe. But some things never change. When the cowboy rode into the pages of American history, he left behind a legacy that lives within the hearts of us all.

—*Ralph Compton*

Chapter 1

Marshal Asher Thrall had his feet propped on his desk and was about to take a sip of coffee when the door burst open. In rushed a boy not much older than ten who excitedly gasped his message.

"Marshal! Marshal! You've got to come quick!"

Ash took the sip, set down the cup and folded his hands in his lap. "Calm down, son. Get your breath back."

Over at the other desk Deputy George Blocker looked at the boy in annoyance. He was writing a report on an arrest he had made and the tip of his tongue poked from the corner of his mouth as it always did when he had to spell. "What the hell set your britches on fire, boy?"

"Be polite," Ash said.

Blocker started to swear and caught himself. "I will never understand why you always have to be so nice to folks."

Ash tapped the badge pinned to his shirt. "This is why."

"There's nothing that says a lawman has to act like a

parson," Blocker said huffily. "Hell, we deal mostly with the dregs. We should treat them the same way they treat us."

"We deal with honest citizens too."

"There's no such critter, Ash. Everyone does things they shouldn't. It's just that most don't get caught."

Ash chuckled. "I wish I may be shot if I ever become as cynical as you."

The boy couldn't stand still. A ragamuffin with no shoes and a dirt-smeared face, he was fidgeting fit to bust his britches. "Didn't you hear me, Marshal? You've got to come right away. She says it's important."

"Who says?"

"Abigail."

Deputy Blocker grunted. "Abby Mason? The whore?"

"The what?" the boy said.

Ash shot Blocker a glance that shut him up before he could reply. "Do you mean Abby over on Fremont Street?"

"Yes, sir. That's where we live, my folks and my sister and me. Abigail lives a few doors down." The boy's teeth flashed white in his dirty face. "She's the nicest lady. She always gives us hard candy."

"Why did she send you, son?"

The boy lost his smile. "Oh. She's in trouble. She says there's a bad man at her place. A real bad man. She says you've got to come quick and arrest him or he might hurt her."

Deputy Blocker threw in, "Want to bet it's some drunk who tore her bedsheets with his spurs?"

Ash swung his long legs to the floor. "She give you a name, son?"

The boy scrunched up his face. "Yes, she did. But I've plumb forgot, I ran here so fast."

"Think," Ash prompted. "Think of when she was telling you to come here. What did she say?"

"I was playing out front of her place. She came down the stairs and took me by the arm. She acted all nervous. Then she said to fetch you." The boy bit his lower lip. "What was that name, darn it?" Suddenly he smacked the desk. "Now I recollect. It was Shar-something."

"Shar-something?" Ash repeated.

"Sharkey! The name was Sharkey."

Ash slowly rose until he towered over the desk and the ragamuffin. "Ben Sharkey? Was that it?"

"She didn't say the first name. All she said was for you to come quick. She gave me two bits, it was so important." The boy opened his left hand. "See?"

"All right. I want you to go home. Don't go anywhere near Abby's. Go straight home and stay there. Understand?"

"Yes, sir."

Ash went to the gun rack on the opposite wall and took down a scattergun. He opened a drawer under the rack and carried a box of shells to his desk. Breaking the scattergun open, he commenced loading it.

Deputy Blocker put down the pencil. "Well, now. So there's something to this? Every time you take out that howitzer it means you expect trouble."

"You heard the boy. It's Ben Sharkey."

"The name means nothing to me."

Ash slid a shell into the second barrel. "It would if you'd ever been up Kansas way or other parts north. He's as mean as they come, George. Killer, rustler, robber—you name it."

"What's he doing in Texas?"

"We'll ask him." Ash snapped the shotgun shut.

"Bring a rifle. We have to hurry. It'll be dark soon and I need to send a telegram first."

"A telegram?" Blocker was making a habit of repeating everything Ash said. "Who to?"

"You'll find out."

The sunset was spectacular. Vivid streaks of red and orange mixed with splashes of pink. Most of Mobeetie's good citizens hardly noticed. Main Street was busy. Dust rose from under the wheels of a clattering buckboard. A dog lifted its leg at a hitch rail. A young woman holding a pink parasol fluttered gaily past storefronts.

The telegraph office was near the bank. Ash strode in and set the scattergun on the counter with a thump, causing the owl-eyed man behind it to give a start.

"Be careful with that thing, Marshal. Is it loaded? It might go off."

"I need a telegram sent, Sam. I need it sent right now."

Sam Baxter said stiffly, "That's what I'm here for." He produced a form and a pencil. "Where am I sending it, and to whom?"

"To the Texas Rangers in Austin."

Ash and Deputy Blocker left the telegraph office. By now only the crown of the sun remained. They walked down Main to Fremont and stopped at the corner.

"How do you want to handle this?" Blocker asked. "Bust in the door and catch him by surprise?"

"Maybe have Abigail take a bullet?" Ash shook his head. "Our job is to safeguard lives, not get bystanders killed."

"You sure do take this job serious," Blocker remarked. "Don't get me wrong. Everyone thinks you're about the best lawman this town ever had, but sometimes you get too caught up in doing what's right."

"We took an oath," Ash reminded him.

"Sure, we pledged to uphold the law the best we can. You take it one step more. You act as if you have to be perfect."

Ash scanned Fremont to the far end. Most of the buildings were frame houses. A few had ROOMS FOR RENT signs out. Times were hard and folks did what they could in order to make ends meet. Holding the scatter-gun low against his leg, he tugged his hat brim down, pulled his jacket over his badge, and headed up the street on the side across from Abby Mason's apartment.

Deputy Blocker was at his elbow. He had put his hand over his own badge. "Trying to hide that we're lawmen?"

"The tin won't make a difference to Sharkey. Not where I'm concerned," Ash answered.

"I don't savvy."

"He knows me."

Blocker didn't hide his surprise. "Why didn't you say so sooner?" He paused. "Say, that's right. You were in Kansas for a spell. You wore a badge up there too. Is that where you know this curly wolf from?"

Ash nodded.

"In what way do you know him? Did you arrest him? Did you play cards with the man? What?"

"I shot him."

Blocker stopped in his tracks. "The hell, you say. Care to spill the particulars? Or do I walk into this with blinders on?"

"All you need to know is that Ben Sharkey is as bad a killer as John Wesley Hardin. He hasn't killed as many, but it's not for a lack of trying. When I ran into him up in Salina he hadn't gone completely bad yet, but he tried to stab a fellow lawman and I took him into custody. I had to shoot him to do it."

"You shot him and you arrested him and he just happens to show up in another town where you are marshal?"

"It's been four years. The judge went easy on him and let him off. The last I heard, he'd drifted up to Wyoming and was plaguing the people there." Ash peered under his hat brim at the window to Abby's apartment. The curtains, backlit by a lamp, were drawn tight. At the side of the house were stairs. A horse was tied to the rail.

"That must be his," Deputy Blocker said.

Ash kept going to the end of the block. Halting, he scratched his chin. "All right. This is how we'll do it. You take this side and I'll take the other. Go from door to door and warn everyone to stay inside until we say it's safe to come out. Do it quietly."

"That's an awful lot of bother to go to," Blocker criticized. "I still think we should sneak up and kick in the door."

"We do it the safest way for everyone." Ash set to work. Most of the houses had small yards and picket fences. A few had dogs. One mongrel barked furiously until the owner hushed it. Ash was worried that Sharkey would hear and look out, but the curtains that covered Abby's window stayed shut.

Only one person raised a fuss. Crotchety Mrs. Brubaker shook her cane at Ash and said, "Stay indoors until you say different? I should say not. If I want to come outside, I will."

"It's for your own good, ma'am. There might be

shooting, and you wouldn't want to be hit by a stray bullet, would you?"

"Marshal, when you've lived as long as I have, you learn a thing or two. Such as when your time comes, there's not a blessed thing you can do about it. We can't hide from the Almighty."

Ash tried another tack. "I would breathe easier knowing you were safe."

"You want to protect me from myself, I take it. But since when is the law our nursemaid? Each of us has the right to live or die when as we see fit. Mollycoddle folks and you turn them timid."

"I'm asking nice."

"Yes. Yes, you are. That's the only reason I don't shoo you off my property." Mrs. Brubaker hobbled inside and shut the door. From within came, "I voted for you in the last election, you know."

Ash sighed and went down the walk to the gate. A few more homes and he was done. He waited for Blocker at the corner.

Darkness had fallen and more windows were lit. It was the supper hour. The aroma of cooked food was heavy in the air.

Ash's stomach rumbled, reminding him he hadn't eaten since breakfast.

Deputy Blocker rejoined him. "All done," he announced, sounding annoyed. "*Now* can we get this over with?"

The dun tied to the stairs pricked its ears at their approach. Its nostrils flared and for a few anxious moments Ash thought it would whinny. He patted its neck and said softly, "There, there."

"You have a way with horses just like you do with people," Deputy Blocker praised.

The stairs were oak planks. Ash put each foot down slowly and applied his weight by degrees rather than all at once. The landing was small, barely five feet square. He trained the scattergun on the door and placed his thumb on the hammers. Holding his ear to the door, he listened.

"Hear anything?" Blocker asked.

Ash glared at him. Gingerly he grasped the latch and lifted. The bolt hadn't been thrown and the door swung in on silent hinges. He eased inside.

A short hall led to the parlor. He took a step and heard a slight jingle. Not from his boots; he wasn't wearing spurs. He wanted to kick himself for not having Blocker take his off.

The deputy wore a sheepish look.

Ash motioned for him to stay put. Wedging the scattergun to his shoulder, he glided to the end of the hall. The parlor was empty. Perfume tingled his nose and he almost sneezed.

A trail of clothes led to the bedroom; a dress, a man's bandana, a lady's chemise, a man's shirt, a lady's stockings and garters, and finally a pair of scuffed brown boots.

The bedroom door was closed. Ash pushed his hat back and carefully pressed his ear to the wood. He heard giggling and then Abby Mason's squeak of a voice.

"You must be joshing."

Another voice, a raspy growl, stirred Ash's memory.

"I'm paying you, aren't I? You've done the one and now you can do the other."

"The way you want to do it," Abby said teasingly. "It's so deliciously wicked."

"Yes or no, woman? I don't have all night."

"It will cost you extra."

"A whore with standards. Now I've heard everything."

"My body is how I keep food on the table. You get carried away and I'll be out of work for a month."

Poised on the balls of his feet, Ash tensed. He flung the door wide and sprang into the bedroom, cocking both hammers as he moved. The twin clicks and the twin muzzles were enough to freeze the two people on the bed. Then Abby Mason jerked a sheet to her chin and bleated in fright.

The hard-faced man on the bed, though, did the last thing Ash expected. He calmly rose onto his elbows and just as calmly smiled, and then he said the strangest thing.

"I can't tell you how happy you've just made me."

"Get up and get dressed," Ash commanded. "Do it slow and keep your hands where I can see them."

"Whatever you want, Thrall. You've caught me good and proper," Ben Sharkey replied, and did another strange thing: he laughed.

Chapter 2

The stage depot wasn't a depot at all. It was a small room on the side of Buxley's general store. It had a bench for the people to sit on while they waited and a stove to cook the soup Buxley's woman served the travelers to keep them warm in the winter.

Only one person was on the bench when Marshal Asher Thrall brought his limping prisoner in. The stranger wore a black suit and a string tie a lot like Asher's own, and was shuffling a deck of cards. A frock coat was folded on the bench beside him.

"Don't believe I've made your acquaintance." Ash moved his jacket so the badge on his vest was plain to see. So was the Remington in the holster high on his hip.

The young man stopped shuffling and looked up. He had a boyish grin complete with dimples and curly hair most girls would love to run their hands through. "That could be because this is the first time I've passed through this gob of spit."

"Here, now." Ash would have to agree that Mobeetie wasn't much as towns went, but it was *his* town.

The populace had duly elected him town marshal and he took his job seriously. "I'll thank you to talk nice about the folks who pay me." He smiled to lessen the sting.

The young man's blue eyes flicked to the prisoner and then back to Ash, and he smiled. "No insult meant, Mister. Me, I'm as peaceable a gent as you ever met."

Ash chuckled. Most any hour of the day or night Mobeetie was as quiet as a cemetery and as dull as a handful of dirt. He liked it that way. "I gather you make your living at games of chance?"

The young man made a fan of the cards. "I admit it. Gambling is in my veins."

"On Friday and Saturday nights there are lively games over at Turner's Saloon," Ash mentioned. "Of course, there's hardly ever more than ten dollars in the pot, but to folks hereabouts that's a fortune."

"Hell, Marshal." The young man grinned. "The stakes I play for are a lot higher."

"Can I sit down?"

Ash had almost forgotten about his prisoner. "Sure, Sharkey. Take some of that weight off your feet."

The young gambler snorted in amusement.

Sharkey wasn't nearly as amused. Scowling, he plopped down, the shackles on his wrists and ankles jangling. "If there is anything I hate more than tin stars, it escapes me."

"I've treated you decent."

Sharkey regarded him coldly, then nodded. "Yes. Yes, you have. I'll give you that. Of all the lawdogs I've ever tangled with, you've been the fairest. It's a shame."

"What is? That I'm conscientious about my duties?"

Sharkey scratched the stubble on his chin. His clothes

were speckled with dirt and grime, his hair hadn't been combed in weeks and when he raised his hand to push his short-brimmed brown hat back on his head, a dark stain showed under his armpit. "Life is a damn shame, Marshal."

"Is that so?"

"Smirk if you want, but I know what I'm talking about. It's a shame we're born only to die. It's a shame some of us are poor and others are rich. It's a shame a body can't do as he or she pleases without other folks poking their noses in."

"That's a fine one coming from you."

The young gambler was listening intently. "What exactly did this hombre do, Marshal, if you don't mind me being curious?"

"I didn't catch your handle, son."

"Grant. The same as the president." The young man grinned. "Not that he's kin or anything."

"Well, Mr. Grant, let me introduce Benedict Sharkey. As lawbreakers go he is near the top of the heap. He has murdered. He has robbed. He has stole money from little old ladies. . . ."

"Only once," Sharkey said. "My poke was empty and she looked prosperous."

"In fact, think of a crime and it's likely Mr. Sharkey has committed it. He is wanted in three states and two territories. A week ago I caught him in the altogether over at Abigail's."

"Who?"

"Our local harlot. She is long in the tooth, but she is experienced and she is smart enough to conduct her business quietly so as not to raise the ire of her church-going sisters." Ash never saw the harm in what Abby did for a living. Truth was he liked her. They had an agreement: so long as she was discreet, he would pretend not to notice the steady stream of men who paid her a visit.

"You caught this fierce man killer with his pants down?" Grant slapped his leg and laughed.

"I am commencing not to like you," Sharkey said.

Ash stepped to the doorway and squinted against the harsh glare of the afternoon sun. A vagrant breeze whirled tiny dust devils in the street. Hooking his thumbs in his gun belt, he rocked on his heels. "Pay him no mind, Mr. Grant. I embarrassed him and he doesn't like being a laughingstock."

"No, I don't," Sharkey declared. "But your turn will come, and when it does folks will be laughing a lot harder at you than they have at me."

"What is that supposed to mean?"

Sharkey didn't reply.

Ash shrugged. "You can't blame them for laughing. You were caught not just with your pants down, but plumb off. I played it smart. I took you when all you had on was skin and hair. Otherwise you'd have filled your hand with your six-shooter and maybe me or my deputy would have been shot."

"I can't wait to tell this one," Grant said.

"You do and I'll see you in hell," Sharkey snapped, and started to rise.

"Sit back down," Ash commanded, placing his hand on the Remington. "What did I tell you in my office? You will behave until I turn you over to the marshal from Cheyenne."

"It must be nice," Sharkey said.

"What?"

"To wear that tin. To tell people what to do." Sharkey turned to the young gambler. "You have no idea who this badge toter is, do you?"

"Is he somebody famous?"

"Not like Hickok, but he is fairly well-known." Sharkey placed his hands on his knees. "Marshal Thrall here comes from Arkansas. He fought for the Yankees during the war and when he came home his own pa didn't want anything to do with him. So he took to trailing cows to Kansas. He wound up in Salina and met a friend of his from the war who offered him a job as a deputy. One night he shot a drunk who pulled a knife on his friend. He didn't shoot to kill, mind you. He shot the drunk in the leg."

"How is it you know all this?"

"When a man cripples you so that you'll limp the rest of your born days, you're not liable to forget him," Sharkey said. He rubbed his right leg and swore. "I was the drunk."

"Now you know the real reason Mr. Sharkey came to Mobeetie," Ash told the gambler. "He hasn't forgiven me."

"Not then, not ever."

"I was doing my job." Ash leaned against the jamb and stared down the street. Only a few hardy souls were abroad in the heat. Three pigs were rooting about near a horse trough. "I should think you'd be grateful I didn't shoot to kill."

"I am. I truly am," Sharkey declared. "Because now I can do to you as you did to me."

"You are awful optimistic," Ash said. "They want you in Wyoming for four murders, and the judge there is a hanging judge." To the east, the empty haze told him the stage was going to be late.

Sharkey stretched his legs and the chains clanked. "Oh, I doubt I'll have to wait that long."

"Planning to break out of jail when you get there, are you?"

"No. I'm planning on not going to jail at all." Sharkey paused. "You see, it was all worked out in advance so there wouldn't be a mistake."

"What was worked out?"

"Everything," Sharkey said, and wagged his shackled wrists. "The whore. This waiting room. Since I'm not wanted in Texas, I knew you would see to it that I got to where I was wanted."

"You honestly expect me to believe that you knew Abigail would send word to me that you were staying at her place?" Ash scoffed. Men like Sharkey had a hard time admitting their mistakes.

"I paid her to."

"What?"

"I paid your town tart to get that message to you. Then I laid back and waited for you to show up."

For a second Ash almost believed him. "You're trying to make me out to be a dunce but it won't work."

"She wanted two hundred dollars but I only gave her a hundred," Sharkey related. "I had to promise her not to tell you, but I want to see the look on your face when the truth sinks in."

Ash laughed. "I have to hand it to you. You can make up a story with the best of them."

"There's nothing to make up. It took me a while to find out where you went after you left Salina. Your old friend Marshal Quait wouldn't tell me. I had to persuade him. I came straightaway, me and my boys, and I laid my plans real careful." He smiled smugly. "I've always been clever that way."

"Crow a little more, why don't you?"

"You're not paying attention, lawdog," Sharkey criticized. "I'm making it as plain as plain can be and you stand there like a dumb ox that doesn't know it's about to be poled."

"I'm tired of your game," Ash warned. He liked to think he was a tolerant man but there was only so much he would abide.

"Do you hear him?" Sharkey said to the young gambler.

"I hear both of you," Grant answered. He stood and shrugged into his frock coat.

Sharkey had more to say. "He accuses me of being full of myself when he stands there and denies what is right in front of his eyes."

"We could show him."

Ash wasn't sure he had heard correctly. "What was that?"

Grant nodded at the holster on Ash's hip. "That's a nice Remington you've got there."

"I like it," Ash said, still puzzled.

"I like Remingtons too. Any pistol good enough for Frank and Jesse James is good enough for me." Grant slid the deck of cards under his frock coat and when his hand reappeared he was holding a nickel-plated, pearl-handled Remington pocket pistol. He pointed it at Ash.

Ash stiffened. "Here now. What in hell do you think you're doing?"

"He sure is thick between the ears," Grant said to Sharkey.

"Anyone who makes their living being shot at can't be too bright," Sharkey agreed. He crooked a finger at Ash. "Hand over the key if you don't mind and even if you do."

"Like hell I will."

The click when Grant thumbed back the hammer of his pocket pistol was unnaturally loud in the small room. "I'd do as he wants. You'll go on breathing a little longer."

Ash looked from his prisoner to the young gambler and back again. The truth hit him with the force of a physical blow. "You two are in cahoots."

Sharkey pointed at the young man. "This here is my sister's boy, Lonnie. He's been riding with me about a year now. You might think he's green, as young as he is, but he's killed a dozen or more and he's only starting out."

"Is his last name really Grant?"

Lonnie answered for himself. "Hell, no. That was a little joke on my part. If you had any brains you might have caught on." He took deliberate aim at Ash's face. "Want me to get it over with, Uncle?"

"You shoot him and I'll shoot you," Sharkey said. "He's mine to kill and mine alone." He stood and held out both hands, palms up. "Give me the key, Thrall. These bracelets of yours are an aggravation."

Ash stared into the muzzle of the pocket pistol and did the only thing he could under the circumstances: he gave the key to Sharkey. Out of the corner of his eye he watched the street, hoping someone would happen by, see what was happening and get help.

"The rest of my boys are outside of town waiting for me," Sharkey said as he freed himself. "Some of them took me for loco, letting myself be caught like I did. But I needed your guard down. I needed you to think you had the better of me when all the time I had the better of you."

Ash was hoping Lonnie would lower the pocket pistol. His skin crawled at the thought of lead exploding from the end of the barrel and ripping through his body. "So, what now?"

"What do you think?"

"You're fixing to take me with you, aren't you?" Ash guessed. So long as he went on breathing he could escape and come back with a posse.

"I admit the notion tempts me," Sharkey said. "Some men would like nothing better than to hear you beg and scream and cry. But me, I favor an eye for an eye. A man punches me, I punch him. A man knifes me, I knife him." He extended his hand to Lonnie and Lonnie gave him the Remington pocket pistol. "A man shoots me, I shoot him."

Ash stabbed his hand for his revolver. He had it halfway out when the pocket pistol boomed and his right leg exploded with pain. He fell to his knee and tried to draw. Another boom and his shoulder felt as if he'd been kicked by a mule. He was dimly aware that Lonnie was laughing, and of the acrid odor of gun smoke. Then Sharkey stepped up to him and pressed the muzzle to his sternum.

"Time to die, you son of a bitch."

Ash started to jerk aside when it felt as if a red-hot poker were being thrust through his chest and his world faded to black.

Chapter 3

Mobeetie, Texas, had the buffalo to thank for its existence.

When the buffalo hunters had killed off most of the buffalo up north, they came south to kill off the rest. A settlement sprouted, a place where the buffalo hunters could buy supplies and bring their hides to ship to points east. The place needed a name so it was called Hide Town.

It didn't stay Hide Town long. About the time a post office was installed, someone suggested they needed a more dignified name. Sweetwater was proposed, since the settlement had been built on the banks of a creek.

So Sweetwater it became, until it was learned another Texas settlement had beaten them to the name.

While wrangling over a new one, it occurred to someone to ask the Indians what they called the creek.

The Indians called it Mobeetie.

Now Mobeetie was a small but thriving town. Along with the post office there was a general store and a bank and saloons. They had a town council.

They also had something a lot of small town didn't: their very own sawbones.

Doc Peters was reading a copy of the *Kansas City Medical Journal* when he heard a pounding on his door. He liked to keep up on the latest medical doings and got the Kansas City journal sent to him along with the *Boston Medical and Surgical Journal*, the *New York Medical Journal* and the *Louisville Medical Journal*. It made for a lot of reading, but Doc Peters wasn't married and could spend his evenings as he pleased.

The pounding irritated Doc. Everyone knew he closed for an hour at noon.

His mornings were taken up with patients. After hours of listening to complaints of bellyaches and fevers and toenails that wouldn't grow straight, he needed that hour to rest. No one was to bother him unless it was an emergency.

Setting the journal on the kitchen table, Doc adjusted his spectacles and went down the hall to the front door. He was wearing the same tweed suit he always wore. Or rather, one of the four tweed suits he owned, all the same shade of gray as his hair and his mustache.

Doc Peters opened the front door and was shocked when Floyd, the barber, excitedly grabbed him by the front of his shirt. "See here. What do you think you are doing?"

Floyd had on the apron he always wore when he cut hair. He was so choked with emotion he couldn't talk. He jabbed a finger at the street.

"Calm yourself, man. Take a few deep breaths and tell me what has you in such a dither."

"The marshal's been shot!"

Now it was Doc who gripped him by the shoulders. "How bad is he? Where can I find him?"

"Over at the depot room," Floyd answered. "He's on the floor. Doc, they shot him three times. He's bleeding like a stuck pig."

Alarm goaded Doc into moving faster than he had in many a month. He collected his black bag and his hat.

Shouts were being raised. People were converging from all directions. Floyd kept grabbing him and pulling him until finally Doc shoved his hand away. "Stop that."

"I can't help it. I like Ash. Everyone does. He lying there dying, Doc. We have to hurry."

"What do you think I'm doing?"

A crowd had gathered. Necks were craning. Mrs. Biddle, who stood barely five feet in shoes with two-inch heels, was trying to see over the shoulder of Ed, the blacksmith, who stood six feet eight barefoot.

"Out of the way! Out of the way! Doc is here! Let us through, will you?" Floyd yelled while shoving right and left.

Muttering and a few curses greeted this rough treatment but it was short-lived. Floyd gained the doorway and then stood aside for Doc to enter. "Brace yourself."

Doc was about to tell him of the horrors he'd seen. About the time a drunken freighter was run over by his own wagon and shattered bones stuck out of the freighter's ruptured flesh. About the time a farmer was cleaning a shotgun but forgot it was loaded and blew the top of his head off, spattering brains and hair and gore all over the ceiling. Or about the awful morning Doc went to deliver a baby that came out strangled by its own umbilical chord.

Then Doc saw Marshal Asher Thrall.

Doc composed himself and went on in. "Close the

door," he said over his shoulder. "Don't let anyone in unless I say."

"Yes, sir."

Doc stood and quietly studied the scene: the empty benches along the walls, the stove splotched by red drops, the walls and the floor splotched too, the tall, broad-shouldered form of Ash lying on his back with a bullet hole in his shoulder and another in his leg and what appeared to be a third in his chest.

Someone had shot the marshal to ribbons.

Doc winced as he bent at the knees. He felt for a pulse and grunted when he found one. It was weak but it was steady. He pried open one of Ash's eyelids and examined the pupil.

He could tell just by glancing at them that the shoulder and leg wounds didn't merit immediate attention. That chest wound, though ... Powder burns on the shirt told him the gun had been pressed against Ash's chest when the shooter fired.

Quickly, Doc unbuttoned Ash's blood-soaked shirt and peeled it wide open. A surprise greeted him. There wasn't a hole. There was a furrow and *then* a hole. As near as he could figure, the slug struck at an angle and then penetrated. Apparently Ash had been turning when the gun went off.

Exercising great care, Doc slipped a hand under the big lawman and felt for the exit wound. It was half a minute before he conceded there wasn't one. Another surprise. At that range most slugs would have gone clean through.

"Well, now," Doc said out loud. He opened his black bag and got to work. First he brought out his stethoscope. Feeling a pulse was fine but it couldn't compare to listening. The heart was still beating steady enough but he thought he detected a slightly erratic quality. Mentally putting it aside for the moment, he selected a probe. Resembling a large sewing needle, it was nearly a foot long. He gripped the tiny ball of metal at the top and slowly inserted the tip into the hole. He needed to know exactly how deep the slug had gone. With luck, the wound was shallow and he could easily extract the lead.

To his dismay, Doc determined that the hole curved slightly, adding proof the slug went in at an angle. He couldn't get the probe far enough in to make contact with the lead. Against his better judgment he tried to force it but stopped when Marshal Thrall groaned.

Doc drew the probe out. He wiped it on a cloth and placed both in his bag and closed it. Rising, he went to the door and was reaching for it when it opened, framing a red-faced tobacco-chewing slab of muscle. "Deputy Blocker."

"I just heard, Doc," the deputy rumbled. "I was out to the Tanner farm. Someone stole one of their horses." He glanced past the physician and his mouth dropped. "God, no. Is he dead?"

"Not yet. I might be able to save him if we can get him to my office quickly so I can operate."

"Say no more." Blocker wheeled and marched outside and began bellowing for men to bring something to use as a litter and for everyone else to make room or by heaven he would bust heads.

Doc emerged and squinted in the glare. He consulted his pocket watch. "I'll go on ahead and prepare."

"We'll be right there," Blocker promised.

Doc started off but stopped. "Be careful with him.

Don't jostle him more than you have to. Whatever you do, keep him on his back. Don't roll him over or place him on his side. Understood?"

"You're the sawbones."

Doc nodded and hastened to his office. He had a lot to do to get ready. His examination room doubled as his operating room. It couldn't hold an unlit candle to the operating rooms he had read about in the journals. The table was wood and not metal. The lightning wasn't as bright as the journals recommended. Most of his equipment was old, but "old" didn't mean "useless."

He had a surgical kit. He had a scale. He had scalpels and probes and scissors. He had surgical saws and bone saws. He had beakers and vials and bottles. He had surgical thread and splints. In short he had everything a doctor needed, including a bottle of whiskey. He poured three fingers into a beaker and swallowed it in two gulps.

Doc held out his hand. It was steady enough. When he was younger it was steadier. Old age had a habit of wearing down the body and fraying at the nerves until a man was a shadow of his former self. He hadn't fallen that far but he had moments when his insides quivered and his hands shook.

Surgery was always the worst. It was all well and good to read about internal organs and correct operating procedure but it was something else entirely to cut another human being open and have their warm, wet intestines ooze over your fingers.

Doc shook his head. He must stop thinking about that part of his job and concentrate on the here and now.

He went to a corner cabinet and took out his surgical

kit. Made of wood, it had a tray for probes and scalpels. Remove the tray and underneath was a saw for use when amputating arms and legs as well as a hammer for testing reflexes and a drill.

Doc laid out the instruments he would need. He placed a pile of clean towels at one end. Bandages went next to the towels. He was scrubbing his hands when voices and a commotion announced the arrival of his patient and an entourage of twenty or more.

Six men, Deputy Blocker and Floyd the barber included, brought the marshal in on a door. Where they got the door Doc couldn't begin to guess and didn't bother asking. "Excellent timing, gentlemen. I am just about ready."

"Do you want him on the table?" Deputy Blocker asked.

"Unless you prefer I operate on the floor."

"That was a joke, wasn't it?" Blocker shook his head. "You think things are funny that no one else does."

"When you get to be my age," Doc said, "you don't take life nearly as seriously as you used to."

Floyd said, "Those are strange words coming from a man who deals in life and death."

"I only deal in life," Doc corrected him. "I took an oath to that effect. For death you want the undertaker."

They set the lawman on the operating table and Doc shooed them out except for Deputy Blocker.

"I need your help stripping him."

"You want me to undress Ash?"

"We'd ask him to do it if he was in any shape to try."

"I've never undressed a man before."

"You undress yourself, I'd warrant."

"That's different."

"Not to me it's not. One naked body is pretty much

the same as every other. Most I'd as soon forget seeing."

Deputy Blocker brightened. "Say, that's right. You get to see ladies naked all the time."

"It never occurs to you, does it?" Doc asked as he set to work removing the marshal's jacket and shirt.

"What?"

"That women only come to see doctors when they're not feeling well. When they have aches and pains. When they have broke bones. When they have diseases. They're not at their best. They're bitter and irritable and more often than not tired from a lack of sleep. The only thing they want is to get better. Asking them to take off their clothes is an affront they can do without."

Blocker was tugging at one of Thrall's boots. "What's your point?"

Doc Peters sighed. "Nothing. Keep at it." He was amused to note that the deputy never once looked at the marshal's body after all the clothes were removed.

"I thank you for your help. You can leave now."

"Don't you need someone to hand you stuff?"

"Are you giving up your badge to become a nurse?"

"Are you loco? I'm a man. Men don't do nurse work. It's not in our veins."

"You are a wonderment, Deputy. But do you know a retractor from, say, your boot?"

"A what?"

"Out you go."

Doc threw the bolt so he wouldn't be interrupted. He washed his hands and dried them. He cleaned all three wounds, confirmed the shoulder and leg wounds could wait, and bent over the lawman's chest. From a score of various probes he selected one with a wooden handle and a long curved tip. Inch by slow fraction of an inch he inserted it into the bullet hole and was surprised at how far in it went before he felt the scrape of metal on metal.

As was his wont, Doc talked to himself as he worked.

"I don't like this. I don't like this at all. I've never had a slug this deep before. Not where the patient lived anyhow."

Doc slid the probe out and dabbed at drops of blood that welled out.

"Who did this to you, Ash? How did you let yourself get caught like this? Usually you're so careful."

The lawman might have been a marble statue for all the life he showed.

Doc sorted through his scalpels. He had some of different sizes and shapes. Each was suited to a specific task or specific part of the body. He chose a heavier one, for when a lot of muscle had to be cut and delicacy wasn't an issue. Holding it poised over the furrow the slug had made, he stared at the pale face of the town's protector.

"I can't guarantee anything. I'll do my best. Sometimes, through no fault of my own, that's not good enough." Doc touched the scalpel to skin. "Let's hope that this time it is."

Chapter 4

Ash Thrall woke up with his head pounding. He opened his eyes and regretted it when the pain became worse. Closing them again, he took stock. He was lying on his back. It felt as if a great weight were on his chest. His mouth and throat were as dry as a desert. Swallowing hurt. Licking his lips, he cracked his eyelids again.

The room was unfamiliar. He was in bed, a blanket drawn to his chin. Brown curtains were drawn and a shaft of sunlight splashed over a folded quilt. A dresser stood against the opposite wall.

On it sat a tray and on the tray was a hypodermic needle and a bottle.

A stab of comprehension caused Ash to try to sit up. The pain that racked his body was almost unbearable. He gritted his teeth to keep from crying out. As it was, a groan escaped him. He sank down again and waited for the agony to fade.

"You've finally come around."

Ash looked up at Doc Peters and mustered a smile. "I figured this was your room. Frankly I'm surprised to be alive."

"Frankly so am I." Doc came over and pulled up a chair that Ash hadn't noticed. "When I say it's a miracle you're still breathing you can take that as fact."

"How long have I been here?"

"Five days."

Ash blinked and without thinking went to sit up again. This time he couldn't keep from crying out.

"I'd lie still were I you," Doc advised. "We need to have a talk, you and me. I must explain your condition."

"How's that?" Ash found it difficult to concentrate. "I hurt so much I can hardly think."

"The morphine must have worn off. Sorry. I had to go deliver a baby and just got back." Doc rose and went to the dresser. He filled the hypodermic. Tapping the needle so that a drop trickled from the tip, he came back and pulled the blanket away, exposing Ash's arm. "This will smart a little."

Ash was in too much agony to care about a pinprick. He had never used morphine before and he was surprised at how quickly a blissful feeling of well-being spread up his arm and down his body. The pain evaporated like dew under a warm sun, leaving him floating on clouds of pure pleasure. "Damn."

"What?"

"This stuff is better than booze."

"Don't like it too much. They say some folks get addicted." Doc took the hypodermic and set it on the tray. Instead of returning, he leaned against the dresser and folded his arms. "Now for our talk. First the good news. Your leg wound and the wound in your shoulder posed no complications. They will heal nicely. But the other one." Doc stopped.

"You look so grim."

"For a reason." Doc Peters paused. "We've known each other how long now, Asher?"

"Ever since I came to Mobeetie. About two years, give or take," Ash responded. His voice had an odd dreamlike quality, as if he was talking into a root cellar.

"Time flies, doesn't it?" Doc didn't wait for an answer. "We've gotten along pretty well. You're not as heavy-handed as our last lawman. You don't pistol-whip drunks for the hell of it or treat everyone as if you're better than they are."

"I do my job is all." Ash was feeling so good, he was tempted to try to bound out of bed.

"You do it well. Everyone in the community agrees. Nearly everyone likes you, me included. Which makes what I have to say next all the harder."

Ash forced himself to ignore the rapturous sensation brought on by the morphine and focused on what the aged physician was saying. "Spit it out, Doc. I'm a big man."

"Bigger than most," Doc said. "But big isn't everything. Goliath was bigger than David and David brought him down with a small stone. Life is about to do the same to you."

"You're making no sense."

Doc frowned. "There's no good way to say this so I'll come right out with it." He sucked in a breath. "You're dying."

Ash blinked. He looked down at himself. "Am I bleeding inside of me? Is that why my chest feels as if a mule is sitting on it?"

"It's not a mule. It's a slug." Doc came to the chair. "I couldn't get it out, Ash. I tried. Honest to God, I tried. But it was deflected by a rib into your pericardium. Do you know what that is?"

Dazed by the revelation, Ash stared blankly.

"Asher?"

"What? Oh. No, I don't."

"The pericardium is a tough muscle that surrounds your heart. The slug is lodged fast. That heavy feeling you're experiencing—how did you describe it? A mule sitting on your chest? It's the slug scraping your heart."

Ash touched a hand to the blanket over his sternum. "You couldn't cut it out? Or use tweezers or something?"

"You're not listening," Doc said. "It's *scraping your heart*. With every beat it penetrates a fraction farther."

The full implications hit Ash like a physical blow. "Wait. You're saying that it's working its way deeper? That pretty soon it will enter my heart and that will be the end of me?"

Doc placed a hand on Ash's shoulder. "I'm afraid so. As to whether it will be tomorrow or six months from now, there's no telling. A lot depends on how active you are and your constitution."

"Active?" Ash repeated.

"The more you move around, the more you exert yourself, the faster your heart will beat and the faster the slug will work its way in. My advice is to plant yourself in bed and only get up when you have to. You'll last longer that way."

"How much longer?" Ash bleakly asked.

"I can't say. You could buy yourself six months. You could buy yourself none."

"Hell."

"I'm sorry. I wish I had better news. I did my best." Doc slowly stood. "It won't be an easy death. It won't be easy at all." He went out.

Despair washed over Ash. Here he was, not even

forty, and before he knew it he would be pushing up sunflowers. He'd always known he might die a violent death. Lawmen on the frontier rarely died peacefully in bed. But Ash never expected anything like *this*: a slow, lingering, painful-as-hell end he didn't deserve.

"To hell with this." Sliding his elbows under him, Ash levered up. So simple to do yet it exhausted him. He propped his shoulders against the headboard to rest.

Ash thought of Claire, of the fourteen months they spent as man and wife, of her terrible, terrible death by consumption and his vow to never marry again. Thank God he hadn't, he told himself. Leaving this world was bad enough. Leaving a wife and kids would be unendurable torment.

Doc came back in carrying a periodical. He sat in the chair and showed the cover to Ash. The *Boston Medical and Surgical Journal*, the title read. "I thought I would show you this."

"I'm not much of a reader," Ash admitted. He could wrestle with circulars and officials forms and wanted posters, but that was about it.

"Only one article is of interest to us." Doc opened to the page in question.

"This one here about a Dr. Phillip Brewster, one of the leading surgeons in the country. Can you guess what his specialty is?"

Ash wasn't a lawman for nothing. "Heart surgery."

"He's operated on more hearts than anyone. Quite frankly, he's your best hope, perhaps your only one. What I propose is for you to go to Boston and let him try to save you where I couldn't."

"Do you really think he can?"

Doc Peters hesitated. "I won't lie to you. Your chances

are slim. It could be you'll die on the operating table but the important thing is you'll have done all you can."

"Boston," Ash said.

"You make it sound like you have to travel to the ends of the earth. By stage and train it shouldn't take you more than a couple of weeks. The trip will exhaust you, but if he can help you, if he can get the slug out, if there are no complications . . ."

Ash held up a hand, cutting him off. "If, if, if. It sounds to me like I could go to a lot of trouble and die that much sooner."

"You could, yes. But why not look at the bright side?"

"I need to think about it."

"Of course." Doc rose and pushed back the chair. "I'll leave you be. Rest and mull it over. There's no rush. You won't be strong enough to get out of bed for another two weeks, if then."

"That long?"

"Count your blessings you're even alive."

Ash didn't see where he had much to be thankful for. Essentially he'd be walking around with a death sentence over his head. Not a noose or a firing squad, but a fate every bit as final. The lead would penetrate his heart and his heart would stop or burst and that would be that.

Closing his eyes, Ash tried to relax. The morphine helped. It brought on the most wonderful feeling he ever experienced. Pure bliss was the only way to describe it. His veins pumped honey, his body tingled with pleasure, his brain soaked in delight. He never wanted it to end.

Ash's chest, though, still felt as if a great weight were pressing down. He shifted to make himself more comfortable. It did no good. The heavy sensation persisted.

Ash thought about the sawbones' idea. Boston was a long way from Texas.

He'd hate to go to all that trouble only to die on the operating table. Provided he even made it there. The stage ride alone might kill him. All that bouncing and jostling was enough to make healthy men and women ill. "What would it do to someone in my condition?" he asked out loud.

Then Ash thought about Ben Sharkey, about the ruse he had fallen for. He remembered the expression on Sharkey's face when he squeezed the trigger. God, how Ash would love to pay Sharkey back. His trigger finger twitched at the prospect.

It seemed to Ash he could do one of two things. He could risk the trip to Boston, which might kill him, and if it didn't, could then risk being put under the surgeon's blade, which also might kill him. Or he could spend the time he had left doing what he most wanted to do.

Sunlight had faded from the bedroom window when Doc Peters returned bearing a tray with a small bowl of chicken soup. He sat on the edge of the bed and ladled a spoon into the soup. "Open up. We need to get some food into you."

"I'll feed myself, thank you very much."

"You can't and you know it. You're not strong enough yet."

Ash sought to prove him wrong by reaching for the tray. Almost instantly his chest spiked with pain. Not only that, his stomach roiled and bitter bile rose in his throat. Grimacing and wheezing, he let his arm drop.

"I warned you," Doc said. "It will take a good long while for you to be able to move about. Even then you won't be your old self. You'll have to take everything nice and slow. On the stage ride you'll want to bundle in blankets to cushion your body."

"I'm not going to Boston."

In the act of lifting the spoon, Doc stopped. "What? Why not? Didn't I make it plain that Dr. Brewster is your only hope?"

"A slim hope, Doc. Your own word."

"Yes, but . . ."

Ash looked down at his chest. "I could die with every breath I take. Why not make the time I have left count for something? Why not die doing what I should have done years ago in Salina, Kansas?"

Doc put the tray on the bed and sat back. "I'm not sure I follow you."

"The man who did this to me. Ben Sharkey. He's a killer through and through. As long as he goes on breathing he'll do to others what he did to me. I can stop that from happening."

"Surely you're not suggesting that you plan to go after him? Deputy Blocker told me that the man who shot you headed north with a younger man right after the shooting. Blocker led a posse clear to the county line but couldn't catch them. By now this Sharkey could be anywhere."

"I can find him. I'm good at manhunting."

"Think, man. You are talking about days and weeks in the saddle. All that jouncing could do you in as readily as a stage ride."

"I have been thinking, Doc. All afternoon. I want my death to count for something." Ash stared at the gray of twilight out the window. "If I can find Ben Sharkey, I save the lives of all those he's likely to kill in the months and years ahead."

"By 'find' do you mean arrest him and put on trial?"

"I can't go on wearing a badge. I'd be next to useless." Ash shook his head. "Let's just say that the next time Sharkey and me meet, only one of us will ride away."

Doc grew somber. "I'm surprised at you, Asher. They have a word for that. You might have heard of it in your profession. They call it murder."

"What do you think he's done to me?"

"An eye for an eye and a murder for a murder? How can you throw away all the years you've worn a badge for something so trivial as vengeance?"

Forgetting himself, Ash went to move and the weight on his chest became a crushing anvil. He lay still until it subsided enough for him to say, "It's not trivial to me. I see it as justice being done."

"The slug grinding at your heart might kill you before you can track him down."

"Maybe," Ash conceded. "The important thing is that I get to have a say in how I go out of this world. Not many of us do."

Doc Peters sighed. "This justice of yours will prove fatal. You know that, don't you?"

Asher Thrall nodded.

Chapter 5

The ring of horseshoe on rock was much too loud. Ash rode with his hand on his Remington, his hat pulled low to keep the glare of the sun out of his eyes. In the heat of summer the hills were brown and dry. He had passed the last ranch more than a week ago.

The west part of Texas was a stark land of rattlesnakes and scorpions. Home to coyotes and cougars. Apaches roamed the region too, and Apache warriors would like nothing better than to come on a lone white man where no lone white man in his right mind should be.

Ash lifted the reins to spur up a hill, and gasped. That awful feeling was back, the terrible weight on his chest that wasn't a weight at all but the pressure of the slug on his heart. For almost a month after he was shot the pressure and the pain had been nearly constant. It had been almost more than he could endure. If not for the morphine he might very well have done something he never, ever thought he would do.

The morphine. Ash glanced at his saddlebags. He

had enough to last a spell. Without it . . . he shook his head.

Just like that, the pressure went away. Ash lifted the reins and continued his climb. It deviled him how the attacks came and went with no way to predict. He'd hardly felt a twinge since sunrise.

From the top of the hill spread a maze of more hills crisscrossed by washes and ravines. A harsh land, as inhospitable as any on earth. A land where outlaws hid with little fear of discovery by the law.

Ash looked down at the spot on his shirt where his badge used to be. He wasn't the law anymore. He was an ordinary citizen. Legally, he had no right to do what he was doing. Bounty men hunted other men but he wasn't after bounty. He didn't give a damn about any reward money that might be on Ben Sharkey's head. He just wanted Sharkey dead.

Ash remembered how persistent Doc Peters had been in trying to talk him out of it. In particular, one talk stuck in his mind. It had been about the eleventh or twelfth day he was bedridden and he had just finished a bowl of stew.

"Can we talk?" Doc had broached the subject.

"I owe you my life. You want to talk, we'll talk."

Doc had carried the tray to the dresser and come back to the chair. "I wish you would stop saying you owe me. I didn't do anything."

"I'm breathing, aren't I?"

Doc had run his fingers through his hair. "It's about this plan of yours. Please reconsider."

"No."

"Why spend the time you have left in misery? Sit in a rocking chair somewhere and savor what life is left to you."

"We've been all through this," Ash had responded. "I've made up my mind. I'm not gong to sit around feeling sorry for myself when I can make a difference."

"That's noble of you—," Doc had begun.

Ash had interrupted with, "I'm being as selfish as hell. Blowing out Ben Sharkey's wick will save however many folks he's bound to kill if he goes on breathing but I'm not doing it for them. I'm doing it for *me*."

Doc had drummed his fingers on the chair. "Very well. Let's say that by some miracle you succeed. You find this Sharkey and you do whatever you aim to do to him. What then?"

"How do you mean?"

"What about after he's dead? Have you thought that far ahead?"

"No," Ash had admitted.

"I advise you to come back to Mobeetie and take it easy for as long as you have left. The people here like you. You've been a fine law officer. Just the other day the mayor was saying how you're the glue that holds this town together. You know its reputation."

Indeed, Ash did. "The toughest town in Texas" was how Mobeetie had once been described. Hardly a month had gone by without a shooting or a knifing. It got so bad the town council fretted that law-abiding folks would be afraid to move there, and hired him. "Mobeetie will get along fine without me. They'll pick a new marshal and life will go on."

"You underestimate your worth."

"Sorry, Doc. I've got it to do."

On that note their talk had ended. They'd had others, but Ash refused to be talked out of his quest.

Soon after Ash was finally up and about, he had turned in his badge. He insisted on walking to the marshal's office without help. Deputy Blocker was flabbergasted by the news.

"You're doing *what*? I can't accept your badge, Ash. You need to go see the mayor or the town council. They're the ones who pinned it on you."

"Explain for me." Ash had taken off his tin and reverently set it on the desk.

"I don't know what to say. There aren't any words."

Ash had gone over and held out his hand. "There's this."

The council had asked Blocker to fill in while they made up their minds whether to offer him the position permanently or to hire someone else.

Ash spent the next day outfitting for a long spell in the saddle and off he went. Now here he was, a moving speck in the middle of vast emptiness.

The roan pricked its ears and raised its head.

Ash gazed out over the bleak landscape and saw nothing to account for his mount's sudden interest. He started down the hill and stiffened when gray tendrils caught his eye—wisps of smoke, maybe a quarter of a mile off. It could be the men he was after.

It could also be Apaches.

A dry wash hid him until he was near enough to smell the smoke. Drawing rein, Ash dismounted. He braced for more pressure in his chest and was relieved when there was none. Tugging his Winchester from the saddle scabbard, he stalked forward.

Voices told him they were white men.

Ash wormed to the crest of a wash. Below, hunkered around a campfire, were four men as scruffy as goats and as dirty as pigs. Each was an armory. Rifles were within quick reach.

Ash quietly worked the Winchester's lever. Just as

quietly he rose and moved toward them, the Winchester level at his hip. They were talking and joking and didn't realize he was there until he was almost on top of them. Then a greasy-haired specimen with yellow teeth sprang erect, crying out, "We've got company, boys!"

Ash covered them but didn't say anything.

The four glanced at one another and then at him and the man who had stood said, "Well, say something, damn it. Where the hell did you come from? You must be part Injun to sneak up on us like you did."

"No need to point your artillery at us," said another.

"We're friendly," claimed a third.

Ash sidled to the right so he had clear shots at all four. "Where do I find Ben Sharkey?"

Again they glanced at one another. A sly look came over the man on his feet.

"What was that handle again, Mister?"

Ash fixed the Winchester on him. "Pay attention. I'll only say this once. Ben Sharkey is hiding out somewhere in these hills. I figure you four know where. Spare yourselves and tell me."

"Listen to him," taunted the last of the bunch.

"Who do you think you are marching in here like this and holding us at gunpoint?" demanded the one on his feet.

"I'd hoped we could do this easy," Ash said. Inwardly he wrestled with his conscience. As a lawman he'd never harmed another soul unless he was given no choice. But he wasn't wearing a badge now. He could do whatever he pleased.

The only thing was, what he wanted to do was something he would never do when he was wearing a badge.

The man who had stood showed his yellow teeth in

a smirk of contempt. "There's four of us and only one of you. Why don't you skedaddle before you get us mad?"

Ash took another sidestep, his gaze on the three by the fire so that the one who had stood wouldn't guess what he was up to. When he was close enough he lunged, slamming the Winchester's stock against those yellow teeth. There was a distinct crunch. The man screeched and fell to his knees, blood and bits of broken teeth dribbling from his mouth. The other three started to rise but Ash trained the Winchester on them.

"I wouldn't if I were you."

"Damn your hide!" a bearded man snarled.

"I'm going to ask again," Ash said. "Where do I find Ben Sharkey?"

"What makes you so sure we know him?"

A quick step and Ash brought the stock crashing down on the man's head. The crown of the man's hat flattened and he folded at the waist and keeled onto his side, unconscious.

Fear showed on the last two. The skinniest gulped and splayed his fingers.

"Don't hit me, Mister! I'll tell you whatever you want."

"Grimes!" the fourth man spat.

Grimes swore, then said, "What's Sharkey that we should bleed for him? He doesn't ride with us. He hides out in the badlands the same as we do, and that's all. We don't owe him a thing."

"It's not right to give him away," the fourth man insisted.

"Since when did you get morals?" Grimes retorted. He faced Ash. "Mister, I don't know who you are and I don't care. You want Ben Sharkey, you're welcome to him." He pointed to the west. "There's a cabin about a day's ride. It's hard to find but there should be tracks. It's where those of us who fight shy of the law lay low sometimes."

"The four of you are wanted men?"

Grimes licked his thin lips. "I thought it's Ben Sharkey you're after."

Ash had another decision to make. These men were outlaws, as he'd suspected. He'd be doing Texas a favor if he took them in. It would delay his hunt, though, and the little time he had left was too precious to squander. "I'm leaving. Stay where you are." He started to back into the dark.

The man on his knees looked up. His chin was slick with blood, his mouth a ruin. Hate blazed from his dark eyes. "You're not going anywhere, you son of a bitch!" With that he clawed for a six-shooter.

Ash shot him in the face. He did it without thinking, as instinctively as breathing.

The man thrashed on the ground and kicked a few times and was still.

"Anyone else?" Ash asked.

"You had no call to do that," said the one who had argued with Grimes. "You had no call at all."

"Let him leave," Grimes urged.

Ash continued backing away. When he deemed it safe he turned and ran to the roan. He shoved the Winchester into the scabbard and forked leather. Reining around, he turned west.

Loud voices betokened a heated argument. Grimes and that other man were still at it. They seemed to be disputing over whether to come after him.

Ash held to a trot until he was sure they weren't. Belatedly he took stock of his feelings. He had killed another human being. He thought he would feel shock or be deeply upset but he wasn't. He felt a sort of elation.

All lawmen wondered whether they had what it took to squeeze the trigger. Some didn't, even when their lives were at stake; they couldn't find it in them to take another life. Those who had bedded down their first man, as the saying went, were considered the best of the tin wearers.

Ash gave a slight start. He kept forgetting. He wasn't a lawman anymore. The killing he had just done was murder. Granted, it was in self-defense, but it was still murder.

Ash didn't care. He would do whatever he had to in order to put an end to Ben Sharkey. Maybe that was wrong, he told himself, but he didn't care. All he had to do was touch his chest to be reminded of why.

Toward midnight Ash stopped. He stripped the saddle and saddle blanket and made a cold camp. As much as he would like some coffee, the glow of a campfire could be seen for miles and Apaches had sharp eyes. He untied his bedroll and spread out his blankets and soon was on his back with his hands folded on his chest, eager to rest his weary body.

He was lying there, doing absolutely nothing, when he had another attack.

One moment he was fine; the next it felt as if a bull had stepped on his chest and was bearing down with all its weight. The pain was terrible. When it got even worse he took deep breaths, in and out, in and out, as Doc Peters had recommended.

It was supposed to help but it hardly ever did.

Ash hated the attacks. He waited for the torment to subside but this was a bad one. It went on and on until finally he couldn't take it anymore. He managed to sit up and groped for his saddlebags. The morphine and hypodermic were in a kit made of black leather. He could hardly see to open it. Fortunately he always kept the hypodermic ready for quick use. All he had to do was expose his forearm, locate a vein and jab the needle in. The needle used to sting but he had become so accustomed to injecting himself that he barely felt the prick.

Delicious rapture spread up his arm and down his body. Gratefully, Ash sank back, the kit in his lap, the needle still in his arm. The pain, the awful pressure, were gone.

Ash touched a fingertip to his chest and smiled. For a while everything would be fine. More than fine. He used to like to drink brandy and whiskey on occasion and enjoyed the good feeling they gave him, but that was nothing compared to this.

Ash remembered visiting a Chinese opium den once while searching for a thief, and recalled seeing people lying in states of stupor. At the time he'd wondered why they would do that to themselves. If opium was anything like morphine, now he knew.

Ash smiled and gazed at the stars. Soon his quest would be over. Afterward he might do as Doc Peters suggested and sit on a rocking chair for the rest of his few remaining days. Just so long as he had enough morphine to last until the end came.

The stuff was pure ecstasy.

Chapter 6

The cabin had seen better days. The roof sagged and the front door hung crooked. Smoke curled from a stone chimney, proving someone was in there. A single horse, a grulla, was tied to a peg in the front wall and stood dozing.

From an outcropping above and to one side, Ash scanned for signs of others. Ben Sharkey supposedly had five or six men with him. Either most of the gang were off somewhere or Grimes had lied to him and whoever was down there had no connection to Sharkey at all.

Ash worked lower. The only window was covered by part of what looked to a pink sheet, of all things. There was little risk of his being spotted. Still, he hugged cover. Near the bottom he eased onto his belly. He was only a few yards from the cabin when without warning the pressure returned.

Ash stopped and bit his sleeve so as not to cry out. As it always did, the pain grew worse. Ash dug the fingers of his left hand into the dirt and prayed for

the pain to go away. He hadn't bothered to inject morphine when he woke up and now he was paying for his
mistake.

Gradually the pressure eased. The agony faded.

Ash almost got up and went to his horse to inject.
When he could move, he crawled to the side of the cabin
and rose into a crouch. He was weak from the attack
and could barely stand.

From the front came the scrape of the door. Someone
emerged. They were whistling the tune to "Little Brown
Jug."

Ash crept to the corner. A quick peek sent a tingle
through him. Wedging the Winchester to his shoulder,
he boldly stepped into the open.

The young man who had called himself Grant and
pretended to be a gambler was saddling the horse. He
was still wearing the black suit and string tie. He had
just thrown a saddle blanket on the grulla and was
about to do the same with his saddle. Either he sensed
something or Ash made a slight noise, because he stiffened and spun.

"Lonnie, wasn't it?" Ash said.

Caught holding the saddle, there was nothing the
younger man could do except what he did; he blurted,
"Damn."

"Set it down slow," Ash directed.

Lonnie obeyed.

"Poke your hands at the clouds and turn around.
Again, nice and slow. So much as twitch wrong and I'll
give you one of these pills."

"How the hell did you find this place?"

"Did I say you could talk?" Ash approached and
jammed the Winchester against the small of Lonnie's

back. Reaching around, Ash relieved him of the Remington pocket pistol, which he tucked under his own belt. Ash stepped back. "You can turn around."

"My uncle will be mad, me being caught like this."

"Speaking of which, where is he?"

Lonnie shook his head. "Go to hell."

Ash motioned at the open front door. "Suppose we go inside. You first. Walk backward and keep those hands high."

Lonnie looked over his shoulder to keep from tripping. As he stepped over the jamb he suddenly stopped and gazed past Ash. "Uncle Ben!" he hollered. "Look out! It's that lawdog you shot!"

Of all the tricks and ruses ever invented, it was one of the oldest. Yet Ash fell for it. He whirled, and no one was there. He spun back around to find that Lonnie had bounded inside and was slamming the door after him.

Ash threw himself at the door, ramming into it shoulder first. It proved to be as rickety as it looked. There was a crash, and slivers and dust flew every which way. Ash wound up on his side on a dirt floor.

A shaft of sunlight illumined Lonnie. He had an axe in his hands and was sweeping it over his head.

Ash rolled just as the axe arced down and it thudded into the dirt an inch from his ear. He kicked out, felt his boot connect, and heard Lonnie yelp. Then he was up on one knee and had the rifle level. "Drop it or die."

Lonnie winced and tottered. "You about busted my knee, you bastard!"

Ash raised the sights so that Lonnie's left eye filled them. "I won't tell you twice, boy."

Hissing like a stuck snake, Lonnie cast the axe down. "I almost had you," he boasted.

Ash stood. The hell of it was, Lonnie was right. He'd been unforgivably careless and nearly paid for his blunder with his life. Glancing about, he discovered a table with three legs and a pair of chairs that appeared fit to fall apart if anyone so much as sneezed. "Take a seat."

Hobbling and cursing, Lonnie did as Ash wanted, and glared. "What now, you son of a bitch?"

Ash slid the other chair a good six feet and straddled it, resting the Winchester across the top. "Now we wait for your uncle to show."

Lonnie laughed. "He's long gone and he's not coming back."

"You expect me to believe he up and left you?"

"I am to join him in . . ." Lonnie stopped. "Damn me. I almost gave it away." He studied Ash. "How is it you're still breathing? I saw him shoot you with my own eyes. You should be dead."

"Some men don't die easy." Ash let it go at that.

"My uncle sure thought he made maggot bait of you. He was drunk for a week, celebrating."

"How many ride with him these days?"

"I plumb forget," Lonnie lied, and chuckled.

"Have your fun while you can," Ash told him. "Once I no longer need you, you won't be laughing."

"Threats like that might work on kids and old women but I don't scare easy," Lonnie declared. "You're a marshal. You don't go around killing folks for the hell of it."

Ash motioned at his shirt. "Do you see a badge?"

Lonnie tilted his head, his eyes narrowing. "Did you leave it back in Mobeetie so you could come after us on your own account?"

"You're not as big a simpleton as I thought," Ash

said. "Tell me where your uncle got to and I'll let you light a shuck."

"Go to hell."

Ash shot him in the leg, the blast thunderous in the cabin's confines. Lonnie howled and fell. Clutching his leg, he rolled back and forth, spewing obscenities. Ash patiently waited for the tantrum to subside. When it did, when Lonnie was spent and gasping and covered with blood and dirt, he said, "Get back on the chair."

"Drop dead."

Ash aimed at his other leg. "You're not a quick learner, are you, boy? I am. I'm learning I like this."

"You like shooting people?"

"I like shooting scum like you." Ash wagged the barrel. "My patience isn't what it was."

Practically shaking with rage, blood dripping from under the hand he had over the wound, Lonnie sat up and slid to the chair, leaving a scarlet smear in his wake. "I can't get up on my own."

"You do, or you don't get up at all."

Lonnie blistered the air with more swearing, but he made it onto the chair. "I'll never tell you anything now."

"That's fine. We'll sit here a spell."

"What are you up to?" Lonnie asked through clenched teeth.

Ash held the Winchester over the back of the chair with one hand and rubbed his chin with the other. "I figure you were on your way join Sharkey and your other friends. When you don't show up, they'll come look for you."

"You've got it all wrong. They're on their way to see about robbing a bank. I was going home to see my ma."

"Sure you were." Ash didn't believe him. As young

as Lonnie was, he'd been riding the high lines with his uncle for a while now and was as hard as they came. "I bet you haven't been back to see her in ages."

Lonnie snorted. "Shows how much you know. My ma and me have always been close. Pa died when I was little and she looked after me and my brothers all on her own. I'd do anything for that lady."

"You'd steal and kill for her?" Ash sarcastically asked. "Is that why you hooked up with your uncle?"

"You've got her all wrong. She begged me not to go off with him but I wanted to repay her for all she's done for me and my brothers."

Now it was Ash who snorted. "Repay her with money you stole from law-abiding folks?"

"I've been saving my share," Lonnie said. "I have enough now that she can buy a new wagon and new dresses and such. Things she's always wanted but never had the money for."

"Your mother the saint won't mind how you got it?"

"Don't you dare insult her again. She'll never know it came from me. I'm giving it to one of my brothers and he'll get it to her and say he won it in a poker game."

"You have it all thought out."

"I'm not as dumb as you make me out to be."

Ash nodded at the spreading scarlet pool under Lonnie's chair. "You're dumb enough to bleed to death for a man who isn't worth dying for."

Lonnie glanced down and his Adam's apple bobbed. Drops of sweat peppered his forehead. He pressed both hands to the wound in an effort to staunch the flow. "I feel awful queasy."

"You'll feel a lot worse before long."

Grimacing, Lonnie gouged a thumb into the bullet

hole. "Damn it. It just won't stop. You've got to bandage me or let me bandage myself."

Ash didn't respond.

"I'm no use to you if I'm dead."

"You're no use at all except to tell me where your uncle is," Ash enlightened him.

"You were a lawman."

"So?"

"So you can't just sit there and let me die."

Ash considered that. Once the boy would have been right. Once he would have done all he could to save him and bring him in alive. "I'm not sure myself what I'll do."

"You're trying to scare me." Lonnie licked his lips and squirmed.

"You don't get it, boy. You don't savvy what this is about."

"Yes, I do. You're mad at my uncle for shooting you and you won't rest until he's behind bars."

"I won't rest until he's dead." Ash pushed his hat back on his head. "You keep thinking of me as a badge toter when I'm doing this for me. For weeks I laid in bed in more misery than I've ever been in and all I thought about was how much I want your uncle dead."

Lonnie's pant legs was soaked and his boot was caked with crimson. His face had become as pale as a sheet and his lips weren't the right color. "My uncle respected you, you know."

"That's a good one."

"He did. He was mad about you crippling him, but he told me that as tin stars go, you were as decent as they get."

"So he hunted me down anyway."

Lonnie held up a dripping hand. "Please, Mister. I don't want to die."

"No one ever does." Ash marveled at how little emotion he felt. He wondered how that could be.

"Do I need to beg?"

"All you need to do is tell me where to find your uncle."

"You'll bandage me."

"I'll bandage you."

"Then take me to a doc?"

"I'll bandage you."

Lonnie was shaking. He bowed his head and his shoulders slumped and he said in a small voice, "My uncle went to Selby. Honest to God he did."

Ash gave it thought. It made sense. Selby was a small settlement near the border, the hub of a farming community. It had a general store and a bank and not much else. The bank would be easy pickings. "How many gunnies does your uncle have helping him?"

"Five. *Now* will you help me?" Lonnie's teeth commenced to chatter. "I'm cold. I feel like I'm freezing when it's summer out."

"It's all the blood you've lost." Ash got up and walked out. He went around the corner and to the rocks to where he had concealed the roan. Sliding the Winchester into the scabbard, he climbed on. Clucking, he tapped his spurs.

He was out of the rocks and a short way from the cabin when a sharp cry brought him to a stop.

Lonnie was a shambling ghost. His red hands were held out in appeal and tears streaked his cheeks. "*Please!*" he wailed. "For God's sake, don't leave me like this!"

Ash reined around. He rode back at a walk. When

he got there Lonnie was on the ground, convulsing. Ash stayed on the roan and leaned on the saddle horn.

No blood came from the wound; there wasn't much left in the boy's body.

The spasms ended and Lonnie lay on his back, gulping air. His lips had gone from blue to purple. "You miserable bastard."

"I'm obliged for the pocket pistol. A man can always use a hideout."

"Miserable, rotten, stinking bastard."

"I'll take your horse too. I'll sell him and use the money for supplies." The mention of money reminded Ash of what Lonnie had said about his mother. He reined the roan over to the grulla. Bending, he opened Lonnie's saddlebags. There it was, right on top, stuffed into an old sock. He counted it and was amazed. There was more than two thousand dollars. "I'm obliged again, boy."

Lonnie was silent.

Ash placed the bundle in his own saddlebags, snagged the grulla's reins, and reined over to the still form. He stared down into the lifeless eyes and he smiled.

"I'll give your uncle your regards."

Chapter 7

Tombstones jutting from the prairie. That was how Selby's dozen or so buildings looked from a distance. They were lined up in a row like graves in a cemetery. The comparison was heightened by the lack of life. The heat had driven everyone and everything—except for several horses tied to hitch rails—inside or into what little shade there was. A panting dog peered out from inside an upended rain barrel. A pig rested under a porch.

A man in an apron stared out the window of the general store as Ash rode up. Ash stiffly dismounted, then stretched. He tied the roan and the grulla to the rail and noticed the trough was dry. Slapping dust from his jacket, he went into the store. A tiny bell jangled over the door.

"How do you do?" the proprietor greeted him.

"I'm hot as hell and thirsty enough to drink a lake dry," Ash replied.

The man offered a polite grin.

"Where can I get water for my horses? I've come a long way and they are wore out."

"So I noticed." The man pointed at a frame house

past the bank. "See that house? It belongs to the mayor. See that metal tank on stilts at the side of the house? It's fed by one of the few wells still working and he will let you have water for fifty cents a gallon."

"Pay for water?" Ash had never heard of such a thing.

The portly man nodded. "We haven't had enough rain for pretty near a year now. The farmers are worried their crops will wither and die, and if that happens the town will wither and die too."

Ash gazed toward the bank. Whoever built it wasn't much for fancy; it was a squat block of stone and wood. "Have there been any other strangers in town the past few days?"

"You are the first I've seen in over week." The man held out his hand. "I'm Walter, by the way. Walter Obermeyer. You can call me Walt."

"Do you have law here, Walt? Or do you rely on the county sheriff or the Rangers?"

"We rely on ourselves." Walt cocked his head. "Why do you ask? Are you in some sort of trouble?"

Ash debated telling him. Walt would no doubt spread the word and the townsfolk might take it on themselves to arm and wait for Sharkey and his men to arrive and blow them to hell. He couldn't have that. He wanted to kill Ben Sharkey himself. "Just curious." To change the subject Ash said, "I noticed you haven't gotten around to building a saloon yet."

"We never will. We are a God-fearing town, Mister. Drink is the devil's lubricant. It brings nothing but misery and lawlessness."

Ash would dearly love a whiskey even though Doc Peters had warned him about mixing morphine and alcohol. Doc said to go easy or there might be complications. Ash realized he'd neglected to ask what those complications might be. "I commend your morals but it's a shame."

"I have jugs of water and tea and there's coffee on," Walt said. "I also have eats." He gave another of those polite grins. "I'm the closest thing to a restaurant Selby has."

"I'll be back." Ash went out and untied the horses. He led them to the mayor's house and opened a gate in a picket fence. He hadn't taken more than a few steps when the front door opened and out bustled a small man in a suit that was too large. He wore a bowler and had a waxed mustache.

"I'm Mayor Quilby. Can I help you?"

Ash nodded at the water tank. Under it was a trough. "Your storekeeper told me I can get water for my animals."

"Did he tell you I charge?"

"That he did," Ash said sourly. It bothered him to have to pay when he was here to help the town.

"Then come ahead. I'll open the spout. How much do you want?"

Ash fished money from his pocket. He stood in the shade of the tank with the roan and the grulla. Dipping his hand in the trough, he wet his neck and his face. The water had a musty scent but was wonderfully cool.

"Mind if I ask your name?" the mayor asked.

Ash saw no reason not to say.

"You are welcome to stay as long as you like, Mr. Thrall. Keep in mind we are not one of those rowdy towns where every evil under the sun can be had."

"What makes you say a thing like that?"

Mayor Quilby looked Ash up and down. "No offense, but you have the air of a tough character and tough characters generally are—how shall I put this?—more free-spirited than most folks."

"By 'tough' you mean 'mean,'" Ash said in annoyance. No one had ever compared him to the kind of men he used to arrest. "Hell, if I was I'd bust your teeth for bringing it up."

"I told you no offense was intended. I was only letting you know we don't go in for those sorts of things." Mayor Quilby wheeled. "Enjoy your water. I'll be inside if you want more."

Ash decided he didn't like the little rooster. He was about to say a few choice words, but stopped. What is happening to me? he wondered. He was much too irritable. He figured it must be the heat. Cupping a hand, he sipped the water. It had a metallic taste and he spat it out.

When the trough was empty Ash took the horses to the last building in Selby, the livery. The double doors were open, the shade inside a welcome relief from the relentless sun. Only one stall was occupied, by a cow. "Anyone here?" he called out.

From the back shuffled a man with white whiskers. He used a cane thick enough to serve as a cudgel. "What can I do for you?"

"I'd like to put these animals up," Ash informed him." Any chance I might be able to sell the grulla? I'll throw in the saddle if I'm offered enough."

The man scratched his whiskers. "I have no need for a horse. Can't think of anyone who does. But if you stay the night I can put out the word and maybe one of the farmers will be interested."

"You'd go to that much trouble?"

"For a dollar I will."

"You folks hereabouts sure do love money."

"Can't live without mammon," the old man said. "Need it for our vices. I have two. Tobacco and coffin varnish."

Ash's interest perked. "I thought this is a dry town. Where do you get your drinks?"

The old man reached behind him and produced a flask. Uncapping it, he took a sip, then held it out to Ash. "A swallow is free. Any more than that and I'll have to charge you."

"A swallow it is. I'm obliged." Ash grinned as the whiskey burned down his throat and exploded in the pit of his stomach. Reluctantly he gave the flask back. "You drink good whiskey."

The old man chuckled. "Don't tell the mayor. He's a teetotaler and thinks the rest of the world should be the same."

"One of those."

"Oh, he's a good man at heart. He always does what he thinks is best for the town."

Ash handed over the reins. He was bone weary. "I could use some sleep. I don't suppose you rent out the hayloft?"

"Now there's an idea. Why didn't I think of that?" The old man winked. "Climb on up if you want. I'll strip your animals and rub them down but it will cost you extra."

"It won't surprise me if I leave this town broke."

Ash made the old man promise to wake him if any strangers showed up.

Then, braced for another attack, Ash scaled the ladder. He made it to the top without incident. As a precaution he opened the hayloft door and piled hay near it so he could see the entire length of the street. He placed the Winchester and his saddlebags next to him.

Lying on his back with his head in his hands Ash wondered how long it would be before Ben Sharkey showed. He hoped to high heaven the boy hadn't lied. Not when it would take weeks if not months to track Sharkey down.

Ash needed the hunt to be over with. He didn't possess the stamina he used to. He tired too easily. Doc Peters had warned him that might be a consequence and once again the sawbones was right.

Ash stared at his chest. It appeared normal. No one could tell by looking at him that a fingernail-sized chunk of lead was slowly, inevitably, boring into his heart. He almost regretted not going to Boston to see the famous surgeon. Then he thought of Ben Sharkey and how much he yearned to curl Sharkey's toes and his regret faded.

A man had to have his priorities.

On that ironic note Ash drifted into limbo. He dreamed he was being chased by a bull buffalo, only the buffalo was made of lead. It clanked as it ran, its hooves so heavy they sank into the earth. He flew with all his speed but the bull slowly gained. Just when it was about to trample him he woke up with a start and lay panting, his body covered with sweat.

That was another thing. Ash was having a lot more nightmares than he ever did. Doc Peters hadn't mentioned he would but it had to be due to his condition.

Ash gazed down the dusty street—and couldn't believe his eyes. Six horses were tied to the hitch rail in front of the general store. Six horses caked with dust from miles on the trail.

Swearing, Ash sat up. He jammed on his hat and moved to the ladder. The old man was nowhere in sight. Ash should have known better than to rely on him.

Quickly descending, he moved to the double doors.

Selby was as quiet and still as a cemetery. As Ash looked on a farmer came out of the bank and walked to a wagon. Presently both rattled out of town.

Four men came out of the general store and watched it leave. The stamp of the hard case was on each face. Each had a revolver on his hip.

Sharkey's men, Ash reckoned. He was proven right a moment later when the door opened again and out strolled a fifth two-legged wolf and Ben Sharkey himself.

Ash snapped the Winchester to his shoulder but he didn't shoot. He might not kill with the first shot. Better to wait until they were closer.

Sharkey had his thumbs hooked in his gun belt. He favored spurs with large rowels and they glinted in the sun as he came out into the middle of the street and moved toward the bank. Three of his men flanked him. The other two stayed in front of the general store.

They were about to rob the bank.

Ash centered his sights on Sharkey. They were coming in his direction; another dozen steps and he would shoot Sharkey where the man had shot him. He wished Sharkey could suffer as he was suffering, wished that by some miracle his slug would lodge in Sharkey's heart as Sharkey's damnable slug had lodged in his. He thumbed back the hammer and lightly curled his finger to the trigger. He was set.

The pain hit him like a hammer blow to the chest. The pressure was worse than ever and Ash doubled over. He tried to take aim but he couldn't straighten. His blood began pounding in his temples and he thought he would be sick.

Ash needed morphine. The kit was up in the hayloft

in his saddlebags. He turned and tried to walk to the ladder but had managed only a couple of steps when he fell onto his side. He looked for the proprietor. Desperate, he used the Winchester as a crutch and rose halfway. The pressure proved too much.

Ash groaned. He hated being helpless. From down the street came shouts and a commotion. Guns boomed. A woman screamed.

Ben Sharkey had struck the bank.

God, no, Ash thought. He pushed against the ground but he was too weak to rise more than a few inches. He had to lie there and listen to the uproar as the man who was to blame for his helplessness, the man he had come so far to kill, blasted his way out of Selby.

From the sounds of things some of the townspeople were fighting back. Rifles cracked. A shotgun mimicked a cannon.

It occurred to Ash that someone might make a lucky shot and bring Sharkey down. He groaned louder, not because of the pain but because he feared his vengeance would be thwarted. He clawed at the dirt and got nowhere.

Another scream pierced the air. A horse whinnied. The gunfire reached a crescendo as hooves drummed and someone shouted, "Stop them! They took all the money!"

Pouring sweat, Ash crawled. The pressure had eased a trifle, enough that he made it to the bottom of the ladder. He reached up, took hold of a rung and sought to pull to his feet but only made it to his knees. Exhausted, he rested his forehead against the ladder.

Hands gripped his shoulders, gentle hands that turned him and propped him up. "Are you shot, Mister?" the old man asked.

"No," Ash got out.

"What's wrong, then?"

"Sick," Ash said.

The man pressed a palm to his forehead. "You look awful. Rest easy and I'll fetch help." He rose and limped out on his cane.

Ash's craving for morphine became overwhelming. He hooked an elbow over a rung and thrust himself erect. He would swear his chest was about to explode. He raised his right boot, then his left. Clinging by one hand, he swayed. The kit was so near yet so far. He vowed that from now on he would keep it with him always. The hypodermic, at least, filled and ready to be injected. He climbed higher and it taxed him to where the livery spun and his head seemed to turn inside out.

"I don't deserve this," Ash protested his fate. Undaunted, he raised a boot ... and fell. His strength completely gave out. He landed hard on his left shoulder. Pain on top of pain now, and him a travesty. It was enough to make him sob in frustration and humiliation.

"Not this way," Ash said, and would have sat up except for a black wave that washed over him and left him floundering in despair.

Then came nothing, nothing at all.

Chapter 8

They told him that if he ever came back to Selby they would shoot him. It was a hell of a thing to say to an ex-lawman.

Mayor Quilby had summed up their sentiments in a manner befitting a politician. "We're appalled and shocked at your behavior. You knew these men were coming to rob our bank. Yet you didn't say anything. You didn't warn us. You rode in and slaked your thirst with our water and boarded your horses at our livery, but not one word. You took advantage of our hospitality but kept quiet about our peaceful community being in dire danger. Now the clerk at our bank is dead and a farmer is dead and three others are gravely wounded. For a small town like ours this is a calamity and it didn't have to happen."

Ash had been sitting in the livery at the time, regaining his strength. He had told them everything when they revived him. A stupid thing to do, now that he looked back on it. He had been in so much pain, mentally he wasn't quite himself.

Eight or nine people were there with the mayor, and

the looks they gave him were looks of utter and total contempt. The mayor had gone on.

"No, this horror didn't have to happen. You're as much to blame as this Sharkey desperado because you had it in your power to prevent it. Why didn't you? I'll tell you why. You didn't warn us because your revenge was more important to you than our lives. That you were a marshal makes it all the more reprehensible. Lawmen take oaths to uphold the law. They protect lives. They watch out for the innocent. You threw all that aside for self-interest. The blood on the floor of our bank and in our street was shed because you are a despicable human being."

The words stung. Ash had tried to get them to understand but they kept on giving him those disdainful looks. Finally he recovered and the liveryman saddled the roan and the grulla and the good townsfolk of Selby escorted him to the edge of town and sent him on his way with a warning to never, ever come back.

"You just don't understand," was Ash's parting remark.

Now it was the middle of the afternoon and he was following the trail left by the outlaws. It was plain enough that a ten-year-old could do it. He hadn't had an attack since he left Selby. In his jacket, ready for use, was the hypodermic, just in case.

Ash saw the bodies on his way out of town. They were laid out in front of the bank. The clerk had been a little mouse, the farmer a burly man of the earth with a beard down to his waist. Ash had felt nothing. Why should he when he didn't know them? A woman was on her knees, wailing over the dead farmer, and other women were trying to comfort her.

Ash's conscience pricked him but he shrugged it off. He had done what he had to.

The trail led to the northwest, toward the border. Ash guessed that Sharkey was getting the hell out of Texas before the Rangers showed up. Sharkey was as mean as they came but he was no fool. No one ever tangled with the Texas Rangers and won. Oh, a Ranger was killed now and again, but other Rangers always dealt with the killers. They were death on horseback for lawbreakers, and Sharkey knew it.

Ash was glad he hadn't sold the grulla. By switching horses when one or the other tired, he was covering twice the ground. He aimed to overtake the outlaws before too long, a tall order given his affliction.

Evening found Ash miles from anywhere, alone in the vastness of the rolling hills. He made camp in a dry wash so his fire wouldn't be seen. He craved coffee but water was scarce and he didn't know how long his canteen had to last. Supper consisted of jerky and a few Saratoga chips he'd come across in Lonnie's saddlebags.

The gray of twilight gave way to the pitch mantle of night. Stars blossomed and the breeze picked up. Off among the hills a coyote yipped and was answered by another.

Ash gazed at the stars and listened to the cries. In the vastness of things he was a miserable little speck. What did it matter that he was hovering at death's brink? It mattered not one tiny whit.

Depressed, Ash munched and settled into his blankets. For some reason he thought of the women he had known.

There had been Darcy. Sweet, nimble, playful Darcy, who at sixteen had been his first love. Her ripe body held such promise that Ash almost married her. Wanderlust had proven stronger than plain lust and he struck off to see the world, leaving her heartbroken.

After Darcy came more fallen doves than Ash could remember even if he cared to. He'd gone through a spell where he visited every bawdy house he came across. He'd been up to his armpits in whores and loved it.

The luster wore off the faded roses, though, and Ash had cast about for a steady bed warmer. That was when he met Claire. She worked for her father at a feed and grain. Ash had nearly collided with her as she was coming out of a millinery, and he was smitten at first sight. She was quiet and shy and much too thin but there was something about her that stirred him where no other woman ever did. He courted her and won her heart. The happiest day of his life was the day she stood in front of a parson and said "I do."

Ash had his future all worked out. They would have kids and raise their family in a nice home and grow old together and die.

Six months after they were wed the coughing began. At first she coughed only a little. She tried herbs and her grandmother's remedy but the cough persisted and became worse. Ash tried to talk her into going to see a doctor. She insisted it was nothing and she would be fine.

Then she began coughing up blood.

Consumption, they called it. The doctor said it killed thousands every year. No cure existed although a dry climate was supposed to lessen the torment. Ash wanted to take Claire to Arizona but she insisted on staying in Kansas, where she had friends and was comfortable.

Ash did all he could. He stayed by her side the last couple of weeks when she was bedridden and too weak to lift a cup to her lips. He'd held her cold hand and looked down at her and wanted to scream.

Claire wasted away until she was a breathing skeleton. Her skin clung to her bones and her eyes were sunken pits. Yet through it all she smiled and told him how much she loved him and thanked him for being the best husband any woman could have.

Burying her was the low point in Ash's life. He went on a binge, drinking himself senseless every night. He visited bawdy houses but for the life of him he couldn't remember a single woman he bedded. He was trying to forget but it didn't work. Some sorrows ran too deep.

A friend pulled him up by his bootstraps. That friend happened to be the town marshal in Salina, and once Ash was sober and stayed sober, the friend pinned a deputy's badge on him.

Ash liked enforcing the law. He liked helping people. He gave up the bawdy houses and hardly ever touched a bottle and life was good again. Deep down, though, was an emptiness that could never be filled. It didn't help that everywhere he went, everything he saw, reminded him of Claire. Finally he decided a change of scenery was in order. He drifted south into Texas and fate brought him to Mobeetie, a town in need of a lawman.

Since then he'd enjoyed a steady job and a steady life. He was reasonably content. He figured to stay on as marshal until he was ready for a rocking chair.

Then along came Ben Sharkey.

Ash was so engrossed in his past that he was slow to react to the crunch of a twig. Belatedly, he sat up. Something was out there in the dark. An animal, he reckoned, although animals generally shied from campfires. He started to turn and glimpsed a streak of movement out of the corner of his eye. Heaving off his blanket, he grabbed for the Winchester but he barely got hold of it when a heavy body slammed into his with the impact of a battering ram. He was hurled onto his back but scrambled up and clawed for the Remington revolver.

A second attacker came at him from behind. The first inkling Ash had was a blow to his back that nearly snapped his spine. Flung forward onto his belly, he twisted and had the Remington half out when a kick sent it spinning from his fingers. He pushed up onto his elbow, only to receive another blow from the side that smashed him to the earth, dazed and gasping for breath.

Ash looked up. There were two of them, swarthy and stocky, with black hair down to their shoulders. He took them for Comanches but they might be Apaches or some other tribe. He'd had little dealings with Indians and couldn't tell one from the other.

Their faces were cold, almost hateful. Bows were slung over their backs and they had long-bladed knives in their hands, which fortunately they hadn't used. One of them bent and jabbed him and said something in their tongue that brought a wicked grin to the other.

Ash realized they'd deliberately taken him alive. They could easily have killed him. He envisioned the tortures they might inflict and swallowed. They were two cats who had caught a mouse and they would make the mouse squeak before it died.

"White man," the warrior bent over him said in guttural English.

"Indian," Ash replied.

"You pick wrong night, wrong place, eh?" The warrior jabbed him again, harder.

"Why did you attack me?" Ash asked. "I'm not your enemy."

"You white," the warrior said, as if that alone were ample reason.

"You attack all whites? Even when they've done you no harm?" Ash was stalling.

The warrior raised the knife close to Ash's eyes. "Whites take land. Whites kill buffalo. Whites say only good Indian dead Indian. I say only good white dead white." He sliced the tip into Ash's cheek.

Ash flinched but showed no fear. Blood trickled over his chin to his neck.

"I'm a lawman on the trail of an outlaw. Kill me and you'll have the army after you."

"Law-man," the warrior repeated, his brow puckered. His friend said something in their tongue and the warrior answered. He poked Ash in the chest. "You law-man?"

"That's what I just said." Ash slid his right hand to the inner edge of his jacket.

"You hunt other whites, eh? That what law-man do?"

"There is more to wearing a badge."

The warrior poked him in the shirt. "Badge, yes. Where metal star or metal circle? Whites who hunt other whites wear badge."

"My badge is in my saddlebags. I can show you if you want." Ash went to rise and received another prick.

"Not care you law-man," the warrior said. "All whites bad. All whites only good dead."

Ash's hand was under his jacket. He had done it so

slickly, they hadn't suspected. "Tell me something. How many whites have you and your friend killed? Or am I your first?"

The warrior grinned. "It twelve winters I kill first white. Bluecoats attack village. I kill soldier with arrow. I kill whites everywhere. White men. White women. White small ones. Kill strange man who wear black clothes and carry big"—the warrior paused to find the right word—"carry big book."

"You killed women and children and a man of the cloth? If anyone has it coming, you do."

"Coming?"

"The reaper," Ash said. Drawing the pocket pistol he shot the warrior between the eyes. The force whipped the warrior's head back. The other one wasn't close enough to use his knife and spun to run off. Ash put two slugs between his shoulder blades and watched the body convulse and twitch.

"It's a good thing I started carrying Lonnie's hideout," Ash said to the horses. He had been lucky. Very lucky. Or as that man of the cloth might say, Providence had a hand in his deliverance.

Ash couldn't stay there. The pair might have friends not far off, friends who heard the shots. Reluctantly he saddled both animals. He doused the fire with water from his canteen and with dirt. Since he'd ridden the roan last he climbed on the grulla. "You'll get to rest later," he promised.

Ash imagined a horde of redskins rushing toward him and used his spurs.

At night the hills reared like squat toads. Sounds came out of them: the snarl of a cougar, the bleat of a doe, hissing and rustlings and once the ululating scream of God knew what.

Ash wasn't overly worried. He would be far away before the dead warriors were found, if they ever were. He took a fix by the North Star and headed to the northwest. In the excitement his fatigue had evaporated. He felt as if he could ride all night.

Ash pushed on for half an hour and changed his mind. He had a long day in the saddle tomorrow.

The next flat spot he came to he reined up.

Intermittent cries continued to pierce the night, predator and prey in their orgy of blood and flesh.

Once more Ash settled in, his saddle for a pillow, the Winchester at his side. He was amazed that in his fight with the warriors his chest hadn't bothered him. The pain was so unpredictable. There was no rhyme or reason to when it struck.

As if to prove him correct, the pressure returned, the worst so far. Ash bore it as long as he could and then he resorted to the morphine, eagerly plunging the needle into a vein.

The wonderful morphine.

Ash sank back and bit his lower lip, waiting for it to take effect. He didn't have to wait long. The pressure eased, or he had the illusion it did, and the pain was no worse than a dull ache.

Holding the hypodermic in his palm, Ash ran a finger over it from plunger to tip. He held up the morphine and said in earnest, "I don't know how I'd get by without you."

From then on, Ash vowed, he wouldn't.

Chapter 9

It was a decrepit hovel in the literal middle of nowhere. Ash would have sworn it was abandoned if not for the horse at the hitch rail and the small corral out back with several more horses dozing in the heat. A wagon was parked nearby. The sign said TIMBERLY'S. His nose told him it was a saloon.

Ash was upset. He'd lost the trail. Rocky ground was to blame, ground so hard there were no tracks, not so much as the scuff of a hoof. He'd spent half a day roving in ever wider circles, and nothing. Now he was pushing to the northwest in the hope Sharkey had continued in that direction.

Ash climbed down and arched his back to relieve a cramp. He left the Winchester in the scabbard and went in. The smell curled his nose, the odor of whiskey and beer mixed with other, fouler reeks. The place was so dark he stopped to let his eyes adjust.

A long plank on stacked barrels ran the length of the back wall and served as the bar. Two tables and a few chairs were to one side. The man behind the bar looked as if he rolled in dirt every morning and was scratching himself. He introduced himself as Oscar, then raised the tips of his fingers to his nose and sniffed.

"What'll it be, Mister?"

"Whiskey." Ash had not had a drink since that sip in the livery and he dearly yearned for more. The man set a glass in front of him and reached under the plank and produced a bottle. "Give me that." Ash took it and opened it himself. He swallowed, smacked his lips and said, "I'll keep this."

Oscar chuckled. "Whole weeks can go by and I don't see a soul, but now in the past few days I've had you and the others before you."

Ash tried to sound calm when he was vibrating with excitement. "Others, did you say?"

"A wild and wooly bunch. Rode in here and got all liquored up and played cards and whored for three days. They had come a long way and needed the rest, Ben told me."

"Ben?"

"Oh. Sorry. The boss, I guess you'd call him." Oscar leaned on his elbows and lowered his voice. "They claimed to be a cow outfit. But between you and me, if they were punchers I'm the Duke of London. More likely they rode the high lines, if you know what I mean."

"They've moved on, have they?" Ash hid his disappointment.

"Just this morning." Oscar slapped at a fly on the plank and missed. "All save for one."

Ash almost choked on the whiskey he was swallowing. Coughing to clear his throat, he said, "There is one still here?"

"They took turns poking Big Ears Alice. One had her three times or more and then wanted another dip. Their

boss said he could catch up and him and the rest left."
Oscar jerked a thumb at a doorway to the back. "The
one who didn't is back there now, the randy goat. Between you and me, he's got peculiar taste in women.
She's as ugly as a stump and just lies there when you
poke her."

Ash was hardly listening. Setting down the glass, he
drew his Remington and cocked it.

"Hold on. What do you need that for?"

Ash pointed it at him. "Stay right where you are and
keep your mouth shut. I have business with that gent
in the back."

"I don't want no killing."

"What I do depends on him."

"I hate cleaning up blood. It gets all over everything
and half the time the stain won't come out."

Ash wagged the Remington. "Stay still and keep
quiet. Don't buck me or you'll regret it."

"I don't much like being threatened."

Staying to one side of the doorway so he wasn't silhouetted against the dim light, Ash peered down a
short hall. The door at the end was shut. From beyond
it came a rhythmic creaking.

"Who the hell are you, anyway? What is this about?"

"I said to hush." Ash crept toward the door. A voice
reached him, a woman's. He couldn't quite make out
what she was saying.

The creaking grew louder. Bed springs, unless Ash
missed his guess. He placed an ear to the door.

"That's it, baby. Nice and easy. We want you to last
this time. There's never any need to rush with sweet
Alice."

Ash gripped the latch. He eased it until it clicked,
then slowly pushed.

The room had a bed and a small table with a lamp and a chair. It reeked worse than the saloon. On the bed were the man and Big Ears Alice. The man had his back to the door. Both were buck naked. The woman's dress and corset were in a pile. The man's clothes had been flung every which way. The bed creaked to the grind of the man's hips. Ash could see Alice's face over the man's shoulder and she appeared downright bored. She caught sight of him at the same instant and her eyes widened. She had the good sense not to cry out.

"Maybe you better hurry, sweetie."

Her customer grunted.

Ash sidled around. The man looked to be about forty, with bushy brown hair and a mustache but no beard. He was well muscled except at the gut where he had a pot. His eyes were closed and he was lost in the moment. Ash let him keep at it.

Alice stared at Ash. "That's it, Cleve. Make your sweet Alice happy. You're so big and strong. I swear, I never met a man like you in all my born days."

She stifled a yawn.

Ash sat in the chair and trained the Remington on Cleve.

"That's it, honey. Yes. Yes. Like that. I'm almost there. Just a little bit more."

Cleve became a steam-engine piston.

Ash fought down a laugh. He winked at Alice and she grinned. Her teeth weren't half bad.

"Yes. Yes. Oh yes. Oh, Cleve. Can you feel it? Can you? Now honey. Oh, now."

Cleve turned red in the face and thrust madly. He gasped a final "Uhhh!" and collapsed on top of her, sucking air like a bellows. "Alice, you are the best," he said sleepily.

"Thank you, sugar. But I wouldn't doze off right now if I were you."

"Why not?"

"We have company."

Cleve's eyes snapped open. They were brown and beady and narrowed in anger when he saw Ash. Slowly sitting up, Cleve declared, "Mister, you better have a damn good reason for coming in here."

"I do," Ash assured him.

"You couldn't wait your turn?"

"It's not the lady I'm interested in. It's you." Ash cocked the Remington. "You ride with Ben Sharkey. I'm trying to find him. Tell me where he is and I'll leave you to your pleasure."

Cleve showed no fear. "Are you the law?"

"I was once," Ash admitted. "Not anymore."

"Why are you after Ben, then?"

"He shot me. I aim to return the favor." Ash aimed at the man's foot. "You have until I count to five."

"Go to hell. Ben Sharkey is my pard."

"One."

"Ben and me have ridden to hell and back again. I'd walk through burning brambles for him."

"Two."

Alice tried to slide out from under Cleve but he wasn't budging. "Damn it. I don't want to be shot too."

"He's bluffing," Cleve told her. "No lawdog, ex or otherwise, shoots unarmed people."

"Three."

Cleve shook a fist. "It won't work. Save it for them as is green behind the ears. I'm going to get up and pull my britches on." He placed his right foot on the floor.

"Four."

Cleve put his other foot down, his arms out from his

sides. "See? I am behaving. Now you can holster your six-shooter and we'll talk about this civilized-like."

"You should borrow Alice's ears. They work better than yours," Ash responded. "Five," he said, and fired.

The slug caught Cleve in the ankle and went all the way through. Bone, blood and skin spattered the floor and the underside of the bed. Cleve screeched, fell onto his side and clutched his leg. Swearing and snarling, he rolled wildly about, spittle dribbling from his mouth.

Alice shrank against the wall and pulled the blanket to her chin. "Darn it, Mister. Oscar will make me clean that up."

Ash cocked the Remington again. He didn't think Cleve would hear it over the cussing but Cleve stopped thrashing and gave him a venomous look.

"I will see you dead for that if it's the last thing I ever do. So help me God, I will."

Ash aimed at the other foot. "It's not smart to threaten someone who is holding a pistol on you when you're unarmed and bare-assed and bleeding like a stuck pig." He stood. "To be fair I will ask you one more time. Where is Sharkey bound?"

Cleve spat at him.

"I have sometimes wondered," Ash said patiently, "if outlaws don't leave their brains in their diapers. This time I'll only count to three. Unless you're partial to crutches, you should start wagging your tongue."

"Mister, I'd rather die than help you."

"One."

Big Ears Alice extended an arm toward Cleve. "Tell him, for God's sake. I don't want you shot again."

Cleve gave her a kindly look. "Thank you for your concern."

"Concern, hell. It'll just make a bigger mess and be more work for me. Don't be a jackass. Do as the man wants."

"Two," Ash said.

Cleve squared his shoulders and sneered. "I'm no weak sister. I've been kicked by a stallion and had my leg broke. I've been bit by a dog down to my wrist bone. I've been stabbed by a redskin and lived to blow out his wick. I've been shot once before too. Do your worst."

"It's your foot," Ash said, and shot it.

At the blast Cleve did more flopping and swearing and bleeding. When he exhausted himself, he lay quaking in agony and hissing through his teeth. He stopped hissing to say, "Kill you, kill you, kill you."

Ash cocked the Remington.

"Now you just hold it right there!" Cleve shouted, holding out a scarlet-smeared hand. "You have shot me enough for one day."

"Ben Sharkey."

"All right. All right." Cleve sagged and bowed his head. "I know when I'm licked." The next instant he hurtled across the floor at his pants. He flung them aside, exposing a gun belt and a holster with an ivory-handled Colt. Like lightning he snatched the Colt out and up and swung around.

Ash shot him in the head. He was so mad at being thwarted that he went over and shot him twice more between the eyes. Then he kicked the body, not once but several times.

"He can't say you didn't warn him," Big Ears Alice said.

Ash made for the door.

"What's your hurry, big man?"

"I'm not in the mood." Ash hadn't been since he was shot. He didn't rightly know why.

"I was wondering how much the information you want is worth to you," Alice said. "Fifty dollars, maybe?"

Ash still had the money he had taken from Lonnie. He had been debating with himself over whether he should spend it or return it. "Are you saying you know where I can find Ben Sharkey?"

"I heard them talk. I know where they're headed." Alice held out her palm. "But it's not free."

"I can't afford fifty," Ash lied.

"How much can you afford?"

"Ten."

Alice snorted. "Hell, that's hardly worth the bother you've put me to. You killed stupid there. You made a mess of my room. The least you could do is make it worth my while."

"Twenty is as high as I can go and at that I'll be broke." Ash realized he was making a habit of stretching the truth lately, something he never did when he wore a badge.

"I suppose that will have to do." Alice let the blanket sag, inadvertently showing most of her bosom. "Everyone is always telling me I'm too kindhearted for my own good."

"This better be the truth."

"As God is my witness," Alice vowed. "I heard Ben Sharkey say that Texas had become too hot for him. He robbed a bank and he shot a lawman dead and . . ." She stopped. "Say, was that you? You don't look dead to me."

"Get to the damn point."

"You don't have to be a grump about it. I said I'd tell

you and I will. Sharkey and his men are interested in having a grand time. They're heading for a place where the whores wear finery and the whiskey is imported and they can live high on the hog for as long as their ill-gotten gains last. I do mean high. A mile up, to be exact."

Ash knew of only one city that fit. "Denver."

"Denver," Big Ears Alice confirmed. She showed more of her bosom. "Now that you know, can I interest you in a poke?"

Chapter 10

The gateway to the Rocky Mountains, fittingly enough, was at an elevation of 5,280 feet. The Mile-High City, everyone called it.

A stepping-off point for gold and silver seekers, it was famed for its crisp mountain air and clear mountain water.

Denver was famous for other aspects too. Its lawless element, for one thing.

While cow towns like Dodge and Abilene were written about more often in the newspapers, Denver's lovers of illicit pastimes thrived in their own special part of the city.

It was known as the Street of a Thousand Sinners, in reality a lust-and-crime-plagued district of four square blocks. Bawdy houses and gambling dens abounded. No one had taken a census but it was estimated that more than a thousand fallen doves plied their sensual wares in those four blocks. Add in the gamblers, footpads, confidence swindlers, toughs and badmen, and it was no wonder it was said that if someone wanted a foretaste of hell, all they had to do was visit the Street of a Thousand Sinners.

Denver had its law-abiding element, too. The fact was, the law-abiding outnumbered the lawless by a substantial margin. The rest of the city had little crime and was safe to visit any hour of the day or night.

Denver had done as many cities and towns did: they denied their dark underbelly by confining it to a small area, effectively hiding their vices from those who preferred to pretend vice didn't exist. Politicians could crow they had made the streets safe. Churchgoers could go to and from their houses of worship secure in the knowledge that the taint of sin wasn't in plain sight. As the saying went, out of sight, out of mind.

All of this went through Asher Thrall's head as he rode down Holladay Street. Holladay was the hub of the vice district. He had heard about it but never visited it before, and he had to admit, it was a wonderment to behold.

A bubbling stream of humanity plied the streets and boardwalks. Many were women in bright dresses and bonnets who were taking time off from their pastimes of parting randy men from their money and doing what most women everywhere most liked to do: shop. The men were a mix of townsmen and dandies, miners and cowhands and others.

There was a city ordinance against wearing firearms and Ash saw none in evidence. He wasn't fooled. Most men carried a weapon. He had unbuckled the Remington revolver and placed it in his saddlebags but under his jacket was the Remington pocket pistol he had taken from Lonnie.

Ash was weary. It had been a long ride. Most of the

way he had to endure the blazing summer heat. It didn't help that his attacks were more frequent and lasted longer. More and more he relied on the morphine. So much so, he was running low and needed to get his hands on more.

Ash had injected before riding in. A pleasant sort of dreaminess had him in its grip, a sense that all was right with the world.

The gaudy signs delighted him. There was Lizzie Preston's, where a young lady stood on the porch welcoming visitors with a smile. The House of Rose had a rose garden out front. On the wide front door of the House of Mirrors hung a gilded mirror. Perhaps the most elegant establishment, and certainly the most famed of the bawdy houses, was Mattie Silk's. It was rumored that Mattie's clientele included many of the city's most prominent and more than a few high in state government.

Not to be outdone, the gambling houses were riots of bustle and noise. The Palace Variety Theater and Gambling Parlor was one of the more ornate. The Progressive Club catered to the rich. The Cricket Club, run by two gents from England, was known for its elegance.

Ash drank it all in. He wondered why he had never visited places like this before. Most of his adult life he had stuck to the straight and narrow. He'd always done what he believed was right. Oh, he'd visited ladies of ill repute but not when he was married. Those were minor steps off the primrose path. Never once did he wholeheartedly plunge in.

The thought troubled him. Here he was, on the brink of eternity, and there was so much of life he hadn't tasted, so much he hadn't done. He watched two ladies stroll by arm in arm and was filled with regret.

Ash caught himself and reined to a hitch rail. He mustn't second guess himself. That path could lead a man to blow his brains out. Climbing down, he looped the reins. His rifle in one hand and his saddlebags over his shoulder, he went up a short flight of steps and through a door. Above it was a sign: FRANNIE'S BOARD-INGHOUSE. ROOMS BY THE DAY, WEEK OR MONTH.

Across a small but lavish parlor was a counter. Behind it stood a buxom brunette with broad hips and full lips. She bestowed a friendly smile, and when he put his hand on the counter, she put her hands on his.

"How do you do? All that dust, you've come a far piece."

Ash was about to inform her he came all the way from Texas but that might not be a good idea. "That I have, ma'am. I'd be obliged for a room. One that won't cost me a lot and is private."

"All our rooms are private," she said, and her finger caressed a circle on the back of his hand.

"Would you be Frannie?"

"Indeed I would. Frannie Crowse. I came here seven years ago and stayed to make my fortune."

"Have you?" Ash teased.

"Not quite." Frannie laughed. "But I have enough squirreled away that I won't lack in old age."

Ash took on a room for a week. He let her know he might stay longer and she said that wouldn't pose a problem. It was comfortably furnished, with a wine red carpet and red draperies and a painting of a nude woman in a revealing pose.

Frannie noticed his glance. "She's some looker, isn't she? You wouldn't know it to look at me now but I was a lot like her when I was her age."

"I took you for twenty-two at the most," Ash said.

"Oh, I like you." Frannie patted his cheek. "I'm twice that, but keep it between us. A few of my customers think I'm Venus in the flesh."

"Tell me something. If you just got to town and had a full poke to spend, where would you head?"

"Are you talking about yourself? You gave me the notion you don't have much money."

"Some friends of mine came on ahead of me." Ash made up another story. "I didn't think it would be hard to find them but now I see I was wrong."

"Mister, you could look for a month of Sundays and not come across them. I wish you luck." Frannie tapped her chin, then rattled off a list of establishments he should visit. "Anything else?"

Ash remembered his supply of morphine. "As a matter of fact, there is. Where's the nearest sawbones?"

The doctor's shingle was a small board with PHYSICIAN scrawled on it.

Ash used the brass knocker. He was mildly surprised when a pretty young woman in a white uniform opened the door. "I thought this was the doctor's."

"It is, sir. Please come in."

A foyer led to a waiting room. Several other patients were seated on a plush bench. Ash waited his turn, and when he was finally admitted, shook the hand of Dr. Wilson, a younger version of Doc Peters, complete with spectacles. Ash explained about the shooting and the pressure. Wilson had him strip to the waist and examined him. When he said Ash could get dressed, Ash responded with, "So you can see why I need more morphine. I'm running low and wouldn't like to make do without."

Dr. Wilson was taking notes. He stopped writing and leaned back in his chair. "Before I prescribe more I have a few questions."

"What about?"

"You."

"Me? What do you want to know? If you don't believe what I've told you, you can check with Doc Peters or George Blocker."

"Oh, I believe you. Your wound, your irregular heartbeat, the lividity of your skin and other factors confirm your account. No, what I want to talk about is the morphine."

"I don't savvy," Ash admitted.

"How long have you been using it?"

"About two months. A little more."

"When you first started how often did you use it?"

Ash shrugged. "Twice a day, if that. It depended on the pain. Some days were worse than others."

"How often do you use it now?"

"Three or four times a day but again it depends on the pain." To justify his need, Ash went on. "But you've got to understand. The attacks come one after the other and the pain has gotten a lot worse. A few times . . ." Ash hesitated. "A few times I thought about ending it."

"I see." Dr. Wilson wrote something down. "Would it be safe to say that without the morphine you wouldn't want to live?"

"I don't have long left as it is," Ash said bitterly.

"I am sorry about that. I truly am. There's nothing I can do to help you in that regard. Your Doc Peters was right. You'd need the best surgeon there is, and there are no guarantees."

"I've been all through that." Ash didn't care to go through it again.

"Yes. Yes. I'm sorry. Back to the morphine." Wilson paused. "Did Doctor Peters discuss the tolerance factor with you?"

"The what?"

"The ability of the human body to tolerate various substances. Physicians call that tolerance. It's a fundamental medical principle."

Ash gestured in irritation. "Make it simple, Doc. I never got around to reading a dictionary."

"Sorry. It works like this. The more of a given drug a person uses, the more their body becomes used to it."

"Like whiskey, you mean?"

"An excellent example, yes. Someone who has never let liquor touch his lips will get drunk on one glass. If that same person keeps on drinking day after day, he builds up a tolerance to where he needs to drink an entire bottle to feel the same as he did when he had that first glass."

"Morphine is the same?"

"I'm afraid so. The more of it you use, the more your body becomes accustomed, and the more you'll need to cope with the pain." Wilson frowned. "It's a vicious cycle. Eventually you could reach the point where no amount of morphine helps."

"I doubt I'll live that long."

"Perhaps not. But there is something else to consider. Have you ever heard of soldier's disease?"

Ash grinned. "The one men get from women?"

Dr. Wilson smiled. "Not a sexual disease, no. Soldier's disease has to do with morphine. During the war between the North and the South thousands of soldiers were wounded. Some lost arms. Some lost legs. To cope they were given morphine. After the war they went on using it. Even when the pain from their wounds had gone away, they went on using it."

In a burst of intuition Ash divined the reason but he asked anyway, his mouth suddenly dry. "Why?"

"They couldn't live without it. They became addicted, Mr. Thrall. The morphine became everything to them. They didn't eat enough. They didn't sleep enough. Gradually their bodies wasted away but they didn't care. All they wanted was morphine."

Ash digested the revelation and let a wry smile curl his lips. "You say it took a while? I won't have to worry about it, then."

"There's evidence to suggest the addiction takes hold quickly. No one knows exactly how many doses, but I dare say that two months of use might be enough."

Ash didn't say anything.

"I took morphine once myself," Dr. Wilson related. "I was chopping wood and missed a swing and cut my leg. The morphine killed the pain, as I knew it would. It also did more." He seemed to grope for words. "It made me feel glorious. Like I was floating in a tub of pure rapture, if that makes any sense."

"It does."

"I realized then and there how easily those soldiers became addicted. Or how anyone else could." Wilson gave Ash a pointed look.

"Once again, Doc, I won't live long enough for it to matter."

"Maybe not. I hope it doesn't matter, for our sake. You have enough to deal with without that. It's not pleasant to go through. You might think it would be, given the pleasure the morphine produces. But most describe it as a living hell."

Ash shuddered.

Dr. Wilson gestured. "So, yes, Mr. Thrall. I'll give you the morphine you want. Against my better judgment, you understand. A normal wound, I wouldn't. Yours isn't normal. You are an exceptional case and merit special treatment."

"I'm obliged." Ash was torn between keen anticipation at getting more and dread at the consequences.

Wilson started to get up but stopped and sank back down. "May I speak freely for a moment?"

"I thought that's what you have been doing."

"You have my deepest sympathy. I know your life has become a living nightmare, but I fear the worst is yet to come."

"Oh?"

Dr. Wilson nodded. "It might become a contest, if you will, to see which kills you first, the slug lodged in your heart or the morphine. You'll need a will of iron to cope. It could well be . . ." Wilson gnawed on his lower lip. "It could well be that the alternative you mentioned a while ago is your only way out."

"The what?"

"Ending it."

"Oh."

Wilson tried to lighten the mood by joking, "Or you might want to pick a fight with the worst killer you can find and hope he does it for you."

Deep in Ash's mind the seed of an idea took root.

Chapter 11

It was worse than looking for a needle in a haystack. At least haystacks stayed still.

Two weeks went by and Ash couldn't find a trace of Ben Sharkey. He went everywhere. He asked bartenders, he asked brothel madams, he asked street vendors. He used he money he took from Lonnie to lubricate tongues and to keep them quiet about the lubricating. He became angry and then frustrated. Either Sharkey's gang had left Denver or he had been lied to and Sharkey never intended to come to Denver in the first place.

Two weeks and one day after his visit to Dr. Wilson, Ash got ready for a night out on the town. He was going to relax and enjoy himself. For one night he would try to forget about Sharkey and forget his vengeance. For one night he would do the things other men were doing. He would drink and gamble and find himself a willing lady.

Ash hadn't had an attack in several days. He had plenty of morphine, courtesy of Dr. Wilson, but he didn't use it that evening. Both physicians had warned him that alcohol and morphine might not mix well, and Ash dearly wanted to get drunk. A man needed to now and then.

Ash took a bath for the first time since his hunt began. He shaved. He put on his best suit. He brushed and polished his boots. He left his Remington revolver and holster in his room but wore the Remington pocket pistol under his jacket. Law or no law, he wasn't going anywhere unarmed.

The streets bustled with Denver's nightlife. Ash breathed deep of the cool mountain air and drank in the sight of the seething sea of humanity. God, it felt good to be alive. Then he thought of the lead touching his heart and bitter regret smothered his elation.

Ash hooked his thumbs in his vest and strolled along, letting whim dictate the direction he took. He passed gambling dens. He passed saloons. He passed bawdy houses where ladies smiled and beckoned and offered him their wares.

It was intoxicating. Excitement bubbled in Ash at the tantalizing prospects the evening held. Those who walked the straight and narrow would say he had strayed off the primrose path and was adrift on the dark currents of sin.

So what? he asked himself. What did he have to lose? He was dying. Besides, he'd never realized how grand sinning could be, how it could get into the blood and fill a person with a zest for life and a hunger for the unknown.

Ash grinned and whistled and was in fine fettle when he came to a saloon tucked between two hotels. Finnegan's, it was called. Owned by an Irishman, Ash reckoned. The exterior was tastefully painted a dark green with brown trim. The door opened onto carpeted elegance. Calling it a saloon was an injustice. This was an establishment for those who took their drinking seriously.

Ash walked to the felt-covered bar and a bartender dressed better than he was came over and took his order. He asked for the best whiskey they had.

Leaning back on his elbows, he sipped and savored while surveying the card games and the faro table and a game of dice. All done quietly, with none of the rowdy behavior one would expect. "I like this place," he said out loud. He liked it a whole lot.

"Do you, now?" asked a man in a distinct brogue. He wore a bowler and a suit and had mutton chops and a bushy mustache. Smiling, he offered a calloused hand. "O'Flynn's the name. I'm a regular. Don't believe I've ever set eyes on you before."

Ash didn't take offense at the man's familiarity. Quite the contrary. He shook and offered to buy O'Flynn a drink and O'Flynn accepted.

"Just passing through, are you?"

Ash was about to explain about Sharkey but changed his mind. To hell with it. For one night Ben Sharkey didn't exist. "Yes. On my way to California," he lied for no particular reason.

"Got the family with you, I'd imagine?" O'Flynn good-naturedly asked.

"Family?" Ash said, and snorted. "God, I'm glad I'm not married. It would make this hell even worse."

"How's that?"

"Nothing," Ash said quickly. He didn't want false sympathy from a stranger.

"I have a family," O'Flynn revealed. "A darling wife and five wee ones. I love them dearly but the wife can be a nag when she's not being darling and the wee ones can drive a man to pulling out his hair. So I come here every evening for a few drafts of the elixir of life and then it's back to the banshees."

Ash laughed. "I envy you."

"I guess I am blessed." O'Flynn drained his glass. "Say, how would you like to join some friends and me for a friendly game? The stakes aren't high and the company is as polite as you'll find anywhere."

"Sounds good."

"Follow me, then." O'Flynn winked at the bartender and walked down the bar and around toward a door at the back.

"The game isn't here?"

"Sure it is. In the back, in a room we'll have to ourselves. We'll play in fine style."

O'Flynn wasn't exaggerating. The room had thick carpet and a mahogany table and soft chairs instead of the usual hardbacks. The four men in the room proved as friendly as O'Flynn. They were dressed in good clothes and were smoking expensive cigars. Ash and O'Flynn claimed chairs and Ash took out his poke. He had plenty of money left and his poke bulged from the wad of bills and the coins.

"Now, me boyos," O'Flynn addressed the others. "This is my new friend, Mr. Thrall. I've invited him to a friendly game and that's what we'll have."

"No problem there," said a round-faced gent whose balding pate gleamed in the lamplight. "We are always as friendly as can be."

For over an hour Ash immersed himself in good company and good whiskey. He won a few hands; he lost a few. He was at ease and content and had no objections when the man with the shiny head suggested they raise the stakes. He won a few more hands and then lost all he had won and began to eat into his poke, only ten dollars or so at a time so he didn't think much of it. Then the man with the shiny head suggested they raise the stakes even more. The others agreed and looked at Ash.

Ash deliberated. He needed the money he had left. He couldn't conduct his hunt without it. Smiling and shaking his head, he said, "It's getting a little too rich for my blood. I'm bowing out."

"Whatever you think best." O'Flynn pushed back his chair. "Tell you what. I should be heading home my own self, so how about we go up front and I buy you a last drink?"

Ash agreed and put his poke in his pocket. He stood and turned and was jolted by a hard blow to the back of his head that pitched him to the floor. Pain made his senses swim. He was vaguely aware of hands on his arms and of another hand groping under his jacket.

"Got it." That was O'Flynn.

"You and Harry deal with him and get back here quick. The night is young yet. We can fleece two or three more sheep."

Ash kept his eyes closed. He figured that they figured he was unconscious.

Two of them carried him out and turned toward the rear of the saloon.

"For a big man he's uncommon light."

"He has a sickly look about him," O'Flynn said. "Noticed it right off but I didn't pry."

"Hope whatever he has isn't catching. I could do without consumption, thank you very much."

"You worry too much, Harry."

"Worry keeps a man breathing."

"Put down his legs and get the door," O'Flynn directed.

"Is it the creek with him, then?"

"We drowned the last one. Another so soon might arouse suspicion. We'll knife this one and leave him in that alley off Colvert Street."

Ash was deposited on the floor none too gently. A door opened and a rush of fresh air helped steady his swirling head. They picked him up, carried him out and set him down again.

"Where in hell is the buckboard?" Harry said. "Doyle was supposed to leave it here when he got back."

"Damn. It's probably out front. Watch our pigeon while I go fetch it," O'Flynn said.

"There's no hurry. No one ever comes back here."

"Even so."

Ash listened to O'Flynn's fading footsteps, then cracked his eyelids. Faint light from windows cast the alley in gray relief. Harry had produced a tobacco pouch and a pipe. Ash marveled at how casual they were about murder and robbery. They'd grown sloppy and it was about to cost them. They hadn't searched him for weapons; he still had the Remington pocket pistol.

Grinding his teeth against the pounding in his head, Ash bided his time to regain his strength. He had been a fool. He'd trusted someone and look at where it got him.

The man called Harry filled the pipe's bowl and replaced the pouch. He went to light the tobacco. A woman laughed somewhere close by and he glanced down the alley but showed no alarm.

Ash slid his free hand under him and went to push up. He couldn't. A feeling of weakness had come over him, whether from the blow or his condition, he couldn't say. He tried again and once more and reluctantly let his muscles relax.

Harry commenced to pace. Puffing clouds of smoke, he walked about ten feet and came back again. "Where the hell is he?" he muttered with the pipe stem in his mouth.

Ash was glad it was taking O'Flynn so long. He attempted to rise once more and this time tingled with delight when his body reacted as it should. He was about to stand and go up behind Harry when clattering and rattling at the far end of the alley signaled O'Flynn's return.

"About damn time," Harry said.

Ash rolled onto his back. The clattering drowned out the click of the pocket pistol's hammer. Holding it in both hands, he aimed at Harry's back but didn't shoot. Harry would be second. He wanted the other one to die first, the one who had played him for a jackass.

Out of the dark materialized the horse and the buckboard. O'Flynn had his bowler pushed back on his head at a jaunty angle, and was whistling. "Here we are," he needlessly announced.

"Took you long enough."

"A parked wagon had boxed it in. They were loading a heavy crate and I had to wait."

Ash aimed at the pale moon of a face between the muttonchops. He fired and had the satisfaction of seeing a hole appear smack between O'Flynn's eyes. Harry spun and clawed a hand under his jacket. Ash shot him in the chest. He had aimed at the heart, but he must have missed because Harry's hand reappeared holding a pistol. Ash shot him again. That should have been enough, but Harry took a staggering step toward him.

"I don't die easy!"

Ash shot him in the face. The lead did the job but Harry fell forward, not backward. Ash threw himself to one side. He wasn't quite fast enough. The lifeless form fell on top of his legs. The man wasn't big or heavy but when Ash went to push him off, his chest flared with pain and the all-too-familiar feeling of pressure.

"No." Ash fought down panic and pushed harder. He had to get out of there. Their friends would come, and if they caught him helpless, they were bound to finish him off.

Loud voices broke out, shouts from both ends of the alley.

Sweat poured from Ash as he exerted his sinews to their utmost. The body rolled off and he lurched to his feet. The pressure persisted, making it hard to breathe. The beat of his heart was like the beat of a sledge on metal.

More voices rose, this time from inside the saloon.

Ash cast wildly about. He had nowhere to hide and was in no shape to run. He took a wobbly step and heard the patter of feet running down the alley. Without thinking he dropped onto all fours and scrambled under the buckboard. None too soon. Legs appeared even as the back door to the saloon was flung wide and out spilled more light.

"What the hell!"

"Two men have been shot!"

Other people spoke, men and women, a babble that grew as more and more arrived, both from within and without.

"Anyone know who these men are?"

"Someone should go for the law."

The crowd kept growing. On hands and knees Ash

moved to the rear of the buckboard. He had been lucky in that the shots hadn't spooked the horse. Noise and commotion didn't seem to bother it.

"Any sign of the shooter?" a man asked.

"He must have run off," speculated another.

Ash peeked out. Most of the crowd ringed the front of the buckboard and the crumpled figures. Few were at the rear and those that were had their backs to him. Holding the pocket pistol under his jacket, Ash eased out. He slowly rose, using the buckboard for support.

The pressure was worse. The pain too. Fortunately no one paid any attention when Ash turned and made for the end of the alley. He had to take small steps. Each threatened to be his last.

Somehow Ash made it to his boardinghouse. He sighed with profound relief when he closed his door behind him. He sat on the bed, opened the kit the doctor gave him and injected morphine. The bliss that soon came over him was wonderful. He sank onto his back and floated on the inner tides of a pain-free sea.

Ash made two decisions then and there. First, he would never again venture anywhere without morphine. Second, he would never again trust another human being. He had learned his lesson at last.

It was dog eat dog in this world. Only a fool believed otherwise.

Chapter 12

Ash woke up and heard snoring. It perplexed him. He didn't understand how he could be awake and snore. In his befuddled state it was a few seconds before he realized it was someone else who was rumbling like an avalanche.

He looked around. He was in his room in the boardinghouse. Pale light framed the window. He figured it must be close to dawn.

Another snore caused Ash to turn. Frannie was on her back, naked as the day she was born, her mouth agape. They must have made love but he didn't remember it. His head felt thick and sluggish. His mouth was filled with invisible cotton.

On the small table was the explanation: an empty bottle of whiskey. He had been doing a lot of drinking lately. A *lot* of drinking. His days and nights were fogs of forgetfulness. He knew he shouldn't but he couldn't stop. It helped with the hurt. Not the hurt of the lead lodged near his heart but the deeper hurt of how damn cruel life was. None of it made sense anymore. Everything he'd taken for granted, everything he'd believed, had been turned on its head.

Ash sank back down. He tried to shut out Frannie's snoring but couldn't. He got up and went to the window. Parting the curtains, he looked out. He had been right. Dawn was breaking. The street was nearly deserted. A milk wagon rattled by. A cat went slinking past. Pigeons had roosted on the roof across the street.

Another snore brought a frown of irritation. Ash went around the bed and cuffed Frannie on her thigh. She mumbled and stirred but didn't wake up. He cuffed her harder.

"What the hell? That hurt."

"I want to be alone."

Frannie smacked her lips and groaned. "Damn. That was some night we had, wasn't it? You're a wild one when you get fired up. I feel as if I've been through the wringer."

"Didn't you hear me?"

"What, you're kicking me out? That's a hell of a note." Frannie slowly sat up. "I don't know as I like being treated like a floozy."

"It's not that," Ash said. But it was. He suddenly couldn't stand the sight of her and wanted her gone.

"Oh. It's that other thing. The bullet."

Ash gave a start. God in heaven, had he told her? "What bullet?"

Frannie smacked her lips again and yawned and scratched herself.

"The one in your chest. The one the doctors can't get out. Amazes me how you can have it in you yet make love like you do. I swear, you acted like you were starved for it."

Ash gripped her wrist. "Promise me you won't tell anyone else."

"Let go. You're hurting me."

"Promise."

"All right, all right." Frannie tugged loose of his grasp. "Damn it. You're a bear in the morning, aren't you? I don't know as I'll let you have me again if this is how you're going to be." She got out of bed and picked up a robe lying on the floor.

"You weren't wearing a dress?"

"Hell. How drunk were you? No, I couldn't sleep and came in to share a few. One thing led to another, and—" Annie grinned. She touched his cheek.

"All in all I had a good time."

Ash went to the door and opened it. "Thanks."

About to tie the robe shut, Frannie frowned. "No need to be so cold. I'm your friend." She patted him as she walked past. "See you later. Try to find your smile."

Ash threw the bolt and went back to bed. He lay staring at the ceiling. It was about time he admitted the truth. He wasn't going to find Sharkey. Not in Denver. He had come all this way for nothing.

Ash closed his eyes. So, what next? he asked himself. It was pointless to stick around. He'd run out of money, and then what? Revenge had driven him for so long that it was all he had. Without it his life was empty. All he was doing was waiting around to die.

Ash remembered what Dr. Wilson had said. A sudden resolve came over him. He got up, filled the washbowl with water from the pitcher and washed and shaved. It had been so long since he used a razor that it was dull. It hurt to scrape off the thick stubble but he didn't care. What was a little pain when he was still breathing?

Ash dressed in his best suit. He donned his hat. He left and made for a restaurant he knew of. Along the way he passed a boy hawking newspapers and bought a copy of the *Rocky Mountain News*. At the restaurant he took a corner table, ordered eggs and bacon and ham, and sat sipping black coffee and reading.

The front page was filled with an account of a stage holdup, the work of the Fraziers, three brothers who helped themselves to the strongbox and all the valuables the passengers had. The *News* lamented that the Fraziers were the scourge of the territory and took the law to task for not bringing them to justice.

Ash's food arrived. He folded the newspaper and pondered while he ate. When he was done he asked the waitress how to get to the marshal's. The streets were filling. He ambled along, taking his time.

As law offices went, it wasn't much. Two desks and a rack for rifles and shotguns and a tired deputy who looked up from *The Black Princess*, an old Beadle's dime novel he was reading. "What can I do for you, Mister? If it's the marshal you need to see, he won't be in for a couple of hours yet. He had to go to the dentist."

"I want to know about the Frazier brothers."

The deputy had gone back to reading but glanced up sharply. "What the hell for?"

"I read about the stage holdup in the morning paper."

"Oh, that." The deputy placed the dime novel, open, on the desk. "Did you know someone who was on it? A passenger was pistol-whipped when he wouldn't hand over his diamond stickpin but he'll live. The rest weren't hurt."

"The Fraziers have been at it a while, I take it?"

"Hell, those three have been terrorizing the territory

for years. Got their start back during the gold rush. They'd hear of someone striking it rich and go rob him. Helped themselves to mine payrolls, marched into gambling halls and took all they could carry, those sorts of things."

"Have they killed many folks?"

The deputy shrugged. "Five or six or maybe seven, the best I can recollect. The marshal would know better than me. He has a head for stuff like that."

"So you'd say the Fraziers are about as mean as they come?"

"There are worse, I suppose, but they are mean enough." The deputy leaned back. "Say, what are they to you anyhow?"

"The newspaper mentioned a reward."

"So that's it. You're a bounty man. There's a thousand dollars on each of their heads but it's not likely you'll collect."

"Why not?"

"The same reason no one else has. The Fraziers know the mountains better than anyone. After they strike they disappear into the high country where no one can find them." The deputy held up a hand when Ash went to speak. "Yes, trackers have been brought in and dogs have been tried and it's always the same. They lose the trail."

"Have you gone after them yourself?"

The deputy blinked. "Up into the mountains? Mister, there's a thing called jurisdiction. You might never have heard of it but it means that the marshal enforces the law as far as the city limits."

"What about the sheriff?"

"His jurisdiction is Arapaho County. Those mountains you see when you walk out that door and look to the west? They're not in it." The deputy smirked at his display of wit.

"Other sheriffs, then?"

The deputy's smirk became a frown. "I don't much like being pestered with so many questions so early in the day. Why is this so important to you?"

Ash decided to own up. "I'm planning to go after the Fraziers. I can use all the information I can get."

"Then I was right. You *are* after the money on their heads."

"No."

"Did they kill kin of yours? Did they rob you or someone you know?"

"No."

"Then why, for God's sake?"

Ash gazed out the window at the flow of people and riders and wagons, and sighed. "I've got nothing better to do."

The deputy rose and came around the desk. "Listen, Mister. Whatever you've been drinking, stop. It's got you addlepated. No one goes looking for the Fraziers without good cause. Or didn't you hear the part about them being killers?"

"Thanks for your help." Ash touched his hat brim. He was surprised when the deputy put a hand on his arm.

"Hold on. Are you hankering to get yourself bucked out in gore? Because the Fraziers will sure as hell oblige you."

"I have it to do."

The deputy looked into Ash's eyes, his forehead furrowing. "Suit yourself. Then listen. Park County is where they've done most of their robbing and killing. Head southwest, up into the mountains. There's a small town called Kester. Ask around for an old Ute who goes by the name of Broken Nose. If anyone can help you find the Fraziers, it's him. He knows the high country as good as they do, if not better. He used to be the best tracker in the whole territory besides."

"Used to be?"

The deputy hesitated. "Like I said, he's old. You might have to talk him into it."

"I'm obliged."

"Save your thanks," the deputy said. "I haven't done you any favors if it lands you in a early grave."

"Not so early," Ash said.

By noon he was ready to ride out. He'd bought supplies and a pack animal to tote them. He wished he'd kept the grulla, but he'd given it to a farmer in a soddy out on the prairie. The farmer had put him up for the night and invited him to supper. The family was so poor that none of the six kids had shoes and the wife owned only one threadbare dress.

Ash vowed it would be his last act of kindness for a while.

The road up into the mountains was well used if rugged. Ash seldom had it to himself. At night he avoided the areas where most camped and picked secluded spots where he wouldn't be bothered. He wasn't feeling sociable.

The mountains were breathtaking. Miles-high peaks reached to the sky, some mantled with snow year-round. Maples and ash were common lower down, spruce and fir higher up. Gambel oaks thrived in the canyons. Golden pea covered the valley floors with bright yellow petals, gaillardias added splashes of color to many a meadow, while the road itself was often bordered by ragwort. Now and then Ash spied bright scarlet flowers that grew in clumps. He had no idea what they were.

Deer were common but stayed shy of the road; too many had fallen to the guns of hungry travelers. Twice Ash spotted elk in the distance. He saw hares and jackrabbits. He grinned at the antics of ground squirrels. Tree squirrels chittered at him from high branches.

The third evening out, Ash glimpsed a pair of coyotes slinking across the road. Shortly thereafter he reined into the woods. A small clearing was suitable for his camp. He gathered enough firewood to last the night and soon had coffee on.

Ash hadn't had an attack in so long, he left the morphine in his saddlebags. He'd begun to toy with the notion that maybe Doc Peters had been wrong. Maybe he'd experienced the last of them. Maybe he'd live to old age, after all.

The crack of a twig brought Ash around, his hand on the Remington.

A man of forty or so, dressed in shabby clothes, froze with his empty hands out. "Have a care there, hoss. I don't mean you harm. As God is my witness, I don't."

"What do you want?" Ash peered into the trees, but the man appeared to be alone.

"I smelled your coffee and thought you might spare a cup." The man stared longingly at the coffeepot. "I'm sorry to impose, but I'm down on my luck." His clothes hung so loosely on his frame that it was obvious he hadn't eaten regular in a long time.

Ash almost told him to turn around and leave. Instead he motioned and said, "Have a seat."

"I thank you." The man smiled and quickly sat close to the fire. "It's nice to know the milk of human kindness hasn't dried up."

Ash thought of his vow and scowled. "It'll be a few minutes yet," he said harshly.

"That's fine. That's fine." The man smiled. "I'm Matthew, by the way. Matthew Waller. I'm on my way to Leadville. The town is booming, folks say, and there are plenty of jobs to be had."

"Denver has plenty of jobs too."

"Leadville is higher and I need high."

"Why?"

Before Waller could answer he broke into a fit of coughing and couldn't stop. Doubling over, he fumbled at a pocket and drew out a handkerchief. Pressing it to his mouth, he suffered a violent coughing fit. When at last the fit subsided and he moved the handkerchief, both it and his mouth were bright red with fresh blood. He wiped it off his lips.

"Consumption?" Ash guessed.

Waller weakly nodded. "Afraid so. That's why I need the high, dry air so much."

"That's what I thought," Ash said, and drew his Remington.

Chapter 13

Matthew Waller recoiled in fear and thrust out his hands. "What do you think you're doing?"

"I can end it for you," Ash said.

Waller cocked his head. "End what?"

"The suffering. The pain. The coughing. The blood. One shot and it's over. One shot and you have peace."

Shaking his head, Waller slowly stood. "I'm leaving. I'm sorry I troubled you."

"I'm serious," Ash said.

"You're insane. I have a wife. We have a baby. I don't want to end it. I want to get a good job so I can provide for them as best I'm able until the end comes."

Ash let his arm dip. "How long do the doctors give you?"

"There's no telling. It could be six months; it could be six years. I'm hoping for the six years. I love my family, Mister, love them a lot." He took a step back. "I aim to go on breathing for as long as I can."

"It doesn't bother you that you're dying?"

"Of course it does. But we all start to die the moment we're born. Our first breath sets us on the road to our last. Me, I'll die sooner than I would have if I hadn't come down with consumption, but the dying is the same whether I'm forty or a hundred." Waller backed to the edge of the clearing and stopped. "The important thing is the living. Long life or short, we shouldn't squander it."

Ash holstered the Remington. "You can come back. I won't shoot you. I promise."

"If it's all the same to you, I think I'll go find coffee elsewhere." With that, Waller wheeled and hastened away.

"Well," Ash said. He opened his saddlebag and took out the morphine kit.

After a few seconds he put it back. From an inside pocket he drew a silver flask, uncorked it and swallowed. The whiskey exploded in his gut with welcome warmth. "Ahhh," he said, and tucked his knees to his chest. He had been sipping all day.

Ash grew drowsy. His stomach growled, but he was in no mood for food. He would turn in early, get plenty of rest and head out before first light. It would be the end of the week before he reached Kester. Not that he was in any great hurry. Time was, he always had a sense of urgency, always felt the need to get things done as quickly as he could. Not anymore.

Ash put a hand to his chest. He was grateful the attacks had stopped. For a while there he never knew but the next day would be his last. He sank back against his saddle and took another swig. "Damn, I'm lonely," he said out loud.

About half an hour had gone by and Ash was on the verge of drifting off when the tramp of feet brought him up on his own. He swooped his right hand to the Remington as half a dozen figures materialized out of the darkness. He was set to draw when he recognized one of them as Matthew Waller. The others wore overalls and flannel and boots and impressed him as being farmers. All except for the man in the lead. Spare and white-haired, the leader wore black save for a white collar, and carried a large book.

"Oh hell," Ash said.

They halted in the circle of light and the parson pointed at Ash. "Is this him, Mr. Waller?"

"It is," Matthew Waller confirmed.

The parson's back stiffened and he raised his voice as if about to launch into a sermon. "Brother, I would have words with you."

"What about?" Ash asked. As if he couldn't guess.

"This man"—the parson jabbed his finger at Waller— "came to our camp asking for coffee. We were happy to show him true Christian charity and offered a bite to eat as well."

"This wasn't my idea," Waller said to Ash.

"Imagine my horror, sir," the parson went on, "when he proceeded to tell us of his encounter with you."

"Go away."

The parson squared his spindly shoulders. "I will do no such thing. I came here to take you to task."

A stocky farmer stirred and wagged a rifle. "We came with him to see that you don't do to him as you threatened to do to Mr. Waller."

Ash sank back down and treated himself to another swallow of coffin varnish. "Life is too ridiculous for words."

"I beg your pardon?" The parson came over to the fire. "I'll thank you to stand and pay attention when I'm talking to you."

"I won't tell you again to go away."

"I'm Reverend Peabody. My flock and I are on our way to the San Luis Valley. Now that the Utes have been tamed, the land they let grow wild can be put to better use."

Ash took the longest swallow yet.

"But that's neither here nor there. I came to ask how dare you treat your fellow man as you treated Mr. Waller? It's obscene, your cavalier disregard for life."

"It seems to me the Almighty has a disregard for it too."

Reverend Peabody was shocked. "Rank blasphemy, sir. Haven't you heard how the good Lord marks the passage of every sparrow? How can you make light of the love he bestows on each and every one of us?"

"Does he bestow pain too? How about Waller's consumption? Did the good Lord bestow that?"

"Have a care, sir."

Ash tried to control his temper, without success. "How dare you. You march in here all high and mighty and preach to me about love and my fellow man. What the hell do you know?"

The stocky farmer came closer. "Here, now. We won't have that kind of talk to a man of the cloth."

Ash didn't take his eyes off the parson. "You say God loves us. Then why does he let us suffer? Where's the love in that?"

"You don't understand."

"I want to, Reverend. So help me, I do." A seething cauldron of emotion washed over Ash. "Explain it to me. Help me to see."

Peabody gestured at the farmers to stay where they were, and squatted. "I don't claim to have all the answers. I used to wrestle with the same issue. Why do bad things happen to good people? Why is there so much suffering on this earth? The Book of Job would have it that suffering is a test of faith. Others say that through suffering we are sanctified in the blood of Christ—"

"Say it plain, Parson. Say it so it makes some kind of sense." Ash desperately yearned to comprehend. He truly did.

"I'm trying," Reverend Peabody replied. "My own belief is that life is like a blacksmith's forge. Just as a blacksmith tempers metal in the heat of his furnace, so does our Maker temper us through our sufferings."

"Hell," Ash said.

"Please be civil. I'm trying the best I know how." Peabody paused. "I sense this is important to you."

"You have no idea."

"The thing to remember is that for all our suffering we also have God's love. He is with us in our afflictions. He suffers as we do."

"You know that for a fact?"

"Scripture says as much, yes," the parson confirmed. "It warms the heart, doesn't it, to know that our Maker suffers as we do?"

"I can't feel the warmth for the pain," Ash said.

"How's that again?"

"Parson, you sit there and tell me that God sticks a knife in our gut and feels the hurt we feel and somehow that makes it right? You call that love? I don't. I call it sticking a knife in our gut."

"We're only human, brother. We can't expect it all to be clear to our small minds."

"So now we're dumb."

Reverend Peabody shook his head. "I didn't say that. I'm only saying that we can't be expected to fully comprehend all there is. There is much about God I don't understand. But there's one thing I'm sure about and that's his love."

"I envy you," Ash said sincerely, and a slight shudder passed through him. "Now I want you to take your farmers and your charity case and get the hell out of here."

"There was no call for that."

"You're not listening, Parson." Ash put the cork in his flask and slid it into his pocket. Rising, he placed his hand on the smooth butt of the Remington. "I won't tell you again. I don't want you here. I don't want the reminder."

"Of what, may I ask?"

"Of what I used to be. Of what I used to believe." Ash shuddered again. "Go, damn it. Or so help me, I'll gun you where you hunker."

Incredibly, Reverend Peabody didn't move. "Surely you wouldn't shoot an unarmed man? A man of God, no less?"

The Remington flashed in the firelight. At the blast, a geyser of dirt spewed an inch from Peabody's foot. The stocky farmer took a step and started to raise his rifle, but froze when the Remington swung toward him.

"I wouldn't."

Reverend Peabody straightened. "Very well. If this is how you want it, we'll leave you in peace."

Ash grunted.

"But before I go I'd like to leave you with a bit of wisdom that might help you in whatever trial you're enduring. Namely, that life is made up of light and dark. Sometimes we get so caught up in the dark we forget there is any light at all."

"Go."

"I'm leaving." Peabody turned and looked over his

shoulder. "I'll pray for you, brother. I'll pray tonight and every night that you come to realize the joy of God's love for us."

"God's idea of love is a forty-five caliber slug and pain. Mine is perfect health and a long happy life."

"You speak in riddles."

"Good night to you, Parson."

The reverend melted into the night and the rest drifted after them. Matthew Waller was the last to go and he said as he departed, "I told them to leave you be but the parson wouldn't listen."

"You're welcome to that coffee if you want."

Waller stopped, his eyebrows nearly meeting over his nose. "You're a strange one. I don't know what to make of you."

"I won't harm you. I promise."

Waller shook his head. "Thanks just the same." He smiled, and the darkness swallowed him.

Ash stared at his Remington. "Just the two of us, eh?" He replaced the spent cartridge and slid the revolver into his holster. Easing onto his back, his saddle for a pillow, he gazed up at the multitude of sparkling stars. "There's some sense to this, is there?" he said, and bitterly laughed.

Ash glanced at his saddlebags. The alcohol hadn't done enough to numb him. He wasn't having an attack but it would sure feel nice to forget for a while.

He reached over and brought out the morphine kit and set it next to him.

One injection was all it would take. He could forget about the parson and the feelings the parson provoked. There would just be the bliss. He opened the kit and took out the hypodermic needle.

"I was mistaken. There's just the three of us."

Ash closed his eyes and groaned. When he opened them they were moist. He swallowed and hastily replaced the needle. Closing the kit, he shoved it back into his saddlebag. "I'm not that far gone yet," he whispered.

Ash rolled onto his side. He drew the Remington and placed it next to his face. "If I had any grit I'd put you in my mouth and end this nightmare once and for all."

For a while Ash lay quiet while his mind raced in inner chaos. The crackling of the fire and the howl of a distant wolf were the only sounds. He held his hand close to the flames to feel the warmth.

"That parson and all his talk about love. He's got a book for blinders and all he sees is what's written on its pages. He doesn't see the real world."

Resentment flooded through him. Not at the parson, at the parson's unshakable faith.

"The man's a fool."

Ash put his hand on the Remington and tried to drift off to sleep. His mind wouldn't let him. He relived being shot, relived the torment, and swore. "If this is the Almighty's notion of love, then God is crazier than I am." He laughed at that, laughed too long and too hard.

Finally, rest came.

Ash awoke feeling different. Not physically, but something inside him had changed, something he couldn't put his finger on. He heated the coffeepot and after a couple of cups broke camp and was in the saddle when the golden crown of the sun set the eastern horizon ablaze.

"From now on I just don't give a damn," Ash said to

the lightening sky. "It's plain as the nose on my face that you sure don't."

He gigged the roan and pulled on the lead rope.

Flowers bordered the road. A butterfly flitted from one to another on gossamer wings. In the trees a robin warbled. A doe and her fawn watched him go by.

Ash barely noticed any of it. Once he would have. Once he would have breathed deep of the mountain air and been happy to be alive. Now he was thinking of the killing he intended to do. He looked skyward again and chuckled at the irony.

"I'm just like you, God. I just never realized it."

Chapter 14

Kester wasn't much of a town. It wasn't much of anything save a collection of shacks and cabins and a paltry few frame houses. It also had the usual saloon and livery, and a small general store that once served as a trading post.

Ash tied off at the hitch rail in front of the saloon. He was in good spirits, all things considered. He still hadn't suffered another attack and was half convinced he was on the road to recovery.

The batwings creaked loudly. Ash walked to the bar and a man smelling of lilac water, a toothpick jutting from his mouth, asked his poison. Ash told him and slapped down an extra two bits.

"What's that for?"

"Information. I hear tell there's a Ute around here by the name of Broken Nose."

The bartender pushed the two bits at Ash. "You don't need to pay me. Just go to the end of the street and head toward the hill to the southwest. On the other side is Broken Nose's place. You can't miss it." He pulled the two bits back again. "On second thought, you might want to give me this and more. Enough for a bottle."

"I'm not that thirsty."

"Not for you. For Broken Nose."

With many Indians on reservations or keeping away from whites so they wouldn't be put on reservations, it was rare to see a teepee. But after Ash followed the bartender's directions and rounded the hill, there one stood. A lodge showing its age by the cracks in the hide and the faded symbols painted on the hide. A pinto was tied to a stake out in front.

Ash drew rein and dismounted. He was about to call out when he heard a peculiar whistling. The flap was open, and he quietly went over and stooped down.

Inside, flat on his back on a bearskin spread out on bare dirt lay an Indian with more wrinkles than Methuselah. His buckskins were as faded and worn as the teepee. The whistling came from his hooked beak of a nose.

Ash entered and nearly tripped over an empty whiskey bottle. More empties were piled to one side, enough to keep a man drunk for months. The reek was worse than a saloon's. Ash nudged the sleeping warrior with his toe but all the Ute did was mutter and smack his lips. "Broken Nose?"

More whistling ensued.

Bending, Ash gave him a shake. "Broken Nose? Wake up. I need to talk to you." He noticed that the old man's nose was in fact not hooked but had once been broken in the middle and when it healed the tip of the nose pointed inward. "Can you hear me?" Ash gave him another shake.

The Ute muttered louder. An eyelid cracked and a

dark eye appraised Ash from boots to hat. "Slit your throat."

"How's that?" Ash wasn't sure he'd heard correctly.

"I was dreaming of a young maiden and you woke me. For that you should slit your throat."

"You speak good English."

Broken Nose closed his eye. "Go away, white man, so I can finish taking her dress off."

"We need to talk."

"You need to talk. I need to dream."

Ash stepped out to the roan and slid from his bedroll the whiskey bottle he had brought. He went back into the teepee and poked the prone Ute with the bottle. "Would some firewater loosen your tongue?"

The right eye cracked open again. "Firewater, hell. That's good whiskey. Congratulations."

"For what?"

Broken Nose took the bottle. "You have loosened my tongue to where it might fall out." He sat up and patted the bottle. "I ran out this morning. This is an omen."

Ash sat cross-legged. He propped his elbows on his knees and held his chin in his hand. "I'm told no one alive knows these mountains better than you."

"Whoever told you spoke with a straight tongue." Broken Nose set to opening his gift. "I was born in what you whites call South Park. I have lived among these mountains all my long life. So yes, I do not boast when I say I know them well."

"Well enough to help me track down the Frazier brothers?"

Broken Nose stopped prying. "What is the word you whites and the Mexicans use? Ah yes. Are you lobo? They are bad medicine."

"It's 'loco,' not 'lobo.' A lobo is a wolf. 'Loco' means 'crazy.'"

"You are crazy, then." Broken Nose snickered and raised the bottle to his mouth. Pausing, he took a deep breath, as if about to plunge into a river or lake.

"I hate you for this."

Ash couldn't decide whether to take him seriously. "Then why are you about to drink?"

"For the same reason I must breathe." Broken Nose swallowed in long gulps, his Adam's apple bobbing. When he finally lowered the bottle, a third of the whiskey was gone. Smiling, he belched and cradled the bottle in the crook of an arm. "I hate all whites for my weakness."

"Oh, sure, blame us," Ash said, half in jest.

Broken Nose shifted and picked up a blanket. Draping it over his shoulders, he took a slow sip and sighed in contentment. "Before you whites came to our land I was happy. I had a good wife. I had children. I lived in a fine lodge and had more than fifty horses."

"That's quite a herd."

"For a Ute, horses are riches, and I was rich. My people looked up to me. They respected me. They asked my advice on important matters. I was high in their councils."

Ash let the old warrior talk. He was in no hurry.

"Then the beaver men came, the whites who trapped our rivers and streams for furs. We traded with them. Furs of our own for guns and knives and . . ." Broken Nose hefted the bottle. "Firewater."

"You got so you couldn't go without."

"Yes," Broken Nose admitted. "From my first swallow. I had never tasted anything like it. When I drank I felt good. I felt happy. I felt strong. I could not get enough." He gazed about the empty teepee. "I would do anything for a bottle. I traded all the furs I had. I traded my horses. I was always drinking. It upset my wife. She asked me to stop and when I wouldn't she took our children and went to live with her mother and father."

"She couldn't stand living with a drunk. Not many women can."

Broken Nose looked at him. "She said it was her or the white man's bottle. I chose the bottle. It's why I hate you. Why I hate all of your kind."

"Where are your wife and children now?"

"That was thirty winters ago. Another warrior took her for his woman and she lived with him until four winters ago when she died. My children want nothing to do with me."

"God and his knives," Ash said.

"Eh?"

Ash briefly mentioned his talk with the parson, summing it up with "He didn't like it when I said God isn't like most folks make him out to be. God isn't love. God is a knife in the gut."

Broken Nose chuckled. "I like that. What you call God, my people call Coyote, the trickster."

They looked at one another.

"Why do you want to die?" Broken Nose asked.

"You know about the—," Ash began, and caught himself. The Ute couldn't possibly know about the lead lodged in his chest. "Oh. You mean the Frazier brothers."

"They kill people."

"So I've heard."

"White or red, yellow or black. They will kill you as

quick as they would kill me or the black man who sweeps out the livery."

"Not if I kill them first." Ash produced a roll of bills. "I'll pay you one hundred dollars to help me find them."

"No."

"It's a lot of money. You could buy enough whiskey to last you the rest of your days."

"You will buy the whiskey."

"Me?"

"The whites in Kester only let me have a bottle at a time." Broken Nose grinned. "They do not like it that when I drink I throw rocks at windows and kick dogs and say things about white people they do not like to hear. They called the sheriff on me."

"And I bet he hauled you before a judge as a public nuisance."

"The judge was a good man. He let me go with a warning. Now I only drink here in my lodge where there are no windows to break or dogs to kick or whites who do not like to hear how whites are."

"How much whiskey will it take to hire you?" Ash was thinking a case, maybe two cases at the most.

"Enough to full a wagon."

Ash threw back his head and roared. "You think awful highly of yourself. Do you honestly expect me to cram a Conestoga with red-eye?"

"The bed of a buckboard will do." Broken Nose smiled. "For what you ask, that is not much."

Ash reckoned that a case of whiskey would cost him between twenty and thirty dollars depending on the brand. "How about brandy instead?" To the best of his recollection, it was going for fifteen dollars a case.

"Brandy is for women."

"Beer, then?" Ash recalled that a case could be had for two dollars.

"I do not drink horse piss." Broken Nose upended the bottle and another third disappeared.

Ash needed the old warrior's help. He was confident he could find the Fraziers on his own but it would take a lot longer. "A buckboard full of whiskey it is. But I want you sober when we head out and you're to stay sober on the trail. Is that understood?"

Broken Nose took another drink and indulged in another belch. "I am sober now."

"We have a deal, then. Let's shake on it."

"A white custom. I prefer my way." Broken Nose spit in his own palm and held his hand out to Ash. "Bend down so I can rub this on your forehead."

Ash didn't much like having spit smeared on him but he had never been particularly squeamish. "This is a Ute custom, I take it?"

"No. I just wanted to rub spit on you. I hate whites, remember?"

Ash grabbed Broken Nose's wrist but it was too late. His brow was wet. Broken Nose laughed, and despite himself Ash laughed too. Once he started he couldn't stop. He laughed until his sides ached. Doubled over, he realized he was the only one still laughing and he glanced up. Broken Nose was studying him.

"Another good omen."

"What is?" Ask asked between gasps.

"You did not hit me."

Ash would have laughed harder but his chest abruptly flared with pain. The pressure returned, returned terribly, and he writhed on the ground in agony.

"What is wrong?"

In too much torment to respond, Ash turned. He

needed the hypodermic. He tried to rise but his chest exploded like a keg of powder. Unable to keep from crying out, he crawled toward the flap. The pain came in waves, each harder to bear than the last. Sweat peppered his body. He was aware of the Ute beside him.

"Are you sick?"

"Saddlebags," Ash groaned, and choked down a scream. He could barely think for the pounding in his head. It was the worst attack ever, far worse than the earlier ones. Digging his fingers into the earth, he sought desperately to reach his horse.

Suddenly his saddlebags were in front of him. Ash fumbled at the flap and got it open. The kit weighed tons. His vision swimming, he opened it. His arms were shaking so badly he couldn't hold the needle still. Somehow he got it over a vein just as a veil of black descended.

Humming woke him. Ash lay still, listening. A wonderful lassitude had come over him, the familiar bliss of the morphine in his blood. The pain and pressure were gone. He touched a finger to his chest over his heart and said, "Not yet, you bastard."

"Are you a doctor?"

Ash remembered the Ute. He moved just enough to see him and the nearly empty whiskey bottle. "What makes you ask that?"

Broken Nose pointed at the needle where it had fallen from Ash's limp fingers. "I have seen the white healer use one of those."

"I'm no sawbones," Ash said. "I need it to get by."

"That happens often?"

"More than I like it to," Ash admitted. He told him about the slug lodged near his heart.

"I was right about you being crazy. You want *us* to

go after the Fraziers, the most vicious white killers in the mountains? Me with my bottle and you with your needle against them with their guns and their knives? They will kill us and leave us to rot."

"You've changed your mind about tracking them?"

"Did I say that?" Broken Nose grinned. "Whites are always saying I am crazy. It pleases me to meet a white as crazy as me. We will hunt them, my crazy white brother. We will hunt them and we will die."

"Why come along if that's how you feel?"

Broken Nose drained the last of the whiskey. "As you whites like to say, it should be fun."

"Damn," Ash said. "I think I'm starting to like you."

"Is that bad or good?"

"I don't want to like anyone these days. It will only make the dying harder."

"Dying is easy," Broken Nose said. "It is the living that is hard."

Chapter 15

The ground squirrel was cute. It scampered every which way, its tail erect, a boundless fountain of vigor and vim. Now and then it stopped and chattered as if offended by the empty air.

"I know how you feel," Asher Thrall said, and chuckled. He was in the grip of morphine, as he had been every day for the past week. He had no choice. The attacks wouldn't stop.

Ash was getting used to them. He was getting used to the morphine too. It had gotten so he actually looked forward to the injections. He looked forward even more to floating in a pool of pleasure.

Now he sat with his back to a pine and watched the ground squirrel, marveling at its silly antics. Or are they silly? he asked himself. Maybe the squirrel had it right. Maybe there was no point to life other than running around and doing nothing of any importance, and then you died.

A profound notion, Ash reflected, and chuckled again. He had hardly ever used words like "profound" before.

The morphine not only helped his body, it helped him think better.

Then out of nowhere Broken Nose was beside him, a half-empty bottle in one hand. "I have been to Kester as you asked."

"And?"

"There is no word of the Fraziers."

"Good."

"It is costing you a bottle a day," Broken Nose reminded him.

"It's my money." Ash wished the Ute would go away and leave him to his bliss. "They need to strike again for us to pick up their trail."

Broken Nose glanced at the ground squirrel. "You admire your little brother."

"There's more to the little bastards than I reckoned," Ash admitted. "I used to think they were as stupid as tree stumps."

"Yesterday you sat and stared at ants."

"I never noticed how hard they work. Work, work, work is all they do. They are more like people than I gave them credit for."

"The day before that you sat and watched the red hawk and its mate fly back and forth over the valley."

"Is there a point to this?"

"You do a lot of sitting."

"I do a lot of thinking too. More than I ever did. I think it's the morphine. It's doing something to my brain."

Broken Nose took a swig and gave a sigh. "I do the opposite. I drink so I will not think. I drink so I will forget the wife I lost and the children and grandchildren who shun me." He grinned. "I drink because I like to drink too."

"I've been meaning to ask," Ash said. "Where did you learn to talk the white tongue so good?"

Broken Nose took a longer swig. "I made the mistake of going to the missionary school. I thought if I was going to drink like a white I should think like a white."

"We're back to thinking."

"You can do all you want. It hurts my head when I think too much." Broken Nose headed for his teepee. "I will be inside forgetting if you want me for anything."

Ash looked for the ground squirrel but it had disappeared. Disappointed, he closed his eyes and drifted on tides of languor. He was so deep inside himself that when someone coughed he was reluctant to open his eyes. He expected it to be Broken Nose. Instead it was a white man, broad across the chest and shoulders, with a square jaw and skin burned copper by a lot of time in the sun. The man wore a high-crowned hat and a slicker and chaps. He also wore a Colt revolver on his right hip.

"I'm Rin Templeton."

The man said it as if it should mean something but the name was new to Ash. "Cowboy?"

"Rancher. I own the Box T, the biggest ranch in these parts. Word has got out that you are after the Frazier brothers."

"Damn." Ash didn't want the Fraziers to hear that he was after them or they might dig a hole and cover it over them. Then again, given their reputations, they might decide to come after him. "I'm not so sure I like that."

"I don't blame you," Rin Templeton said. "But that's what happens when you partner up with a drunk Injun. He told a few folks and they told a few more folks and it got back to me through one of my men who stopped at the Kester saloon."

"Why are you here?" Ash was eager to sink back into the morphine.

Instead of answering Templeton said, "Is there something the matter with you?"

"Why do you ask?"

"You have a funny look about you."

"It's my medicine," Ash said.

"You're sick?"

"I have a condition. It's not anything I talk about."

"I don't blame you. A man's business is his own." Templeton paused. "I'm here to make you an offer. Me and my pistol and my rifle."

"For what?"

"To help you hunt the Fraziers. I am no brag when I say you'll find me more than competent."

"Why would a rancher turn man-hunter? Are you after a share of the bounty money?"

"You can keep all the reward for yourself. I just want the Fraziers dead."

"I'm listening," Ash said.

Templeton's blue eyes glittered like quartz. "Two years ago those sons of bitches rustled some of my cattle. A puncher of mine was shot and died. I chased them for pretty near two hundred miles and recovered some of my cows but the Fraziers got away."

"Now you want revenge."

"I want justice. For a while I offered my own reward but no one claimed it. No one wants to go up against them. Or didn't until you came along."

"I don't know," Ash said. He knew nothing about this Templeton. The man could be a hothead and a nuisance on the trail.

"Why not? I can ride better than most and I shoot straight and I can fend for myself as well as you and better than that drunk Injun."

"I'll thank you to stop calling him that. His name is Broken Nose."

Rin Templeton frowned. "Let's get something straight. I don't like Injuns. My grandpa was killed by Sioux. I tangled with the Utes a few times over the land I claimed for my ranch. They should all be on reservations or dead."

"We don't need your help," Ash informed him.

"I'm not done. I don't like Injuns but I get along with them well enough when they don't give me cause to shoot them. I will be civil with your pet redskin if that's what it takes."

"He's not a dog or a cat. He's a man."

"Fine. Have it your way. He's a man. A man who is nearly always drunk. You need someone who isn't. You need someone you can rely on. You need a man like me to watch your back when your back needs watching."

The rancher was right. Back when he wore a tin star Ash always had a deputy to back his play. "You have a point."

"I can come, then?"

"So long as you understand that I'm in charge. You do as I tell you or you turn around and go back to your cows."

Templeton's cheeks colored and he balled his calloused fists. "I don't usually take that kind of talk but this is your shindig and I admire you for being blunt. Yes, I'll do as you want. I have to ask, though. Do you know what you're doing? The Fraziers aren't amateurs."

"I was a marshal once."

"That tells me nothing. Some lawmen are worth their badge, some aren't. You could have been one of the useless ones." Templeton smiled. "I can be blunt too."

"If at any time you think I'm not fit to lead the hunt, you're welcome to cut and go."

"That's fair enough." Templeton came over and offered his hand.

It was like shaking a block of iron. Ash had an urge to check if his fingers were broken. "How do I get word to you when I'm ready to ride out?"

"You walk over to the other side of that teepee and tell me. I'm making camp there and will stay until we do."

A bay and a packhorse were over by the lodge. A rifle stock poked from a scabbard on the bay.

"You have come prepared. I like that."

"My pa didn't raise slackers. Idle minds and idle hands don't get a man anywhere in this world. It's work and sweat that do." Templeton turned. "Now if you'll excuse me, I'll tend to my animals." His spurs jingled as he walked off.

Ash hoped he hadn't made a mistake. He got to his feet and went to the teepee and ducked under and in. Broken Nose was on the bearskin, staring blankly at the opening at the top. "A man has come."

"The rancher. He is hard, that one. I have seen him a few times. He does not like me."

"You knew he was here?"

"Firewater goes down my throat, not in my ears. I heard him when he was an arrow's flight away and looked out."

"He has asked to join us."

"How did you answer? You told me it would be you and me."

"He's a hard man. You said it yourself. The Fraziers are hard men. We can use someone like him. Hard against hard."

Broken Nose's gaze drifted from the opening to Ash. "What about you, Walking Dead Man? Are you hard enough?"

"What did you call me?"

"The new name I have given you. Your Indian name. Walking Dead Man."

"That's a hell of a handle."

"You told me you could die any time. You are as good as dead, you said. A walking dead man is what you are."

"How about if I start calling you Drunk as Hell. I bet that would stick in your craw."

Broken Nose chortled. "I would like that very much. It is better than the name I have."

"How did you break your nose anyhow?"

"I was kicked by a pony when I was a boy. I have hated my nose ever since. I am not fond of ponies either."

"Do me a favor, then. Don't tell the rancher about my condition and don't call me Walking Dead Man in front of him."

"That is two favors. You have enough fingers to count that high. Or is it your medicine?"

"You can go to hell," Ash said, and laughed. He walked back out and around the teepee.

Rin Templeton had stripped his saddle and saddle blanket off the bay and gotten a fire going. He was on a knee, spooning Arbuckle into a coffee pot. Without looking up he said, "I've changed my mind. Tell me more about your condition."

Ash was taken aback. "You heard?"

"That overgrown tent is paper thin. I could hear the Injun break wind." The rancher stopped spooning. "I've been honest with you. I expect the same treatment. It sounds like this condition of yours could pose a problem."

Resentment flared, but Ash smothered it. "Fair is fair," he agreed. Over two cups of steaming coffee he told about Sharkey and the slug and the morphine. He held nothing back and when he was done he said, "You're welcome to change your mind about tagging along. I won't hold it against you."

Templeton held a battered tin cup in both big hands and sipped, his eyes shadowed by his hat brim. "You have sand, I'll give you that."

"I have nothing to lose is what it amounts to."

"Still," Templeton said. He tilted the cup to his lips. "These attacks of yours. You say they come with no rhyme or reason? You could be doing just about anything and one will hit you?"

"There's no predicting."

"What if you have one in the middle of our fight with the Fraziers? I could find myself alone against the three of them."

"I won't lie to you," Ash responded. "I'll do all I can but you can't count on me. You'll have to watch your own back as well as mine."

"Hell."

"Do you still want to join us?"

Rin Templeton nodded. "I wouldn't miss out for all the tea in China. I buck odds for a living so this is no different."

"You're a rancher, not a gambler."

"You know nothing about ranching. There are diseases that can drop cows like flies. There's drought. There are winter snows that bury them alive. Raising cattle *is* a gamble, each and every day. What's one more?"

"This one could get you killed," Ash pointed out.

"A man does what he has to. I owe the Fraziers for murdering my hand and stealing my cows. I won't back out on account of a little risk."

"It's not little."

"Are you trying to talk me out of it? Save your breath. When I give my word, I keep it. We'll hunt those three sons of bitches together and if we die together, then it was meant to be."

"No," Ash said. "Nothing is ever meant to happen. Things just do and we pick up the pieces and move on."

"Were you this cynical before you were shot?" Templeton grinned as he asked it.

"No. Being a Walking Dead Man will do that to you."

Chapter 16

It was the talk of the territory. The *Rocky Mountain News* called it the most brazen act of lawlessness ever conceived. The *News* exaggerated but they had newspapers to sell.

The facts, as Ash pieced them together, were these: Six days ago three men rode into a small mining camp known as Ute City on the bank of the Roaring Fork River. Ute City wasn't named in honor of the Utes; it was named to spite them. The camp was on Ute land and the Utes weren't happy about it.

An enterprising banker from Denver put up a tent and went into business. He planned to have a building built if the camp lasted but in the meantime the miners and prospectors could place their ore and money in the banker's safe. A team of six sturdy horses brought the safe up from Denver, and the banker bragged that it was the only safe between Denver and the Pacific Ocean. He exaggerated, but he wanted their money.

Word got around, as word always did. So it was that the three men in slickers rode into Ute City on a sunny morning and made straight for the banker's large tent. One held their horses while the other two went in. All three were armed with shotguns. That was how the sheriff later deduced they were the Fraziers. The brothers favored shotguns for close work. As one of them once mentioned to a bystander, "We like the splatter."

The two who entered the tent leveled their cannons and commanded everyone to throw their hands up. The banker threw his up the quickest but one of the clerks reached down instead of up and a Frazier fired. The shotguns were loaded with buckshot and there wasn't much left of the clerk's head. It was later established that the clerk had been reaching for his spectacles, which he needed to see at any distance but not for when he was writing deposit slips and the like.

The safe was closed. The Frazier who shot the clerk demanded that another clerk open it. When the second clerk balked, the Frazier brother blew his left leg off at the knee. That loosened the banker's lips. He eagerly gave them the combination.

The Fraziers took their sweet time filling the burlap sacks they'd brought. Everyone the journalist from the *News* interviewed said how the Fraziers were extremely calm the whole time. They joked and laughed while they were emptying the safe.

The blasts had been heard, though, and men converged from all over. The Frazier holding the horses sought to discourage the curious by firing into the air. Some ran off. The rest resorted to their revolvers and rifles.

The ensuring bloodbath, the *News* proclaimed, was horrific. The two brothers inside the tent rushed to help the brother outside the tent, and in the battle that followed, five men were slain and seven were wounded, two so severely they might not live. As one observer told the journalist, "Bodies were everywhere."

None of the bodies belonged to a Frazier. When the shooting ended and the gun smoke was drifting on the breeze, they calmly mounted and calmly departed Ute City, taking much of its wealth with them.

The *News* was outraged. In an editorial the owner declared,

> Our territory has long had a reputation for lawlessness. Decent and honorable citizens wish it were otherwise. Our minions of the law have made considerable inroads in curbing the violence and crime but plainly more needs to be done. In our territory's pantheon of lawbreakers, the Frazier brothers are at the pinnacle. Steps must be taken to put a stop to their blood-drenched sprees. Call in the army. Call out the militia. Organize vigilantes. As incentive, the *News* is offering a thousand dollars for each Frazier to the person or persons who send the Fraziers to their Maker. The *News* isn't squeamish. Shoot them to death or string them from cottonwoods, but for God's sake rid our territory of this menace.

Ash liked the part about the thousand dollars.

"The trail will be cold when we get there," Rin Templeton commented as the three of them headed out on horseback the next morning. "You know that, don't you?"

Ash nodded. "At least two weeks old but it's the freshest we're likely to have so we'll give it a try."

"What do you say, Injun?" Templeton asked. "Think

you can track the Fraziers after so much time has gone by?"

"My name is Broken Nose."

"You didn't answer me."

"Treat me as you would treat a white man and I will. Treat me as you treat your dog and I won't."

"Damn, you're prickly," Templeton responded. "Why should I treat you as white when to me you're nothing but another redskin?"

"Why should I treat you as red when to me you are another white with his head up his ass?"

Ash drew rein. He fully expected the rancher to turn on the old warrior in a fit of anger. To his surprise, Templeton laughed.

"You learned that from a white man, didn't you? All right. I'll show you respect, but you have to earn it the same as everybody else. Now, can you track the Fraziers after two weeks have gone by or not?"

"It depends."

Ash was interested in the answer himself. "Depends on what?"

"Many things. If it has rained. If anyone knows which way they went when they left Ute City. If they were smart enough to wipe out their tracks or they figured no one would come after them because everyone was afraid."

"That's a lot of ifs."

"Do not give up hope. Horses are heavy. They always leave tracks except on rock. If we strike their sign, I will find them. On that you can count."

"If you say so." Templeton made no attempt to hide his skepticism. "Just so when we catch up to them it comes as a surprise to them and not us."

"Do not worry. I do not want to die."

"Me either."

Ash made it unanimous, adding, "It's important they don't catch on that we're after them. Anyone asks, we're elk hunters and Broken Nose is our guide."

"It's the wrong time of the year for elk," Templeton disagreed. "Mountain sheep would be better."

From Kester to Ute City was a distance of fifty miles as the raven flew, but they weren't ravens. Two ranges barred their way. To save time they avoided the first by swinging to the southwest until they came to Buena Vista and the Arkansas River and then they followed the Arkansas north until they reached Twin Lakes. From there they struck off due west. A hard climb brought them to Independence Pass.

At the summit Ash drew rein and dismounted, both to rest their weary animals and to admire the magnificent view. Below lay a vast vista of forested slopes rolling in green waves to wash against the continental divide. "I've never been three miles above the earth before," he marveled.

Broken Nose tamped the ground with a moccasin. "How can we be three miles above when it is under our feet?"

Rin Templeton snickered.

"When I say three miles above the earth I mean three miles above sea level," Ash explained.

The Ute looked around them with an air of puzzlement. "The water sea or the eyeball see?"

"The water sea."

"There is no sea in these mountains."

"The nearest are the oceans, and they are a long way off."

"Why do you think of them when they are so far away?"

"It's how whites measure how high mountains are," Ash elaborated. "We compare the mountains to the sea."

"I thought my English was good."

"It is."

"I do not understand. Why do you measure a mountain by the sea? Do you compare a chicken to a goat to tell how big a cow is?"

Templeton roared and slapped his leg. "Keep at it. You two are downright comical."

Ash wasn't feeling so comical by the time they reached Ute City. His chest was acting up. Not with the pressure so much as pangs of pain that came and went. He hadn't used morphine for a few days and was sorely temped to, but held off.

Ute City was no different from any other mining camp: a lot of dirt, a lot of tents, a lot of grimy, smelly men, and when the wind was right, the stink of out-houses. It was a wretched example of why Ash liked big towns and cities.

The banker's tent was the largest. Over it hung a long board with neatly painted letters: THE FIRST BANK OF DENVER. Under that was A SUBSIDIARY.

Ash read it out loud.

"I do not know 'subsidiary,'" Broken Nose said.

"It means 'branch.'"

"Like the branch of a tree or the branch of a river?"

"Here you two go again," Templeton said.

The banker was a moon of a man with a puffy face. He sweated a lot and liked to chew on unlit cigars. "Why do you want to know about the robbery?" he asked suspiciously.

"I read about it," Ash answered, which was no an-swer at all, but the real reason had to stay secret.

"Then you know all there is to know." The banker

chewed some more. "Those damn Fraziers. Marched in here bold as brass. I recognized them right away from descriptions I'd read. They are all as big as oxes and have big noses and red hair."

"I don't recollect the newspaper mentioning their first names," Ash said.

"No one knows. All they have ever been known by are the Fraziers or the Frazier brothers."

"Did you see them ride off?"

"Hell, no. I was too busy having the mess they left cleaned up. Blood all over the place, and one of my workers was missing a head. I tell you, I'll have nightmares for the rest of my days."

Ash asked a few more questions but it was apparent the banker would be of no help. They left and roamed the camp, asking people they met about the robbery. Most were eager to talk. Few, though, had seen the Fraziers leave Ute City. One man who swore he did said they rode off to the northwest.

By then the fiery orb of the sun was balanced on the rim of the world.

"I suggest we stay the night and start the hunt at first light," Rin Templeton proposed.

Ash had wanted to head right out but the suggestion made sense. They needed to rest up and his chest was still bothering him. "All right." He looked at Broken Nose. "But no one gets drunk and we turn in early."

They camped near the river in a clearing in the trees. Templeton picketed the horses while Ash kindled a fire and put on coffee.

Broken Nose stood off by himself, his arms wrapped around his chest, his eyes closed, chanting quietly and shuffling his feet in a circle.

"What the hell are you doing?" Ash's chest had made

him irritable. He still refused to use the morphine if he could help it. He had become entirely too dependent on it.

"Singing my death song."

"You expecting to keel over?"

"The Fraziers like to shoot." Broken Nose went on shuffling.

Templeton snorted. "Injuns and their silly ways. What good does singing do you?"

"Shouldn't you be dying when you sing it?" Ash asked. He had heard that somewhere.

"With the Fraziers our deaths will be quick," Broken Nose answered. "I might not have the chance."

"Silly red idiot," Templeton said, then announced, "I'm going to have a drink and maybe play a hand or two of cards. I'll be back early like you want."

"I'll go with you," Ash said. The death chant was making him think of the lead rubbing against his heart, and he'd rather not.

Saloon tents weren't hard to find thanks to tinny music, rowdy voices, and the tinkle of poker chips.

Ash bellied to a plank bar and asked for whiskey. He would have one and only one. His elbow on the plank, he sipped and watched the rancher sit in on a poker game. Doves in tight dresses roamed among the customers, smiling and teasing. Ash didn't notice one approach until a warm hand fell on his arm.

"Buy a girl a drink, Mister?"

She was pushing thirty and the wear and tear showed. Her blue dress could use mending and her shoes were scuffed. She had a nice smile, though, and her hazel eyes were friendly.

"One and only one. I won't be staying long."

"The name is Mabel. It's short for Mabeline."

Ash didn't give her his. He paid for the rye she wanted and they touched glasses and sipped.

"Been up here long?"

"A couple of months. Between you and me, I miss Denver. But I have to do what the boss wants." For a few moments her guard was down and her face mirrored sorrow. "I hate it that life never leaves us any choice."

"You're wrong," Ash said. "So long as we're breathing we always have a choice."

"Easy for you to say. You're a man and can do pretty much whatever you please. Us women don't have it so easy. There aren't a lot of jobs to be had and those that are don't pay much." Mabel motioned. "This job does. I make three times what I would as a seamstress. The hours are too long and the men paw us too much but my kids and me don't go hungry."

"You have children?"

"Three. I had a husband too. He was a miner. He went and got crushed in a cave-in."

A commotion broke out at the poker table and Ash looked to see why.

Rin Templeton had drawn his revolver.

Chapter 17

The last thing Ash wanted was to draw attention to either of them.

The voices and laughter faded, the piano pinged a last note, and all eyes shifted to the poker table.

Templeton pointed the Colt at the man who was dealing. "Shuffle the cards and deal again and this time deal from the top."

The dealer, a gambler in a frock coat and derby, was as rigid as stone, the deck in one hand, a card he was about to deal in another. "I don't know what you're talking about, friend."

"I made it plain enough," Templeton said. "You're dealing from the bottom. Try it again and I'll blow out your wick."

"You haven't been playing but two minutes and you accuse me and make threats," the gambler blustered.

"I have good eyes."

Another player next to the gambler, a miner who looked to have come to the saloon straight from the mine with his dirty clothes and his cheeks smeared brown, cleared his throat. "You've been winning an awful lot of hands, Dyson."

"So I've had a run of luck. So what?" Dyson returned. "Some nights the cards are in our favor. Some nights they're not."

Templeton hadn't lowered his Colt. "When you were done dealing I saw the ace of spades on the bottom of the deck. Show us what the bottom card is now."

"This is stupid," Dyson said.

"Show us."

Dyson turned the cards enough for all to see that the bottom card was the two of hearts. "You were mistaken."

"Turn over your cards."

"The hell I will."

The click of the Colt's hammer was ominously loud. "The hell you won't. I won't be cheated by a tinhorn."

Dyson was mad, his face flushed red, his jaw muscles twitching. "I don't have to sit here and take this."

"You try to leave and you'll walk out with lead in you." Templeton glanced at the dirty miner. "Turn his cards over so we can have a look."

The miner started to reach for them but Dyson grabbed his wrist.

"No one is allowed to look at another player's cards. Ever. That's always the rule."

"I never argue with a cocked six-shooter," the miner said, and tugging loose he flipped the gambler's cards over.

The ace of spades was one of them.

Whispers broke out. Hard looks were cast at Dyson. Next to a horse thief, men on the frontier despised card cheats the most.

Dyson was sweating. He forced a laugh and declared, "I tell you I dealt that card off the top. This gent is wrong."

"My trigger finger is itching," Templeton said.

Dyson regarded the ring of cold faces. "A gent can see when he's not popular." He put down the deck and slowly rose. "But I insist I'm no cheat. As God is my witness." He half turned. He removed his derby and mopped at his brow with his sleeve, saying, "Did it suddenly get hot in here?"

Ash saw the gambler's other hand dip into the hat. He reacted on pure instinct. He drew his Remington and fired just as Dyson's hand reappeared holding a derringer. He fired once. His slug caught Dyson in the forehead, snapped Dyson's head back, and burst out the back of Dyson's skull, spraying hair and gore all over those behind him.

A woman screamed. Men ducked or dived flat on the floor. As smoke curled from the Remington's muzzle, Dyson oozed to the floor. His legs twitched a few times and that was all.

"Land sakes," someone said.

Ash walked over. He frowned at the dead gambler and slid the revolver into his holster. With his toe he poked the derringer lying next to the gambler's limp fingers. "He was going for this."

"We all saw it, Mister," a man declared. "You did right. And damn me, that was some shooting."

Heads bobbed in assent. Someone clapped Ash on the back. He looked at Templeton. "We're leaving."

"I just started to play."

"We're leaving," Ash said again, and without waiting for a reply, he stalked through the crowd to the flap and on out into the cool mountain night. The tromp of boots behind him only fueled his anger. "You damned simpleton."

"Be careful. I don't let any man talk to me like that. What has you so riled anyway? You did what you had to. I'm obliged."

Ash stopped and spun so suddenly that Templeton nearly collided with him.

"Use your noggin. What will happen now? Everyone in there will tell everyone they know about the shooting. It's what always happens."

"So?"

"So word is bound to reach the Fraziers."

"So?" Templeton said again. "No one in there knows who we are or why we're here. To them you're some stranger who shot a cheat."

"I still don't like it." Ash resumed walking. He hadn't gone far when there was a holler and a small man in a fancy suit came hurrying up.

"Hold on there. I'd like to talk to you."

Ash looked for a badge on the man's vest or jacket. "Are you the law?"

"What? Oh hell, no. Ute City doesn't have any. The sheriff comes through now and then, but that's about it." He reached under his jacket and brought out a pencil and paper. "My name is Horace. I work for the *Rocky Mountain News*. I'd like to find out who you are and how it is that you're so slick with your smoke wagon."

Ash glared at Templeton, then said, "Go away."

"No need to be modest. I was there. I saw the whole thing. I've been up here doing a follow-up on the robbery and I'm due to take the stage down to Denver tomorrow."

"Good for you."

"I can put what you did on the front page."

"I'd rather it didn't get around," Ash said.

"Either you've been living under a rock or you're naive. Shootings are big news, Mister. The whole camp will be buzzing about it."

"There's nothing great in killing a man," Ash said. "God kills people all the time."

Horace chuckled. "What a strange thing to say. Are you feeling regret? You shouldn't. If ever a shooting was justified, that was it. I doubt the sheriff will even bother to look you up."

"I refuse to talk about it." Ash went to walk on but the journalist snagged his sleeve.

"Be reasonable. This is how I earn my living. All I want is your name and whether you've ever shot anyone before and maybe where you're from and where you're bound."

"Leave me be, you damned nuisance." Ash pulled away.

Rin Templeton picked that moment to step between them. To the journalist he said, "You have to forgive my pard. He's been feeling poorly of late and he's become a grump. I'll tell you whatever you want to know."

"Don't," Ash said.

Templeton ignored him. "My friend's name is Thrall. He's from Texas. I invited him to my ranch and we decided to go after mountain sheep." He offered his hand and introduced himself. "I own the Box T. Maybe you've heard of it?"

Horace was scribbling away. "Mountain sheep, you say?"

"They don't have them down to Texas. I figured Mr. Thrall would find it exciting to hunt up among the high peaks."

"Are you still going through with your hunt?"

"Why wouldn't we? We can't let a little thing like shooting a no-account cheat spoil our exercise."

"My readers will love that quote. Is there anything else you'd like to say about the incident?"

Templeton hooked his thumbs in his belt and pursed his lips. "I'm not much for gab but I will say this. A man who cheats sloppy shouldn't cheat at all."

Horace grinned. "You, sir, are a geyser of quotables."

Ash had listened to enough. He walked off and was almost to the stand when the rancher caught up.

"I'd say that went well."

"Damn you."

"What are you mad about now? I stuck to the story about hunting sheep."

Halting, Ash faced him. "You told him my name."

"No harm in that," Templeton said. "It's not as if you're somebody famous like Wild Bill Hickok or Bat Masterson. No one in these parts ever heard of a Texas marshal by the name of Asher Thrall, I can guarantee."

"What about people not from these parts?" Ash snapped.

"Who?"

"Someone I don't want to know I'm here but will if he reads the *News* or hears about the shooting from someone who did."

"You talking about the man who shot you. What was his name? Sharkey?"

"That's the one."

"Who cares about him? The important thing is that the Fraziers won't have any idea who you are or that you're after them." Templeton put a hand on Ash's shoulder. "Listen, you need to calm down. Squirt some of that morphine in your veins. You're always in a good mood when you take that stuff."

Ash pushed his hand off. "I'm trying to do without."

The rancher sighed. "You ask me, the longer you do, the grumpier you get. Could be you've reached a point where you can't not have it. I've heard that happens."

Ash remembered both doctors saying the same. He threaded through the oaks to the clearing and over to the fire where Broken Nose was staring morosely into the flames. "What the matter with you?"

"I am too young to die."

"Hell, you must be a hundred." Ash spread out his blanket and set his saddle at the top and tiredly sank down. He glanced at his saddlebags but didn't touch them. "I'll be damned if I will."

"What was that?"

"Nothing."

Templeton was filling a tin cup with coffee. "Pay him no mind, Broken Nose. He's out of sorts."

"Thank you," the Ute said.

"For what?"

"That is the first time you have called me by my name. Usually you call me Injun or redskin."

"That's what you are."

Broken Nose raised his wrinkled face to the rancher. "Do I call you whiteskin or white man? I do not. I respect you. You should respect me."

"Must be something in the air," Templeton muttered, and walked toward the horses. "I think I'll sit over here where I won't have to listen to you ladies carp."

"Why did he call us women?" Broken Nose asked Ash.

"He must think as highly of them as he does Indians." Ash filled his cup and sat back to drink in quiet, but it wasn't to be.

"Are you ready for what is to come?"

"This was my idea, remember?" Ash glanced at his saddlebags a second time and shook his head.

"I have listened to the wind and I have a bad feeling. It is not too late to change your mind. We can forget about these killers and go back to my lodge. I will drink and you will stick yourself with your needle. We will be happy."

"I have it to do."

"Why?"

Ash fidgeted and swallowed and mentally resisted a stronger impulse to reach for his saddlebags. "I've already explained. I want to spend the time I have left doing something that has meaning."

"Killing has meaning?"

"Killing bad men does. Killing men who doesn't deserve to live. Men like these Fraziers."

"There will be others?"

Ash hadn't given it much consideration. Now that he had to, he said, "If I live I reckon there will. There's one man in particular I want to find, but it appears fate has other plans."

"The Shark man you told me about. And after him, who?"

"I haven't thought that far ahead," Ash replied. How could he, when each breath might be his last? "I suppose you think poorly of me."

"No. You forget I am a Ute warrior. I have killed."

"How many coup did you count?"

Broken Nose picked up a stick and poked at a red ember. "You mistake us with the Cheyenne and the Lakota and the Blackfeet. We do not count coup as they do. The Cheyenne think it is brave to ride up to an armed enemy and strike him with a stick and then ride away again. We think it is stupid."

"I figured the Utes were the same."

"When a Ute has to kill an enemy he kills him and is done with it. When he steals a horse, he steals it and does not boast of the stealing later."

"Sensible people, you Utes."

"Not sensible enough." Broken Nose grinned. "If we had more sense we would have wiped out the first whites who came to our land and kept on wiping out those who came after."

"It wouldn't have stemmed the tide. A lot of my kind have taken something called Manifest Destiny to heart."

"What is that?"

"The belief that white people have the right to take control of all the land between the Atlantic and Pacific Oceans. Some say we should go farther and take over Canada and Mexico too."

"Who gave you white people this right?"

"God."

Broken Nose blinked. "It never fails. Is that the expression?"

"What does?"

"Just when I think white people cannot do or say anything crazier than they have, they prove me wrong."

"There's another belief, one I've grown partial to of late."

"That whites should take over the moon and the stars?"

Ash grinned. "No. That this world is what we call an asylum, a home for crazy people, and all of us are lunatics."

"Speak for yourself, white man."

Chapter 18

They were told the Fraziers rode off to the northwest so they did the same.

Ash figured the brothers would stick to the main trails for as long as they could; the going was easier. At some point they would turn off and head for wherever they had their hidey-hole, be it a cabin deep in the woods, a cave in a cliff or some other spot.

For five days Ash and his fellow killer hunters followed a trail that paralleled the Roaring Fork River. Eventually they came to a valley that wound toward Glenwood Springs.

Broken Nose constantly checked both sides, seeking sign.

Ash soon realized that they needed a stroke of luck or their hard effort would be in vain. It had been too long. He asked people they met with, miners and others, if anyone had seen any sign of three redheads on horseback and the answer was always the same: no.

The sixth night they made camp beside a small creek. They were so deep in the mountains that many of the towering peaks around them did not have names.

Ash nursed a cup of coffee and glumly regarded the ink-layered slopes. From on high wafted the howls of wolves and now and again the screech of a mountain lion.

Templeton was equally glum. "We're not going to find them. We might as well admit it."

"I admit nothing," Ash said. "I refuse to give up."

"We could search for a year and have nothing to show for it. I can't stay out here that long. I have a ranch to run."

"You can go home any time you like."

Broken Nose was staring at a mountain to the north. It stood by itself and wasn't part of a range. At its base was the junction with a trail to Glenwood Springs to the northwest and Gypsum to the northwest. "What is that light?"

"Eh?" Templeton said.

The Ute pointed. "Near the top. Do you see it?"

Ash did. A single yellow pinpoint that had to be two miles higher than they were. That they could see it at all was thanks to the clear mountain air.

"It's not a campfire," Templeton declared. "Flames would flicker more."

"A lantern, maybe, or a lamp," Ash speculated.

"A cabin, you think?" Templeton said. "But who the hell would live way up yonder?"

They looked at one another.

"It might be worth a look-see," the rancher suggested.

Ash agreed.

At daybreak they began to climb. The going was steep, the slopes as rugged as only mountain slopes could be. Twice they had to detour on account of deadfalls and once on account of talus. By noon they were only halfway up the mountain and stopped to rest.

Broken Nose was roving about when he called Ash's name and excitedly gestured at the ground.

Three shod horses had passed that way heading up the mountain. The tracks were old but clear.

"It could be them," Templeton said hopefully.

"I'll go on alone and make sure," Ash proposed.

"Why you and not one of us?"

"As I keep having to remind you, hunting them was my brainstorm. I'm in charge."

Templeton frowned and put his hands on his hips. "I don't like it. I have a stake in this too."

Ash turned to Broken Nose. "How about you? Aren't you going to object?"

"You hired me to track, not to fight. I will stay with the horses. If you do not come back I will sell yours for drinking money."

"You better not sell mine, Injun," Templeton declared. "If I die, take mine to the Box T. Tell them I said to give you a reward for bringing it back."

"They might not believe me."

"Just do it. I've had that bay four years now. Sell him, and I swear I'll come back from the grave to haunt you."

"Enough bickering," Ash broke in. He made sure the Remingtons and his Winchester were loaded, and faced up the mountain. "If you hear shots, light a shuck. It'll mean they are on to us."

Ash was sweating profusely after going only a hundred feet. A hundred yards and his chest spiked with pain. He stopped and touched a hand to his shirt over the wound. He'd left the hypodermic in his saddlebags. An attack now would be the worst thing that could happen.

Ash had a decision to make. He looked up the mountain and then down at the trees where he had left Broken Nose and Templeton. He continued to climb.

A quarter of a mile higher Ash regretted his decision. The pain was worse. He had to stop often to catch his breath. He forged on. So far there had been no sign of a camp or a cabin. He needed to rest again so he sat with his back to a fir and placed the Winchester across his legs. A gust of wind sent a slight chill rippling through him.

A sparrow alighted in the fir. It chirped gaily, then must have spotted him because it flittered shrilly away.

Ash breathed deep, wishing the pain would stop. It was as if tiny claws were ripping at his insides. He closed his eyes and willed himself to relax. No sooner did he do so than the brush crackled and he opened them again, thinking a deer or some other animal had happened by. Instead it was a young man with a mane of red hair and a shotgun, which he had trained on Ash.

"Who the hell are you and what the hell are you doing on our mountain?"

Ash nearly jerked the Winchester up but had the presence of mind not to. The shotgun would blow a hole in him the size of a melon. "I'm hunting," he replied. "I didn't know this land belonged to anyone."

"Well, it does." The young man came closer. "You don't look so good, Mister. Are you feeling poorly?"

"I have a condition," Ash said.

"And you're climbing mountains?" The redhead chuckled. "Don't this beat all. My brothers are always saying how I don't have the brains of a turnip, but you have me beat. Who are you anyhow?"

"My name is Jackson." Ash had picked the first one that popped into his head. "What might yours be?"

"Abimelech."

"My God."

"It's my ma's fault. She was powerful fond of the Bible so she named all of us by turning the pages and touching one when the spirit moved her. If she touched a name we were stuck with it."

"I've heard of people doing that."

"My brothers have better names than me and never stop teasing me about it."

"What might theirs be?"

"Jotham and Zebul."

Ash didn't see how they were much better. "You say this mountain is yours? After I rest up, can I visit your homestead? I could use a cup of coffee or just water if that's all you have."

"My brothers don't like strangers," Abimelech said. "They might take it into their heads to shoot you."

"They'd kill a man for no reason?"

"Mister, my brothers . . ." Abimelech stopped. "Jotham is right. I gabble like a goose. Slide that rifle off your legs and set your six-gun next to it. Then stand up with your hands in the air."

"I need to rest a little longer."

"You only think you do. I won't tell you twice." Abimelech wedged the shotgun to his shoulder. "I sort of like you and don't want to make mush of your innards. Do as I say and you go on breathing."

Inwardly, Ash cursed. He should have been more alert, should have spotted Abimelech before Abimelech spotted him. "I'll do as you want. Just go easy on those triggers." He slid the Winchester onto the grass and used two fingers to place the Colt next to it. Then, bracing himself against the fir, he slowly rose. He exaggerated how much pain he was in and when he was erect he clutched his chest and grimaced.

"Is your heart giving out on you? You act just like my pa right before he dropped dead in front of us."

"It's not anything I like to talk about," Ash told him. "Listen, couldn't I stay here and your brothers come to me?"

Abimelech shook his red mane. "They wouldn't like that. They'd beat me for not bringing you and I'm awful tired of being beat. Go around that tree and up the mountain and we'll be there directly."

Ash moved slowly. He hoped Abimelech would make a mistake and he could jump him, but Abimelech stayed well out of reach and always kept the shotgun centered on his back. "Why does your family live so far from anywhere, if you don't mind my asking?"

"Towns don't agree with us. Folks generally look down their noses at us and there's all those can't-do's."

"Can't-do's?" Ash repeated.

"You can't get too drunk or they throw you in jail. You can't fight. You can't cuss when ladies are near. You can't shoot out lights or even shoot into the air. In some towns you can't even carry a gun. When I was little my family got run out of a few places and we got tired of it."

"I'm sorry to hear that," Ash commiserated.

"It wasn't so bad on us menfolk but ma and my sisters always got upset. Ma cried a few times. Pa got mad at her and said it wasn't our fault people put on airs. We are as good as anyone, he'd say, and she should be proud to be a Frazier."

Ash feigned ignorance. "That's your last name?"

"Damn."

"What?"

"No more talking until we get there."

"There" turned out to be a cabin nestled at the foot of a cliff. Whoever built it didn't know much about building. The logs were uneven and had gaps between them. From some logs, the stubs of branches poked out. Mud had been caked in the wider gaps but now the mud was cracked and splitting. To one side was a corral fashioned from saplings. It held seven horses.

There was no door, just an old elk hide that hung down like the flap of Broken Nose's teepee. The window had neither glass nor curtains.

"Stop right there," Abimelech commanded. He raised his voice. "Jot! Zeb! Look at what I found!"

Older versions of Abimelech came out of the cabin. Older, bigger and coarser, their beards tangled mats, so dearly in need of baths they stank. They also carried shotguns.

It was the pair who came out next that startled Ash. Two women, both between twenty and twenty-five or thereabouts. Both with the same red hair and the same big noses. Their dresses were faded homespun, with more patches than a quilt.

The oldest and broadest of the brothers reared over Ash and glared. "Where did you find him, Ab?"

"Sitting by a tree down near where we shot that grouse last week. He was panting and sweating like he is now. He's sickly, Jot."

"Peculiar," Jotham said.

Ash smiled and held out his hand. "I'd be grateful for something to drink. My throat is as dry as sand."

"It's his heart, Jot," Abimelech said. "I saw it with my own eyes. Wouldn't surprise me if he fell dead right where he's standing."

"You don't say." This from the middle brother, Zebul. "Makes you wonder what a man in his shape is doing up here."

"I was hunting," Ash said.

"What?"

"Mountain sheep."

Zebul laughed. "The best peaks to find sheep are to the south. There's none on ours, none at all."

"I didn't know. I'm new to these parts," Ash justified his mistake.

Jotham was rubbing his red beard. "You don't look like no hunter to me. You have the reek of law."

Ash thought fast. "I own a dry goods store in Denver. Came there from Ohio about six months ago."

"You're lying, Mister. You don't talk like you're from back East. I can't say where, exactly, but this is two lies we've caught you at."

Zebul leveled his shotgun. "Step aside and let's be done with him. I have things to do."

To Ash's surprise, one of the girls moved between them. "Not so fast, consarn you. Elisheba and me have got a say, don't we?"

"Out of the way, Jochebed," Zebul said angrily. "You know better than to step in front of a man when he's about to shoot."

Jochebed's dark eyes roved over Ash from his hat to his boots. "I want this one alive a while yet."

"What for?"

"He's not bad on the eyes."

"Oh hell."

Jochebed turned to the oldest brother. "I leave it to you, Jot. You know how long it's been. Can Elisheba and me have him to play with or not?"

Jotham wasn't any more happy about her request

than Zebul. "What do you need him for when you have us?"

"It can get boring, the same thing every day." Jochebed rejoined. "We'd only want him for the night. You can do what you want come morning."

The younger sister, Elisheba, clapped her hands and squealed. "Please, Jot! Please let us play with him."

"Danged women." Jotham glowered at Ash and at the sky and then at his sisters. "You two are a nuisance. You can have him but make damn sure he doesn't get away."

Jochebed grinned. "Sickly as he is, I doubt he'll live out the night."

Chapter 19

Months ago, when Ash told the parson life was too ridiculous for words, he had no idea. Here he was, trussed up like a calf for the slaughter, bound wrists and ankles to a chair in a small room at the back of the cabin. Crumpled blankets were on the floor. The room had a smell that reminded him of a bawdy house.

Ash had been there about an hour. The brothers had tied him and left and no one had come to see him since. He'd yearned to resist, to fight them, but there wasn't a moment when he wasn't staring into the twin muzzles of a double-barreled shotgun.

Ash sat slumped in despair. His chest still hurt and his head hurt and his wrists were chafed from his trying to get loose. He pulled and wrenched in the hope he could, but Jotham had done a good job.

The door opened.

Ash sat up. It was the younger of the two sisters, Elisheba. He noticed she was barefoot and her feet were filthy. "How do you do, ma'am?"

"My, ain't you the polite one?" She came over and

pranced around the chair with her hands clasped behind her back, then stood and giggled.

"Untie me, won't you?" Ash asked.

"Now, why would I want to do a thing like that?" Elisheba giggled some more. "It would only make my brothers and sister mad at me."

"Why have you done this? What do you intend doing with me?"

She was quite the giggler. "My sis and me are going to have fun. When we're through we'll give you to our brothers and they'll have their fun."

"What do mean by 'fun'?"

"With me and my sis it's one thing. With our brothers it's another."

"I've never done you or your family any harm."

"So?" Elisheba crooked a finger and hooked it under his chin. "Sis is right. You're not bad on the eyes. The last one we got to play with was a miner. He was older and uglier and too afeared to amount to much."

"You've done this before?"

"Plenty of times." Skipping and humming to herself, she pranced around the chair again.

"I can't hardly believe this is happening."

"Oh, it's happening, sure enough. But it won't be so bad. Jochebed and me are she-cats. When a man lies with us he doesn't forget."

"What if the man doesn't want to lie with you?" Ash asked, and almost lost an eye when she raked her fingernails at him. He felt sharp stings and the trickle of blood. "You had no call to do that."

"Don't insult us, then."

"All I was saying is that a man should get to choose." Ash flicked the tip of his tongue at a drop of blood on his lip.

"I'm not stupid, Mister. You think my sister and me ain't pretty enough or refined enough. You'd rather have one of those fancy gals who live in town, with their bonnets and ribbons and such."

"I want no such thing."

"Liar. You're a man. Men take it anywhere they can get it. I learned that from my pa and my brothers."

The door opened again and in came Jochebed. "What are you doing in here?"

"Talking to him is all," Elisheba said.

"You heard Jotham. Neither of us is to be in here with him alone." Jochebed inspected the ropes. "We'll take turns. One can have her fun while the other watches that he doesn't make a break."

Elisheba giggled and winked at Ash. "When do we start? I'm ready now."

"After supper."

"Why do we have to wait so long?"

"Don't ask me; ask Jotham. I'd as soon get started now, but you know how he gets."

"He's too damn bossy," Elisheba said.

Jochebed glanced at the door. "Have a care, girl. He ever hears you say a thing like that and he'll bloody your back with a switch."

"The hell he will. He has no right. Only pa did."

"Jotham is head of the family now that pa and ma are gone. Like it or not we have to do as he says."

"It ain't fair," Elisheba complained.

Ash was being ignored and remedied that by saying, "You're not thinking this through, ladies. People know where I am. They'll come looking for me when I don't come back."

Jochebed chuckled. "It'll just be too bad for them if

they do. They'll wind up at the bottom of the ravine like the rest."

"What ravine?"

"Where we throw the bodies. The buzzards always pick the bones clean. It saves us the burying." Jochebed showed no trace of remorse. "I have one of the skulls. I use it for a candle holder."

Ash remembered seeing it on a shelf in the main room. "How can people like you live with yourselves?"

Jochebed bristled like a stuck porcupine. "What the hell do you mean, people like us? We're no different from anybody else. Or is it that we never had no schooling and don't talk proper?"

"This world *is* an asylum," Ash said to himself, and was slapped so hard it was a wonder he didn't lose teeth.

Jochebed reached behind her and flourished a knife with an antler handle. "Call us crazy again, you bastard, and I'll slit you from ear to ear."

Ash did bristling of his own. "Go ahead, bitch. Spoil your fun."

Swearing luridly, Jochebed knocked his hat off. She gripped him by the hair and pressed the knife to his throat. "Call me that again and see if you don't bleed."

Ash didn't care the blade was against his skin. "Threats don't work on someone who is already dying."

Lowering the knife, Jochebed stepped back. "That's right. My little brother says you have the same thing my pa got. But you better be nice to us, Mister. You're not dead yet. We can make your dying a lot worse if you prod us."

Ash was so mad, he forgot himself. "How is it everyone is out to hang your brothers and not the two of you? You're just as vile as they are." He realized his blunder the instant the words were out of his mouth.

The sisters swapped glances and Elisheba said, "Did you hear him, sister? He knows who we are. He's not a hunter like he claimed. We should let Jotham know." She turned, but Jochebed grabbed her wrist.

"Do that and Jot will drag him out and kill him. Our night of fun will be spoiled."

"I hadn't thought of that." Elisheba hungrily devoured Ash with her eyes. "I reckon it doesn't much matter when we tell Jot. This one will die all the same."

Jochebed wagged the knife in front of Ash's face. "You're not wearing a badge so you must be after the rewards. I hate bounty men. We were going to go easy on you on account of your heart, but now we'll do you as we've done the others, and if it kills you, so be it."

"There are worse ways to die than to be forced to make love."

"Not the way my sister and me do it. You'll understand once we bring in the whip and the collar." Jochebed laughed and lightly ran the edge of the blade across Ash's cheek. Then she poked her sister with her elbow and the pair waltzed out, whispering and giggling.

The moment the door closed, Ash sagged in the chair and bowed his chin to his chest. Fear clawed at him. Real fear. He told himself he was being stupid. He was dying anyway. What difference did it make if the lead pierced his heart or the Fraziers did him in? But call it pride, call it the will to live as long he could, it *did* make a difference.

Lifting his head, Ash craned his neck from side to side, trying to glimpse the ropes. As near as he could tell, it was old rope, and old rope wasn't always as strong as new rope. Not that he could snap it. It would take effort. A hell of a lot of effort.

Ash set to work twisting his wrists back and forth. At first they barely moved. The longer he persisted, the more success he had. It hurt, though. God in heaven, it hurt. The pain got so bad, he forgot about the other pain, the pain in his chest. He rubbed and rubbed until he had lost a lot of skin and his wrists dripped blood.

It was funny, Ash thought. For years he'd been in the prime of health. Nary as much as a toothache. Since he was shot, pain had become as much a part of his life as breathing. Now he was in even more.

Desperation made a man do strange things.

Ash tugged and pulled. The ropes weren't slick enough yet. He tried not to imagine how his wrists must look.

It was do or die.

Ash lost track of time. The sisters were due back and he must be free by then. Intent on rubbing, he was bewildered at hearing distant shots, five or six from down the mountain. He cocked his head and listened for more but there were none.

About a quarter of an hour went by. Ash was bleeding bad. He was feeling weak. The pressure in his chest was worse. The last thing he needed was another attack. Not now. It would be the end of him.

Then boots tramped and the door slammed open. In strode all five Fraziers, the three brothers in the lead. Jotham loomed over him, his big hands on his hips, and glowered.

"Who are they?"

"Who are who?"

The blow nearly took Ash's head off. The room swam and he floated in and out of consciousness. The next he knew, his jaw was in an iron vise and Jotham's hate-filled eyes were inches from his.

"Play smart with me and I'll knock your damn teeth out. How many of you are there?"

Ash tried to speak and discovered his mouth was full of blood.

"It hit me that maybe you weren't up here alone," Jotham went on. "So I sent Zebul and Abimelech to scout around."

Zebul nodded and took up the account. "We spotted two men sneaking up this way. One was an old Injun, the other a cowpoke. The old Injun saw us and warned the cowboy and then took off like a rabbit. We swapped lead with the cowboy but he slipped away on us."

Jotham tightened his grip on Ash's chin. "I went down quick as I could to help. We found where you and your friends camped and horse tracks leading down the mountain."

Ash had harbored the notion that maybe, just maybe, Templeton and Broken Nose would rescue him. That hope had been dashed.

"How many of you are there?" Jotham growled. "And don't give me that lie about hunting mountain sheep. You came here after us. You're part of a posse, aren't you?"

"No."

Jotham swore and dug his nails into Ash's flesh. "Don't lie to me, you son of a bitch. You're the law. I know it."

"I used to be. Not anymore," Ash confessed.

From behind Jotham came a squeal. "I knew it!" Jochebed exclaimed. "He's after the money."

"A bounty man," Zebul said in disgust.

"No," Ash said. "I just wanted to kill you."

Jotham's bushy brows beetled and he let go and straightened. "What in hell for? What did we ever do to you?"

"Nothing."

Jotham started to draw back his fist, but stopped. "I don't savvy, Mister. Explain it so I can."

"You'll laugh."

"I don't laugh much. And I wouldn't keep me waiting."

Ash gave it to them plain. "I'm dying. I wanted to do something with the time I had left, something worthwhile, so when I heard about you and your brothers, about all the killing and robbing you've done, I thought, Why not? That Indian and the other man were my guide and my helper."

"That's why you came up here? For real and for true?"

Ash nodded and braced for a beating. To his amazement, Jotham took a step back and broke into peals of gruff glee.

"Just when I thought I'd heard it all!"

"You believe him?" Zebul asked.

"Look at him. He's telling the truth. You can tell." Jotham chuckled.

"What we've got here is a damned do-good. A gent who wants to rid the world of evil like us. Or maybe he's doing it to get in good with God."

"Not likely," Ash said.

Jotham placed his big hand on Ash's shoulder. "We've had tin badges after us. We've had men after the price on our heads. We even had Pinkertons once. But you are a first."

"I'm flattered."

"And do you know what? For this you deserve the best death we can give you."

"Best how? As in quick and painless?"

"Slow," Jotham said. "Slow and hurting. Hurting so much, you'll scream your lungs out. Hurting so much, you'll blubber and beg. I want you to die knowing you're the most stupid bastard who ever lived."

"You might be right," Ash said in self-reproach.

"What about Elisheba and me?" Jochebed asked. "Do we still get to play with him?"

"You do not. We're dragging him outside, tying him to a tree and getting right to it. Zeb, you fetch the skinning knife. Ab, you find the axe. Girls, we'll need your sewing needles for his eyes and his oysters." Jotham patted Ash and grinned. "Let's have us some fun."

Chapter 20

Stripped to the waist, his boots and socks removed, Ash girded himself for the horror to come. They had been true to their word; they'd dragged him out and tied him to a fir tree near the cabin and now they were squabbling over who got to carve on him first.

Ash had hoped for a chance to make a run for it when they brought him out but two of the brothers had seized his arms while the third held a shotgun to the back of his neck the whole way.

The sisters weren't taking part in the argument. They stood to one side, studies in frustration, Jochebed in particular mad they didn't get to play with him, as she put it. Petulantly stamping a foot, she complained, "Jot could let us have him for a few hours at least."

"Don't say that louder unless you want a busted nose," Elisheba cautioned. "Remember the last time you sassed him?"

At Ash's feet lay an axe, a skinning knife and several sewing needles. Plus a hammer. He could imagine the uses they would be put to and held back a shudder.

"Damn your contrary hide," Jotham was snarling at

Zebul. "All this fuss when by rights it should be me. But I'll tell you what. To show how fair I can be, we'll draw sticks. Long stick gets to cut on him first. How would that be?"

Abimelech gathered three sticks. Jotham broke the ends off two of them so they were the same length, leaving the third slightly longer. "Come over here, girl," he said to Elisheba. He had her hold the sticks with the ends poking out and each brother took a turn picking one.

"It's me!" Zebul declared, waving the longest. Chortling, he came over and picked up the butcher knife. "Where to begin? Where to begin?" He jabbed Ash in the side and a scarlet flower blossomed.

Ash flinched. He had made up his mind not to break, but he knew he would. There was only so much a person could take. "Cut me loose and give me a fighting chance."

Zebul was about to jab him again. "No way in hell. You brought this on yourself. Now you can take your medicine." He laughed and the knife flashed and another crimson petal appeared.

"I hope you're tough enough to last the rest of the day and all night, besides," Jotham remarked. "There's nothing I like better than carving on people."

Zebul held the knife down low. "How about I start with his oysters, brother? Like we did that prospector that time?"

"Not yet," Jotham said. "Some can't take the shock. We'll save those for later, after we've chopped off his fingers and toes."

Ash's mouth had gone dry. He began to quake and willed his body to stop. He would be strong for as long as he could.

"I have an idea," Jochebed said. "Why not start with his tongue? He'll only use it to cuss us anyway."

"I like that." Zebul reached for Ash's mouth. Ash jerked his head away but Zebul got hold of his lower lip and about tore it off. "Keep still or you'll only make it worse."

Ash clenched his teeth.

"That won't do no good," Zebul told him. "I'll just cut away the gum and pry out your teeth one by one."

"Do it!" Jochebed urged.

Zebul pressed the blade tip to Ash's lower gum. "Let's see. How about if I start at the front and work my way around?"

All of them were grinning.

Ash swallowed blood and was overcome with dread. Here he'd thought he didn't care if he lived or died. Here he'd thought his zest for life was gone. But he was wrong. He *did* like living. He had the same zest as always. Nothing had really changed.

Zebul had the knife poised to commence. "Any last words?"

Then a rifle cracked and the hand holding the knife exploded, bits of fingers flying every which way. Zebul leaped back and howled, his eyes wide in shock. "I've been shot!" he bleated the obvious.

Another crack and Jotham whipped halfway around. The slug had caught him high in the shoulder. "Find cover!" he commanded.

Like quicksilver rabbits, the Fraziers bounded into the woods. The rifle banged a few more times but as near as Ash could tell, no one was hit. Silence fell.

Ash gazed down the mountain. He had a hunch who had come to his rescue.

Movement alerted him to a Frazier slinking through

the undergrowth: Abimelech, working lower. Ash opened his mouth to yell a warning but closed it again. The Fraziers might shoot him.

Ash tried to break loose. His wrists were welters of agony. Breathless with worry, he waited. The minutes crawled. No more shots boomed. None of the Fraziers reappeared.

Unexpectedly a head and a hat popped into view less than a stone's throw away. Rin Templeton flicked a smile and came toward Ash in a crouch, holding his rifle ready to shoot.

Ash was torn. He dearly wanted to be free but it had to be a trap. The Fraziers must be lying low, waiting for whoever shot Zebul's fingers off to show himself. The rancher was playing right into their hands. "Don't! Get out of here while you can!"

Templeton paid him no heed. Turning from side to side, he came to the fir, reached down, and drew a boot knife.

"Damn it. I don't want you dead on my account."

"The three of them are searching for me below," Templeton whispered back. "I'll have you loose in two shakes of a calf's tail."

"What about the sisters?"

"Those two fillies I saw? I don't know where they got to." Templeton stooped and slashed at the rope and it parted but not quite all the way. He raised his hand to slash again.

Out of a thicket hurtled Jochebed and Elisheba. Jochebed had the axe and her younger sister had the hammer. Screeching like bobcats, they flung themselves at Templeton.

"Look out!" Ash cried.

The rancher spun. He brought up his Winchester but

he did not quite have it level when Jochebed buried the axe in his forearm. The rifle went off, the slug digging a furrow, as Templeton staggered back, blood spurting from a severed vein. He dropped the rifle and clawed for his revolver and had it almost out when Elisheba smashed the hammer against his wrist.

Ash heard the crunch of bone. He lunged to help Templeton and was held in place by the rope. Frantic, he exerted all of his strength, heedless of the torment. The rope broke and he came up behind the sisters as Jochebed swung the axe on high. Templeton was on one knee, his good arm raised to ward off the blow.

"Chop his head off!" Elisheba screeched.

Ash tore the hammer from her grasp. She turned as he slammed it against her temple. With a groan, she buckled.

Jochebed hadn't seen. "You're dead, Mister!" she cried at Templeton. "No one hurts our kin."

The axe arced down. Ash swung the hammer. Wood clacked on wood as the hammer's handle caught the axe's handle and stopped it from descending.

"You!" Jochebed cried, and sprang back. She saw her sister and her face flushed with fury. "If you've killed her, so help me . . ." With that she came at him, a whirl-wind of retribution.

Backpedaling, Ash warded off swing after swing. Some he dodged. A few he ducked. He was well aware that if he didn't end it soon her brothers would show up and end him permanently. She was shrieking and hissing and swearing as if she'd gone berserk. The axe, with its long handle, gave her greater reach and she used it to her advantage, staying well away from him.

From somewhere down the mountain came a bellow. Jotham, shouting that her brothers were coming to her aid.

Ash doubted she heard, so intent was she on chopping him to bits. He tried to spring in close but the axe drove him off. He couldn't get past it. He knew it and she knew it. So Ash didn't try. He feinted and sidestepped and threw the hammer at her face.

Jochebed's howl of pain and rage pierced the rarified mountain air.

She tottered back, her left eye half-shut and bleeding. "You've blinded me!" she screamed. "Damn you to hell, you've blinded me!" She came at him in a frenzy, swinging wildly.

Diving, Ash rolled. The axe swished over his head and he scrambled up and saw that Rin Templeton had drawn his Colt. Templeton was drenched in blood and spurting more. Yet the rancher managed to hold the Colt steady and he fired as Jochebed turned, fired as she hiked the axe, fired as she took a faltering step toward Ash and fired as she fell.

"You may have killed me but I've killed you, bitch," Templeton gasped.

Ash reached to help him. "We have to get out of here."

"Hell," Templeton said. He was looking at the forest.

A twin-barreled howitzer discharged both barrels at once and Templeton's head burst, one ear flying one way and the other ear the other way.

Ash dived again, this time for Templeton's Winchester. Another shotgun went off but the spray of lead whizzed over his head. Flipping onto his back, he took a swift bead on Jotham's chest. The hammer had already been pulled back so he figured there must be a round in the chamber. There was. The slug rocked Jotham onto his heels but he didn't go down.

Gaining his feet, Ash raced into the forest. He reached cover without being shot, and hunkered.

The three bothers were converging on their fallen sisters. They could see that Jochebed was dead. Jotham and Zebul cursed in a fury. Abimelech knelt and lifted Elisheba's head into his lap. She showed she was alive by groaning.

Jotham began reloading his shotgun. "We go after him, you hear? We go after him and we make him suffer for Jochebed more than we have made anyone suffer, ever."

"I don't need an excuse," Zebul declared, holding up the bloody stumps that had once been fingers. "This is his fault. He didn't shoot me but he's the reason they came after us."

"I'll stay with sis," Abimelech offered.

Ash worked the lever and raised the Winchester. He had them. Three shots and it was over. He centered on Jotham's forehead and squeezed—and the rifle clicked. The reason hit him like a ton of rocks. The Winchester was empty. Templeton had used up the rest of the cartridges and hadn't thought to reload or didn't have the time.

Ash didn't have any ammunition on him. Under the circumstances all he could do was retreat deeper into the forest.

"There he goes!"

A shotgun thundered and a tree branch above Ash's head dissolved in a shower of slivers. He was around the trunk before they could try again.

"We're coming for you, bastard!" Jotham bellowed. "You're as good as dead. Do you hear me?"

Ash wondered how it was that Jotham wasn't dead. He was positive he'd hit him dead center. Skirting a rock outcropping, he stopped. Should he go higher or lower? He went up, pumping his legs, seeking a likely spot to spring a surprise.

He held on to the Winchester, empty though it was.

The woods had gone quiet. Now that Jotham's initial rage had passed, the Fraziers were as silent as ghosts.

Ash was sorry for Templeton, but the rancher had been foolish to do what he did. Now Ash would have to go to the Box T and break the news. He'd always hated that chore as a lawman and felt no better about it now.

Above the outcropping was a large log. Jumping over it, Ash flattened. This would do nicely. If they followed his tracks they would be right on top of him before they realized he was there.

To the east a jay squawked. To the west several finches took noisy flight.

Birds didn't spook like that without cause. Ash looked to the west. A silhouette took shape, moving slowly, searching. He pressed low. Whichever brother it was would pass within twenty feet of him. Ash's eyes began to hurt, he stared so hard.

A soft scrape came from the other side of the log.

Ash dared a quick peek.

Zebul was almost to the top of the outcropping. The missing fingers didn't seem to bother him much. He held his shotgun in the crook of his elbow with his other hand on the hammers and triggers.

Ash rolled onto his back, the Winchester on his chest. Gripping the barrel in both hands, he tensed. A shadow darkened the top of the log and then darkened him. Zebul was above him, peering intently into the woods ahead. Careful of the shotgun's muzzles, Ash jumped up and swung. The Winchester's hardwood stock caught Zebul full across the face. The shotgun thundered, the barrels emptying into the ground and not into Ash. Zebul tottered, stunned, and Ash swung again at Zebul's throat.

Zebul toppled. Coughing and gagging, he thrashed wildly about. He flailed, he kicked, he bucked. The convulsions might have gone on, only Ash struck him a third time on the forehead.

Ash was pleased. One more down, one less to deal with. Crashing and crackling alerted him to Jotham, who was charging from the west like a bull gone amok, plowing through everything in his path.

Ash ran. He wished he'd grabbed Zebul's shotgun. Now there was no time. A cry of loss and outrage told him Jotham had seen Zebul's body. Ash flew faster.

He went a short way and glanced over his shoulder, thinking possibly he had gotten away.

Jotham was after him, coming on swiftly, death writ on his face.

Ash vaulted a boulder and sped around a spruce. Ahead was a slope strewn with small rocks. He started up only to have the rocks slide out from under him. He fell onto his right knee, got a hand under him, and went to rise.

Past the spruce pounded Jotham. The instant he saw Ash he threw the shotgun to his shoulder to fire.

"Now you die!"

Chapter 21

Ash threw the Winchester at him. It was the only thing he could think of to do. The rifle struck the shotgun and the twin muzzles swung skyward just as Jotham fired. Ash hurled himself at Jotham. His shoulder caught Jotham low in the legs and upended him.

Ash made it up first. He was weaponless so he resorted to his fists and caught Jotham with a looping right as Jotham started to rise. Incredibly, it had no effect. Roaring like an enraged grizzly, Jotham wrapped his arms around Ash and squeezed.

A bear hug. When done by a strong man, a really strong man, it could squeeze the life out of a person.

Jotham was immensely strong.

Pain shot down Ash's spine. Arching his back, he kicked and struggled. Pressure filled his chest. God, no! he thought. He was having an attack. He would be weak at the very moment he needed what strength he had left. He kicked harder, thrashed harder.

Jotham laughed. It was a cold, fierce, brutal laugh, filled with venom. "I have you now, you son of a bitch."

Ash's vision began to blur. He drove his forehead against Jotham's face, against his mouth and then his nose, and was rewarded with a spurt of blood and a yowl.

"You'll have to try harder than that," Jotham taunted.

"Try this, then," Ash said, and drove his knee up and in. Once, twice, three times.

Jotham grunted and colored. He swayed. He gurgled and teetered. A fourth blow brought a cry and Jotham's arms slackened enough that Ash heaved free. He kicked Jotham in the right knee. He kicked Jotham in the left knee.

Jotham crashed down. Roaring in fury he grabbed at Ash, but Ash skipped aside. Ash saw the shotgun and snatched it up. Swinging it by the barrels, he smashed it against Jotham's head. Again and again he swung, battering through Jotham's outflung hands, striking again and again and again until it occurred to him that Jotham wasn't moving.

His chest on fire, gasping for breath, Ash stopped.

Jotham's head resembled a crushed melon.

Ash went through Jotham's pockets. He found seven shells. Breaking the shotgun open, he extracted the spent shells and replaced them. Grimly he marched down the mountain. His chest was worse but he refused to stop. It didn't help that the world would blur and then come into focus again.

They were still there. Elisheba had recovered and was on her feet. Abimelech was hunkered next to Jochebed, his head bowed, his hand on her bosom.

They heard Ash and turned.

Ash used the first barrel on Abimelech and evaporated half his face.

Elisheba screamed and turned to flee and Ash used the second barrel between her shoulder blades.

Ash reloaded. Belatedly, he realized that was the last of them. The Fraziers were all dead. He stared at Templeton's body, then shuffled toward the cabin. He needed his clothes. He needed the Remington. He needed morphine more than he needed anything.

Ash reached for the door. His chest hammered and the ground and the sky swapped places. The cabin seemed to leap at him and a black cloud swallowed the small part of him that was left.

Sounds. Images. They came and they went. Ash was vaguely aware of swaying. Once he heard voices. Another time he opened his eyes and there were stars above and a figure was huddled by a crackling fire. Someone said something, but he was fading out again.

His return was abrupt.

Ash blinked and tried to make sense of what he was seeing. Poles of some kind, poking through a hole. The smell of alcohol tingled his nose. "Can't be," he croaked.

A form filled his vision. Ash blinked again and saw who it was. "You," he said weakly.

Broken Nose was examining him. "You have come back from the land of the dead. How do you feel?"

"Like hell." Ash had no strength, none at all. His chest hurt but not a terrible lot.

"It has worn off, then. I will give you more."

"What has worn off?" Ash asked, and had his answer when Broken Nose squatted, holding the hypodermic. "You've been giving me morphine?"

"For weeks now." The Ute rolled up Ash's sleeve.

Ash's forearm was speckled with marks. "Where did you learn how to inject it?"

"I watched you."

The familiar prick preceded the familiar bliss. Ash embraced it, cherished it. Then he realized what Broken Nose had said. "Wait. Did you say weeks?"

Broken Nose was putting the hypodermic in the kit. "Twenty sleeps, as my people would say."

"I was out that long?" Ash reached up to scratch his chin in bewilderment and discovered he had the start of a beard. "I'll be damned."

"You were almost dead when I found you. I did what I could and brought you back." Broken Nose smiled. "I must like you to go to all this trouble."

"How did we get to your lodge?"

"We flew."

"What?"

Broken Nose laughed and patted Ash's shoulder. "I made a travois and tied you on it and here we are. Your horse is outside. Your saddle and guns and other things are over there." He indicated the pile. "The man from Denver has been here two times and will come again tomorrow."

"What man from Denver?"

"The one you talked to at Ute City."

"That journalist from the *Rocky Mountain News*? What the hell did he want?"

Broken Nose moved off. When he came back he was holding a newspaper.

"He said now all whites will know of you."

The front-page headline was in large bold type: FRA-ZIERS DIE IN GUN BATTLE WITH HEROIC EX-LAWMAN.

"God, no," Ash breathed.

Broken Nose set the paper next to him. "Read it when you want. You have made the man very happy. He said they have sold a great many newspapers thanks to you."

"How did they find out?"

"When we came down the mountain there were men with wagons. Miners. They asked how you got hurt." Broken Nose grinned. "You know how whites love to talk. Word spread. I could not move very fast with you on the travois and when we got to Ute City a lot of people were waiting to see you. The man from Denver was one of them. He asked me many questions."

It took effort, but Ash sat up. He put the paper in his lap and read the account. It was remarkably accurate. "How did you know all this? You weren't even there."

"I saw everything except what they did to you when you were inside."

Ash looked up. "You watched the whole fight? You saw Templeton get killed? And you didn't help?"

"You did not hire me to fight, only to track." Broken Nose stepped to the pile and returned with a poke that bulged and jangled, a poke Ash never set eyes on before. "This is the money the newspaper put on the Fraziers. I kept three hundred dollars for myself."

Too much was being thrown at Ash too fast. He sank down. "Three hundred is an awful lot."

"Your life is not worth that much?"

Ash let it drop. He should be grateful. He should be thankful to be alive. Relaxing, he sank into morphine-induced pleasure. He welcomed the feeling into every fiber of his being. How long he was immersed in the sensation, he couldn't say. A persistent shake on his shoulder intruded on his ecstasy, but he kept his eyes closed and said, "Leave me alone, Broken Nose."

"It's not the old Indian, Marshal Thrall. It's Horace Smithers, with the *Rocky Mountain News.* Remember?"

Ash reluctantly opened his eyes. "You can leave me alone too."

Horace was ready to scribble. "You don't mean that. Haven't you read the accounts in the paper?" He reached down and showed the copy of the *News* that Broken Nose had given to Ash.

"I've read that one."

"You're a hero, Marshal. Everyone in the territory has heard about what you did. Taking on the Frazier gang and wiping them out. That took uncommon courage."

Ash marshaled his energy. "Let's get some things straight. First, I'm not a lawman anymore. I had to give up my badge. Second, going after the Fraziers was stupid. It got Rin Templeton killed and damn near got me killed too. I don't want to hear I'm a hero when I'm no such thing."

"You're too modest. I know about the slug near your heart. How you are slowly dying. How you went after the Fraziers because you wanted to do something worthwhile before you meet your Maker."

"Hell," Ash said.

"It's in the other accounts."

"What others?"

"You haven't read them? I've done a whole series on you. I dug up all I could find out and guessed a lot of the rest or made it up but I assure you it's all quite flattering." Horace beamed. "I've made you famous, Marshal. Painted you in glory for all the world to admire."

"Hell, hell, hell."

"Why are you so bothered? You should be flattered. People will remember you long after you're gone."

Ash wanted to punch him. "That's where you're wrong. The glory men do is buried with them. Five years after I've been planted not a soul will remember me."

"You're wrong. You'll see."

"Not from the grave I won't." Ash was tired and wanted him to go. "Why are you here, Smithers?"

"I'd like to do a last account. Give it a personal touch. Tell about your life growing up. How you were as a boy. Why you pinned on a badge. The loves you've had. Those sorts of things."

"If I had my pistol I would shoot you."

Horace cackled. "You don't mean that. I like your sense of humor though. It's very droll."

"God in heaven."

"You're a religious man? I'll be sure to put that in. The folks admire a man who speaks adoringly of the Almighty. That's why politicians do it all the time."

"Broken Nose?" Ash called out.

"Yes?"

"Throw this nuisance out."

"Throw him out yourself. I am drinking."

Horace did more cackling. "You two are a caution. Now, then, shall we begin? Where were you born and what were your parents like? What forces molded you as you grew up? Would it be safe for me to write that you value honor above all else?"

Ash had enough. He closed his eyes and turned his head.

"I understand. You're not feeling well. I'll come back when you are." Horace clasped Ash's wrist. "You're a good man. It's rare I meet such a decent human being."

"There is one thing you can write for me," Ash said.

"Really? What? I'll write anything, anything at all."

"You can tell your readers that this world is hell and everyone in it is loco. You can tell them there's no point to any of it. We're born, we suffer, we die. That's all there is."

"Oh, Marshal. I could never write that. My editor would throw a fit and our readers would be offended." Horace stood. "Besides, you don't really mean it. That's the morphine talking."

"Thank you, Smithers."

"For what? My articles?"

"For proving my point." Ash rolled over so his back was to him and listened to the journalist go out. Good riddance, he told himself. "Broken Nose?"

"I am still here."

"I don't ever want to talk to him again. Don't let him into the teepee. Throw him out if he tries to come in."

"You keep forgetting. I am red. He is white. Whites don't like it when a red man is uppity, as you call it. Throw him out yourself. I will hold the flap for you, but that is all I will do."

Ash swore. To hell with Broken Nose and to hell with Horace Smithers and to hell with the whole damn world, he thought. He didn't want anything to do with any of them. He would find a hole somewhere and crawl into it with his morphine. It sparked a troubling thought. "Broken Nose?"

"You are fond of my name today."

"How much morphine do I have left?"

"I would say a week, maybe ten sleeps, and you will not have any."

Panic welled but Ash quelled it. He had plenty of time to get to Denver and get more. "Broken Nose?"

"Where is my candle? I need wax to plug my ears."

"In case I forget later," Ash said, "I want to thank

you for all you've done. For keeping me alive and bringing me back."

"I did not do it for you, white man. I did it for drinking money."

"You are a man after my own heart."

Chapter 22

Life was grand.

Ash spent his days in morphine stupors. In the evenings he roused out of bed and spent most of each night making the rounds of his favorite haunts in the area known as the Street of a Thousand Sinners.

Ash drank, and drank heavily. He had been warned not to but he didn't care. The alcohol helped him forget. He gambled too, but he was careful not to lose too much. He needed his money for other things, namely morphine, whiskey and women.

Ash couldn't get enough of perfumed bodies and perfumed sheets. He gorged on soft flesh and softer lips. Every night it was a new lady. Blondes, brunettes, redheads, short, tall, skinny, not skinny—he had them all and enjoyed the having.

To a casual observer it might seem Ash was another of the many wallowing in the mire. There was more to it. He was living life to the fullest because death was knocking at the door to his heart.

The pain, the pressure, never went way. They were always there, constant reminders that he was dying. He hated it, but there was nothing he could do except live and wait for the inevitable.

Few knew who Ash was. He seldom gave his name. When he did, he made one up. He learned that lesson the first night he was back in Denver and made the mistake of saying who he really was in a saloon. Before he could stop them, men were clapping him on the back and offering to buy him drinks for ridding the territory of the Fraziers. He tried to tell them that he hadn't done anything to merit their praise, that it had been a god-awful blunder, but no one listened. He was a hero, they said.

Ash didn't feel like one. The killing left scars. Often he woke up in cold sweats, torn from slumber by nightmare images of Jochebed being shot to ribbons or him blowing a huge hole in Elisheba or what was left of Jotham's face after he got through smashing it. So what if they deserved to die? Ending their lives hadn't made him feel as if he had done something worthwhile. It made him feel twisted and empty.

So Ash injected and drank and womanized. He lived each moment as if it were his last. He was content even if he wasn't happy. He might have gone on savoring the Street of a Thousand Sinners until the slug in his chest got around to puncturing his heart, if not for an incident that brought him out of himself.

Ash started the evening as he did every other. He shuffled from bed and washed in the basin and combed his hair and dressed.

The new boardinghouse where he was staying was comfortably furnished and the landlady minded her own business. She was on the front porch in a rocking chair when he came out.

"Good evening, Mr. Smithers."

"Evening, ma'am." It had amused Ash to use the journalist's name. "Nice breeze."

"That there is," she agreed.

Ash started down the steps.

"Say, did that man ever get hold of you?"

"What man?" Ash wondered if the real Horace Smithers had tracked him down.

"He wouldn't give his name. He came into the parlor this morning, about ten it was, and asked if you were staying here. Said a friend of his had read about you in the paper and was interested in finding you." The landlady paused in her knitting. "At least I think he meant you. Are you famous?"

"If I am it's news to me," Ash said. "What did this gentleman look like, might I ask?"

The landlady sniffed. "He was no gentleman, Mr. Smithers. He was rude and coarse. Why, he didn't even have the decency to take his hat off in the presence of a lady."

"What was he wearing?"

"I didn't look too closely. His clothes were dirty and he dearly needed a bath. He reminded me of one of those hitters."

"Hitters, ma'am?"

"You know. The men who work with cows."

"Oh. You mean punchers. He reminded you of a cow puncher?"

"His clothes did, yes. But not him. I've seen a few punchers and they are generally young and carefree and almost always polite. This man was older, I'd say in his thirties or forties, and as I told you he wouldn't know polite if it bit him on the ass."

Ash laughed.

"Pardon my language, but he irritated me so. He

wanted to know what you looked like and what room you were in and what your habits were and when . . ."

"Hold on." Ash went over. "He asked all that?"

The landlady bobbed her white-haired head. "He was terribly nosy. I didn't like his eyes. They reminded me of a snake's. Then there was that revolver he had under his jacket in violation of the city ordinance."

"That's all you can tell me about him?"

"I'm afraid so, yes."

Ash thanked her and again started down the steps.

"Oh. There is one more thing. As he was leaving the parlor he sort of chuckled to himself and said something half under his breath. I only caught part of it."

"What did he say?"

"Something about wait until the Shark hears. What on earth could he have meant by that? There aren't any sharks in Colorado."

Ash was jarred to his marrow. "Could the word have been 'Sharkey'? Could that have been it?"

"I honestly couldn't say. I suppose. Really, though, his mother should have taught him better manners."

Deep in thought, Ash drifted along the street. Could it be? he asked himself. It had to. Ben Sharkey had read Smithers' accounts. Sharkey must still be in Denver and wanted to settle accounts.

"Damn," Ash said. Here he had about given up on ever getting his revenge. He headed toward a restaurant he liked and was halfway there when his stupidity hit him like a punch to the gut. Stopping short, he turned to a display window and pretended to smooth his jacket.

Night was falling. Many windows were bright and the streetlamps were being lit. Pockets of darkening gray were broken by shards of light.

Ash scanned the street. No one matched his landlady's description. He walked on, glad he had the Remington pocket pistol. He pulled his hat brim down so
when he glanced in the windows he passed no one
would notice. He'd about decided he was taking a
pointless precaution when he casually looked over his
shoulder.

A figure almost a block behind him darted into the
shadows.

"So," Ash said, and smiled. An old saying popped
into his head, a saying he tweaked. "Good things comes
to those who spend their days on morphine." A silly
joke, but he laughed and rounded the next corner. He
ducked into the first recessed doorway he came to and
slid his hand under his jacket. He didn't have long to
wait.

Boots slapped, and past him ran the spitting image
of the landlady's visitor.

The man rose onto his toes, peered ahead and swore.

Ash gave him an ample lead and swung out after
him. The hunter had become the hunted. Plenty of people were out and about so it was simple for him to nearly
always have someone between him and his stalker. The
man never once glanced back.

For the next quarter of an hour Ash played cat and
mouse. He couldn't believe his luck. Fate had practically thrown Ben Sharkey into his lap. All he had to do
was not lose sight of the man who had been shadowing
him.

The man took to looking into the front window of
every saloon and bawdy house and gambling hall. When
a woman bumped into him, he shoved her so hard she
nearly fell. Plainly he was mad at having lost Ash and
was growing desperate to find him.

Ash could guess why. Sharkey would take it out on the man's hide. That was the trouble with people like Sharkey; they had no loyalty to friends.

Ash had to admit, though, he was a fine one to talk after what he did to the Fraziers. Maybe he wasn't the badman that Sharkey was, but he would be a hypocrite to cast stones.

Ash had always prided himself on living by the letter of the law. Part of it was that as a lawman he had to set an example. The other part was his own nature. He'd long refused to take a life. Only as a last resort, he told his deputies. Look at him now. He'd killed and killed again, women as well as men.

Ash shook his head in disgust. He was becoming a man he didn't know, a man he didn't like.

He looked up and stopped. His stalker was only twenty feet away, peering into the window of a gambling hall. Ash turned away and shammed an interest in a store display until the man hurried on.

Ash debated jumping him and questioning him. A revolver barrel did wonders for loosening tongues. But if something went wrong, if the man fought back and forced him to shoot him, he might never find Sharkey.

By now they were in the heart of the Street of a Thousand Sinners.

Over the hubbub of voices, music blared. Women in enticing dresses or in few clothes at all beckoned from doorways and balconies.

Just when Ash was wondering if the man would ever stop searching for him, he entered a saloon. Ash walked past and on around to the side. There must be a back door, he reckoned. It opened into a hall that took him past a kitchen and a storage room to a door. He opened it.

The saloon was packed. People mingled and talked and joked, having a good time.

Ash tried to spot the man he was after. There were so many. Clouds of cigar and pipe smoke hung heavy in the air like fog. The milling, the comings and goings, made it next to impossible. He was about to step out when he spotted his man over at a table. Three others were there.

Ash's hand swooped under his jacket.

None were Sharkey.

Ash swore. He must wait. He joined some people watching a dice game, his back to the table.

Ash had been so caught up in finding Sharkey that he hadn't thought once about his chest. A sharp pang reminded him. He thought it would go away but it didn't. More morphine would help. The hypodermic was in his jacket but he wasn't about to use it right there in front of everybody.

Ash needed privacy. Although loathe to leave, he went down the hall to the storage room. No one tried to stop him. He took out the hypodermic. Taking off his jacket, he rolled up his shirtsleeve.

"Here I go again," Ash said with a mix of bitterness and anticipation. He located a good vein and jabbed the needle in, flinching at the sting. He slowly pressed on the plunger. Then he leaned back against a wall. Usually it didn't take long. Warmth flooded his body, followed by the welcome sensation of pure pleasure.

God, how he loved it! Anymore, Ash couldn't get through a day without it. He told himself that he could if he really wanted to; he just didn't want to. Why should he when without it he would spend each day suffering the torment of the damned?

The rapturous feeling grew. Ash closed his eyes and

let it claim him completely. Time became meaningless. Only vaguely was he conscious of the wall he was leaning against and the room around him. Were Sharkey to walk in, he'd be at the mercy of a man who had none.

Sharkey. Ash should go back out and watch in the saloon until Sharkey showed up. Sharkey's men were there so maybe he would come join them.

But Ash didn't move. He was immersed in morphine heaven.

The doctors had warned him that morphine was a demon in disguise, but they were wrong. Morphine was a chemical angel. Morphine brought joy and peace. Everyone should use it. Then they'd know. Then the whole world would know.

Suddenly the door opened and in came a man wearing an apron, who stopped short in surprise.

"What the hell. Who are you?"

"Nobody," Ash said.

"What are you doing back here?"

"I'm holding the wall up," Ash said, and chuckled.

The man stared. "You don't look so well. You're not sick, are you?"

"If that was all I was, I'd be the happiest gent alive."

"You don't make much sense."

"Life doesn't make much sense."

"Enough riddles. Off you go. No one is allowed in the saloon after we've closed. The boss is strict about that."

"Sure. I'll go." Ash reached for his jacket. "Hold on. Did you say the saloon is closed?"

"We stay open until dawn. Then we close until noon so we can clean up and get ready for the new night."

"I couldn't have!" Ash said. He ran out and down the hall.

No one was there. The saloon was empty. The front window wasn't dark with night but was growing bright with the light of dawn. He went out and looked up and down the street. The man he had followed was long gone. He had blown his chance to put an end to Sharkey.

"Damn me anyhow."

Ash bent his steps to his boardinghouse. It served him right for losing all track of time.

Once in his room, Ash lay on the bed and curled into a ball. It was just like life to offer him hope and then dash that hope to bits. He should get back up and scour Denver from end to end. Maybe tomorrow, he told himself. Right now all he cared about was the morphine, and the feeling it gave him.

Sharkey and the rest of the world could go to hell.

Chapter 23

The days blurred into weeks and the weeks blurred into a couple of months and Ash spent nearly every minute in his room with his morphine. He injected constantly. He couldn't stand not to. The pressure, the pain, were always there, always reminding him that he hovered on the precipice of oblivion.

Ash seldom bothered to wash up. He never shaved. Every other day or so he shrugged into clothes and went to the nearest restaurant to eat. The food was poorly cooked and the portions were pitifully small but it was cheap, and truth to tell, Ash didn't care much about eating anymore. Or drinking. He stopped downing whiskey. The morphine was all he needed. On the tenth of each month he always went to the doctor for more. Without fail.

Once a week his landlady came to his room for her money. Usually he opened the door a few inches and shoved it out to her and went back to bed.

Came one day, though, when Ash opened the door and she crinkled her nose and sniffed.

"What is that awful odor? That's not you, is it?"

"Might be," Ash allowed.

"You need to bathe. I won't have you stinking up my house. Honestly. You impressed me as so clean-cut. What in the world has happened to you?"

"Life," Ash said.

"Life is for living. You need to get out more."

"This room is as much of life as I care to see. Now scat."

Another month went by.

A knock on his door brought Ash out of bed. He had taken to sleeping in his clothes and shuffled over to open it. He knew who it was. "Just a minute and I'll have your money."

"There's no hurry," the landlady considerately replied.

Ash opened his saddlebag and took out his poke. He loosened the string and upended it over the bed. The coins and bills that spilled out made a pitifully small pile. He counted out his rent and opened the door. "Here you go."

"Good heavens. Have you looked in the mirror recently, Mr. Smithers?"

"Who?" Ash said, then remembered he had taken the room under an assumed name.

"Very funny. But have you? You look abominable. I dare say you would frighten some of my female boarders to death. Please. Clean up and shave or I'll be forced to end your stay here."

Ash sat on the bed and counted the money he had left. It wasn't enough for the next rent. Worse, he was low on morphine and needed what was left for his next visit to the doctor. He could go without food and drink but he couldn't go without morphine.

"How did it all go so fast?" Ash asked the walls. Rising, he went to the basin and looked in the mirror. "My God." He hadn't seen his reflection in weeks. The person staring back at him wasn't him. An unkempt tangle of hair and a shaggy beard made him look as wild as the Frazier brothers. He was so thin his own mother wouldn't recognize him. His cheeks had sunk and his eyes were dark pits. His clothes were a rumpled mess. He raised his arm and nearly gagged. "The old biddy was right."

Ash stared at the bed. He wanted to lie back down and drift on clouds of delight. Instead he poured water from the pitcher into the bowl. A lot of scraping with his razor and a lot of rubbing with lye soap and presently the image in the mirror reminded him more of him—but God, he was thin. Skin and bones and little else.

Ash donned the only clean shirt he had left and a pair of pants. He slipped into his jacket, opened the window to admit fresh air, and went out. The landlady was on the porch, as usual, knitting.

"That's much better, Mr. Smithers. Although I must say, you could stand to eat more." She smiled in her kindly fashion. "I don't mean that as a criticism, mind you. I know you're sickly. You haven't said what ails you and I have no right to pry, but you really should take better care of yourself."

"Do you happen to know the address of the *Rocky Mountain News*?"

"Why, that I do. They used to be over to Cherry Creek but their first building was washed out in the big flood of 'sixty-four. Mr. Byers, the owner, went and bought out a rival paper, the *Commonwealth*, and the *News* had been there ever since."

* * *

A pert young woman at the front counter told Ash that, yes, the *News* did keep copies of previous editions.

"Our archives are up the stairs and to the left. Miss Eddings will gladly assist you."

Ash was about to step on the bottom stair when the last person in the world he wanted to run into came up and cheerfully clapped him on the back.

"Marshal Thrall!" Horace Smithers exclaimed. "What on earth are you doing here? Looking for me, perchance?"

"No," Ash said, and shook hands.

"How have you been keeping yourself?" Horace asked, his eyes betraying his shock.

"As well as can be expected."

"I wondered where you got to. It isn't every day someone becomes famous and disappears. The people of this territory will never forget the service you rendered in wiping out the Frazier clan."

"I'd rather not talk about it," Ash said. He turned to go up but stopped. It might take hours to find what he wanted in the archives and here was a living source of the information he needed. "Say. Maybe you can do me a favor."

"Anything, Marshal. Anything at all."

"Are there any others like the Fraziers? Outlaws with bounties on their heads?"

"The list is as long as your arm. I can write one up for you if you want. Or you can go to the sheriff and talk to him."

Ash would rather not do that. "Give me a name. Who has the highest bounty? Or one of the highest?"

Horace lit with excitement. "Oh, my. You're planning to do it again, aren't you? In that case, the one you want to go after is Marion Judson. He is worth almost three thousand dollars."

Ash's interest was piqued. "What has he done?"

"What hasn't he?" Horace rejoined. "Judson came west during the beaver years. He trapped until the trade dried up and then he prospected for a while, but that didn't suit him so he took to shooting people and helping himself to whatever they had of any value."

As Ash recollected, the beaver trade faded more than forty years ago. "He must be in his fifties or sixties. How many has he murdered?"

"No one knows for sure. The last estimate I heard was more than thirty people. There was a family of settlers. Another time it was a banker's son up in the mountains, fishing. Then there were some Mexicans down Durango way. I wouldn't know them all, but I can look them up for you if it's important."

"Sounds as if he's been killing all over the territory," Ash observed. "How do they know it's him?"

"He puts a rock on the head of each of his victims."

"He does what?"

"You heard right. Judson places a rock on the head of everyone he bushwhacks and robs. No one knows why. The law would like nothing better than to string him up, only he's impossible to catch. He'll be a lot harder to find than the Fraziers."

The money, though, would last Ash months. "Where would I start? Any notions?"

Horace looked around as if to be sure no one was listening. Taking Ash by the arm, he led him away from the stairs. "I might. But if I do you this favor I expect one in return. I want your word that if you catch him you'll come to me with the story. To me and only me."

"That's all?"

"You don't understand what it will mean to me. Men in my profession get ahead by getting news no one else has. By being the first with important stories. That series I did on you exterminating the Fraziers? I don't mind telling you it earned me a fifty-dollar-a-month raise."

"Congratulations."

"Thank you. My point is that I owe you. So I'll share a tidbit I came across a while back when I was writing about one of Marion Judson's murders." Horace looked around again and lowered his voice to a whisper. "Judson has a sister. Her name is Rohesia Kanderwold. She lives up in Estes Park with her husband, an invalid. You might start with her."

Ash pumped Horace's hand. "Thanks. I'll be in touch." It occurred to him as he left the *News* that bumping into the journalist in Ute City has been a godsend. Smithers undoubtedly knew a lot more than most about the various and sundry lawbreakers roaming the territory, especially those with large amounts of money on their heads. The man could keep him in morphine indefinitely.

The thought brought Ash to a stop. A pall of despair fell over him.

He had less than a year to live; that was about as definite as it got.

Still, Ash was elated at the idea of getting his hands on three thousand dollars. It might last until the grave claimed him.

The sun was just peeking above the rim of the earth the next dawn when Ash stepped into the stirrups and rode out of Denver on the road that would take him to Estes Park. It was a long climb. Denver was a mile above sea level; Estes Park two thousand feet higher and seventy-five miles into the mountains. Ash had never been there but from what he'd heard the scenery was spectacular. Estes was a resort where the young went to frolic and the old to rest weary bones.

Ash had bought more morphine the night before. He had enough to last a month if he used it sparingly. He must find Marion Judson quickly so he could get more and use it as freely as he liked.

The mountains were in full splendor. Lower down, deciduous trees fringed the banks of creeks and farm fields. Cottonwoods were particularly plentiful along the waterways. Wooded slopes were broken by boulder-strewn bluffs and tablelands of red rock. Higher up, thick forests of pine were mixed with tracts of firs and occasional aspen groves.

Bald eagles soared among the clouds. Hawks circled in search of prey and buzzards circled in search of carrion. Songbirds warbled and jays squawked.

White-tailed deer roamed the lowlands; black-tailed deer preferred the high country. Twice Ash spotted elk. He'd heard that once buffalo roamed the foothills as well as the plains but they had long since filled supper pots. Most of the grizzlies had been killed off too. It was rare for anyone to sight one these days. Black bears were still around but in far fewer numbers.

As eager as Ash was to reach Estes, he took his time. It would be pointless to ride the roan or the packhorse into the ground.

About the middle of the afternoon Ash had to stop for a spell. His chest was bothering him. The pain would spike and then fade. He had injected that morning and didn't want to use more morphine if he could help it.

Toward sunset Ash camped on a shelf with a magnificent view of the country below. The emerald foothills rolled in waves to the sea of grass that stretched for unending leagues far to the east and the broad Mississippi.

Ash put coffee on. For his supper he heated a can of Van Camp's beans in tomato sauce. He cut several thick slices off a loaf of bread and smeared them in butter from a small tin. With the fire crackling and stars starting to blossom, he dipped the buttered bread in the piping-hot beans and ate with relish.

It was ironic, Ash reflected, how much more he appreciated being alive now that he was dying. He looked around him at the mountains and the foothills and felt the wind on his face and the warmth of the food in his belly, and he almost broke into tears.

Ash didn't want to die. He would give anything to relive that fateful day when Sharkey shot him. He should not have gone to Abigail Mason's. He should have stayed in his office.

Abigail. Ash suddenly remembered Sharkey saying that he'd paid her to send for him. Did she know why? Had Sharkey told her what he was up to and Abby sent the boy anyway? Ash would like to ask her and, if she had, beat her to death with a club.

A coyote was yipping when Ash pulled his blanket to his chin and lay in a cocoon of warmth and contentment. For that moment in time everything was perfect. He wished it could last forever.

Ash touched his chest. Tear welled, and this time he didn't fight it. He quietly wept until he was drained dry. Wiping his nose on the blanket, he stared at the dark sky and asked out loud, "Why me? What did I do to deserve this?"

Ash shuddered. Everything he ever believed had turned out to be wrong. All those years he wore tin, all those years he did his best to live right and do good—and for what? For lingering agony and a slow death?

"I don't know a lot," Ash said haltingly. "I don't know why we're here and what purpose all this serves. But I do know it's not right that people suffer. It's not right that people have to go through what I'm going through. How the hell can you let it? How can they say you care when you put us through hell and we end our days as maggot food?"

The sky didn't answer.

Ash was angry and growing angrier. "It's bunk and bunkum, that's what it is. Only a lunatic would call this life sane. Only a fool could see all the hurting and claim there's some purpose to it." Ash shook a fist at the stars. "Do you hear me up there? Or am I talking to empty air? Prove to me I'm wrong. Give me a sign. Show me there's more to this. Please."

To the north a shooting star cleaved the heavens, burning bright, only to fade into the night.

"That's it? That's your sign?" Ash laughed and couldn't stop. He laughed until his sides hurt. He recollected hearing somewhere that life was a stage and everyone was a player. "If that's so," he told the speckles above, "then the play is a comedy and we are all of us jackasses."

On that bitter note, Ash let himself drift off. His last thought before sleep claimed him was that those who thought life made sense had no sense at all. He was living proof.

Or rather dying proof.

Chapter 24

The toll road up to Estes had only recently been completed. It was considered crucial to opening up the area to settlement.

Not everyone was happy about the idea.

Estes Park was split into factions. There was the Earl of Dunraven, one of the very first to set eyes on the park's natural charms. The earl started a ranch and tried to take control of every square inch of land; he had to settle for controlling six thousand acres. Those acres were soon surrounded by more and more homesteads. The earl wasn't worried. He was confident the harsh winters and short growing seasons would drive the homesteaders off. As added incentive he had their fences torn down and drove his cattle over their lands and through their gardens. His hard tactics and the hard winters might have driven them off if not for the natural wonders the earl so admired.

The homesteaders admired them too. Everyone who saw Estes Park fell in love with the Eden of the Rockies. People from all over the territory came to fish and hunt or enjoy the splendor. They packed into tents because there were no accommodations.

That gave one of the homesteaders a brainstorm. He reasoned that people who came so far just to bide for a short while might be willing to pay good money to have a place to stay. Soon practically every homesteader offered lodging and meals and earned enough to stock up for those hard winters and to put up new fences to keep the earl's cattle out.

The earl was a practical man. He decided that if he couldn't beat them, he would go them one better. He planned to build a lavish lodge to cater to the needs of the visitors and add to his already considerable fortune.

All of this Ash gleaned his first night there. He stayed with a family by the name of James. Their homestead bordered the earl's ranch and James spent most of the evening meal complaining about how the English in general and the earl in particular thought they had the right to take over the world.

"As if that's not enough," James groused on, "you should see the earl cavorting with his lady friends. It's not unusual to see him riding with two or three at once, and all so intimate."

"It's scandalous," the wife said.

James nodded. "They are wickedly naughty, those British. What they need are good spankings when they are growing up."

"Or to spend nights in the doghouse," the wife added.

Ash asked about the Kanderwolds and was informed they had a small cabin near Black Canyon.

"Why they settled there is beyond me," James remarked. "Black Canyon is a dark, brooding place. No one ever goes there. Even the Indians avoid it."

"We tried to talk them out of it," the wife revealed. "But Rohesia wouldn't listen. She didn't want to live near anyone, she said. And her with a husband who can hardly get around."

"The woman is pigheaded," James said bluntly.

"Or it could be she doesn't want to impose on others." The wife came to Rohesia's defense. "She doesn't want nor will she accept pity on account of Arthur." To Ash the wife explained, "That's her husband. A nice enough man. But all he does is sit and stare."

"What happened to him?"

"No one knows. From remarks Rohesia has dropped I suspect a brain fever was to blame." She clucked in sympathy. "That poor woman. She must do so much herself that a husband would normally do."

"She's pigheaded," James repeated.

"Now, now."

"You know I'm right. If she'd had the sense to live near the rest of us, we could help her. As it is, it takes half a day to get there."

It took Ash five hours. He followed the directions James gave him but finding it took some doing. The canyon *was* dark and brooding and heavily wooded, and the trail in not much of a trail at all.

The cabin stood in a small glade. Awash in sunshine, it seemed out of place. Even though it was summer smoke curled from the stone chimney.

A few sniffs told Ash why: food was being cooked. He dismounted and stepped to the front door and knocked.

It was a minute before a reedy voice called out, "Who's there?"

Ash remembered the trick Lonnie had played on him in Mobeetie.

"My name is Grant, ma'am. I'm up here fishing and need a place to stay for the night."

"We don't offer lodging."

Ash had been told she didn't and had his reply ready. "Would it be all right if I camp in the clearing, then? I promise not to disturb you and to be gone in the morning."

"I don't know."

"I've come a long way. I won't be a bother. I promise you won't even know I'm here." Ash thought he heard someone else say something but he couldn't be sure.

"It would only be until morning?"

"Yes, ma'am. I only aim to fish one day and then try another spot. I'll pay you for the privilege if need be. Please, ma'am. My horse is tuckered out and so am I."

Again muffled voices murmured.

"Very well."

Ash thanked her and set about stripping his saddle and saddle blanket and untying his bedroll and spreading it out. He used a rock to pound picket pins into the ground and tied the horses so they wouldn't stray off. The whole time he was aware that the front curtains had parted and he was being watched. He pretended not to notice.

A corral on the far side of the cabin held three horses. One was a fine black stallion.

Ash went into the forest to gather firewood. The woods were unnaturally still and quiet thanks to the high canyon walls that blocked much of the wind. They also plunged the canyon floor into deep shadow for most of the day.

Only after Ash had a fire going and was opening a

can of beans did the latch rasp and the front door inched open. "That you, ma'am?" he said when no one came out.

She emerged, the perfect portrait of an elderly matron, her snow-white hair in a bun, her stout body draped in an ankle-length homespun dress. She had a nice smile and blue eyes. Troubled eyes. "Did I hear you say your name is Grant?"

"Yes, ma'am."

"I'm Rohesia Kanderwold. My husband, Arthur, and I live here." She clasped her hands. "It isn't often we get anyone out this way."

"I can see why. You're as far off the beaten path as you can get."

"So are you, Mr. Grant."

Ash noted the suspicion in her tone. "Ma'am?"

"You say you're up here to fish, but the best streams for trout are clear on the other side of Estes Park."

Ash had his reply ready for that too. "That's not entirely true, ma'am. An old-timer told me of a stream in this very canyon. He says no one has ever fished it. I'll have it all to myself."

Rohesia patted her bun. "You're certainly welcome to do as you please but I fear you've come all this way for little reward. My husband has fished that stream a few times and only ever caught a few fish."

As casually as he could, Ash remarked, "I was told your husband is a cripple or some such."

"People can be so crude," Rohesia criticized. "But no. Arthur spends most of his time in a special chair but he can move around when he has to. In fact, the doctor insists he try and get a little exercise each day."

"Special chair?"

"Wait here. I'll introduce you."

Ash filled a pot with the beans and didn't look up until he heard creaking.

Out of the cabin came Rohesia, pushing a wheelchair. Sturdily built of oak, the chair had oversized wheels that could use greasing.

The man in the chair wore a floppy hat with a wide brim. From under it spilled long gray hair. A blanket had been draped over the lower half of his body. His shirt had a high collar that had been pulled up and covered the lower half of his face. The only part of him Ash could see clearly were his cheeks and his blue eyes.

"Mr. Grant, I'd like you to meet my husband, Arthur," Rohesia introduced them.

"How do you do," the man said, his voice thin and raspy.

"Arthur isn't a cripple, Mr. Grant," Rohesia went on. "He has a heart condition. He must be very careful not to overexert himself. He is also nearly always cold. Something about the blood not circulating as it should. Which is why he is bundled up."

Ash stood and offered his hand. Arthur Kanderwold reached from under the blanket and touched his fingertips but didn't shake. The hand was immediately withdrawn. "Pleased to make your acquaintance."

"My wife tells me you are here to fish."

Ash pointed at the fishing pole and gear he had bought in Denver before setting out. He'd hated to spend the money, but he got them cheap and he needed them to make his lie believable. "I've been told the fishing in Estes Park is excellent."

"That it is," Arthur agreed, "although not many come all the way to Black Canyon to try their luck."

"So your wife was saying. She also said you've fished the stream here so you must know the best spots."

"As a matter of fact," Arthur responded, "I know one that will do nicely. A pool where the canyon bends, about half a mile past our cabin. There's a bank for you to fish from. I've caught a few trout there. It's quiet and peaceful and restful as anything."

"Sounds perfect. I'll head up tomorrow and spend the day."

"I wish you success," Arthur Kanderwold said.

Rohesia coughed. "Well, we can see you've put your supper on. We'll leave you to your meal. Perhaps tomorrow after you come back you can visit and talk a spell. It isn't often we have visitors."

"I'd like that," Ash said. They certainly were proving to be friendlier than he had been led to believe. "It's very gracious of you."

Rohesia smiled. "I get lonely out here sometimes. I'm so far from anywhere, with only the animals and the wind for company."

"You have me," Arthur said a bit gruffly.

"Of course I do," Rohesia quickly answered. "It's just that you are all I have. There's no one else. No women to sit at tea with. No one else to talk to unless it's the rare traveler like Mr. Grant here."

"Take me in. I'm getting cold."

"Yes, dear."

Ash felt sorry for her. But then, she didn't have to live here. Or did she? he wondered. Maybe she wasn't permitted a say in the matter. Shrugging, he sat back down and waited for his beans to cook.

The curtain parted. Someone was staring out at him again.

After eating, Ash stretched out on his back, fully dressed, and pulled a blanket to his chin. Moving slowly so it wouldn't be obvious to the watcher in the cabin, he drew his Remington revolver and held it on his stomach. That was how he slept. The slightest noises awakened him, from crackling in the brush that might be deer to the hooting of an owl.

Ash didn't bother getting up at the crack of dawn. He slept in. It had to be nine or ten when he finally stirred and sat up. Almost instantly a familiar craving came over him. His first act every day was always the same. Holstering the Remington, he turned to his saddlebags. He caught himself just in time and glanced at the cabin.

The curtains were parted.

Ash stretched and stood. He needed an injection, needed it badly. Without one, he would quake all over and his muscles would cramp. But not in front of the Kanderwolds.

Forgoing breakfast, Ash collected the case that held his rod, and the fishing basket. Keeping his back to the front window to block their view, he transferred the morphine kit from his saddlebag to the basket. Then, shouldering the rod case and with the basket under his arm, he sauntered around the cabin to a narrow trail that wound into the canyon's gloomy depths. He whistled and acted as if he didn't have a care in the world.

Once out of sight, Ash went faster. The craving had become a hunger he could hardly hold at bay. His chest wasn't hurting. There was no pressure at the moment. But he had to have morphine. He *had* to. His mouth went dry and he broke out in a sweat. He started to shake. He wouldn't make it to the spot Arthur had told him about. Stopping, he broke open the kit.

"Damn."

Ash had forgotten to fill the hypodermic after using it the day before. He had done that more and more of late, a sign he was becoming lazy. Or was it something else? He was shaking so much that he could barely hold the needle steady. The hunger had become a searing need that tore at him like the claws of a wild beast.

"Hurry, damn you." Ash was being a fumble fingers. He might as well have butter or grease smeared on his hands. It took him twice as long as it should but at last he had the hypodermic ready. Rolling up his sleeve, he held the needle above a vein.

This was the moment Ash lived for, the moment when he was on the cusp of pure heaven. He stabbed in the needle and winced. The wince soon changed to a smile as the morphine coursed through his blood. There was warmth and tingling and the precious pure ecstasy he couldn't do without.

For Ash the feeling was akin to that moment when a man was with a woman and crested in release. He moaned as the morphine took full hold. Slumping onto his side, he immersed himself in the sensation.

Ash would have been perfectly happy to lie there for the rest of the morning. With great reluctance he sat up, put the kit in the basket and continued on.

The trail seldom saw use except for wildlife. It paralleled the stream to the bend Arthur had mentioned. The pool was about ten feet across, the water bathed in sparkling sunlight and so clear that Ash could see the bottom. A quicksilver streak confirmed there were fish.

Ash set down the rod case and the basket and was straightening when a gun hammer clicked.

"Twitch and you're dead."

Chapter 25

Ash turned to stone as a hand groped at his waist and relieved him of the Remington revolver. He heard it thud to the ground.

"Turn real slow and sit real slow."

Again Ash complied. He was extremely calm. The morphine's doing, he figured. When he beheld the man holding an old single-shot Sharps rifle on him, he hid his surprise. The eyes were the same and the gray hair was the same but the man had changed into buckskins. "Marion Judson. You looked different in the wheelchair."

"I scrunch up to hide how big I am."

"And the real Arthur Kanderwold?" Ash asked.

"My sister's husband died about ten years ago. He'd been sick a long time. Some kind of blood sickness."

"Whose idea was it for you to pretend to be him?"

"Rohesia's. She's smart, my sis. She figured that if anyone came looking for me, they'd never suspect an invalid. So when I need to hide out I come here and play the part of Arthur. It's worked real fine."

"She doesn't object to the killing and the robbing

you do?" Ash had his hands at his waist, close to his open jacket.

"Not at all. She feels the same as I do. She hates them as much as me."

"Hates who?" Ash stalled. The longer he could keep the killer talking, the better his chances.

"All the people moving to the mountains. It used to be so wonderful. Hardly a soul anywhere. Just the forest and the valleys and the animals and the Indians. It was paradise."

The implication jolted Ash. "You haven't been murdering folks for their money?"

"Hell, no," Judson said gruffly. "What do you take me for? I do it because I hate what they're doing to the mountains." He gazed about the pristine canyon as a man might gaze fondly on a lover. "You've got to understand. I was one of the first. I came to the Rockies back in the thirties with a fur brigade. I saw these mountains as they used to be before all the people came along and spoiled everything. Them with their cities and towns. Laying waste to the timber. Scouring the earth for gold and silver and coal. It used to be so beautiful but they've made it ugly."

"*That's* why you killed all those people?"

"Can you give me a better reason? They soil the wild places like a baby soils its diaper."

Ash was dumbfounded.

"Back when I started I'd hoped that if I killed enough it would scare a lot of the rest off and they'd go back to wherever they came from. But it didn't work. More and more kept coming and I couldn't stem the tide."

"Yet you kept on killing anyway."

Judson shrugged. "I still had my hate. I couldn't keep it pent up. I had to do something or I'd bust."

"The only thing you could think of was to murder innocent men, women and children?"

"Don't look at me like that," the mountain man growled. "How am I any different from those whites who wiped out whole Indian villages? Or who shoot game for the fun of it and not for the meat or the hide?" Judson spat in disgust. "I hear tell another ten years and they'll have pretty near wiped out the buffalo."

"It's no reason to kill." Ash edged his right hand to the underside of his jacket.

"I can't think of a better one."

"So now what? You shoot me for coming here to fish?"

"No. I shoot you because your name isn't Grant. It's Thrall. You're that ex-lawman who has taken to collecting bounty money. I can read. We get the newspaper late but we get it and I know all about how you found the Fraziers and blew out their wicks."

"The paper never described me."

"No, it didn't. But there's a rumor going around that this Thrall has something the matter with him. The rumor has it he looks sickly." Judson gestured. "If you looked any more sickly you'd be six feet under."

Ash swore. He should have known word would spread. People loved to gossip and he was a popular topic thanks to Horace Smithers.

Marion Judson laughed. "Never thought of that, did you? Never thought that I might figure you to come after me, what with the money on my head. Truth is, I expected you long before this."

Ash bowed his head. No, he hadn't thought of that. He should have. Once he would have. Back before he was shot he always thought one step ahead of those he was after.

"You fixing to cry?" Judson mocked him.

"No," Ash said softly.

"Most of the time when I shoot people I do it because of the hate inside of me. With you it's not hate. It's disgust."

Ash's fingers were under the jacket.

"You sit there and look at me like I'm scum. But you're worse. At least I have a reason. You kill for money. That's all. To fill your poke you take a life. The real scum here is you, not me."

"There's more to it," Ash said. His fingertips brushed the Remington pocket pistol.

"You only shoot wanted men so that makes it noble?" Judson took a step. "I'm going to enjoy this. I'm going to enjoy it more than anything."

Ash chose that moment. He looked up, past Marion Judson at the trail to the cabin. "Why did you bring your sister with you?"

"What?" Judson started to turn.

Ash drew. He had always been quick and he was quick now. He shot Judson in the chest and the mountain man took a step back but didn't go down. The Sharps boomed and Ash felt a searing pain in his left shoulder even as the impact slammed him onto his back. He thumbed back the hammer and aimed and fired a second time. It seemed to have no effect.

Judson roared and charged him, holding the Sharps aloft like a club. Ash scrambled aside and the stock struck the ground where he had been lying. Heaving onto his knees, Ash jammed the pocket pistol against Judson's ribs and fired again. That should have done it. That should have brought Judson down. But the mountain man swung the Sharps and caught Ash across the chest.

The next instant cold and wet enveloped Ash like a glove. He had been knocked into the pool. He came up sputtering, half expecting to be shot as he broke the surface.

Marion Judson was on his side, twitching. He was fumbling with a cartridge, trying to reload.

Ash's feet found bottom. He had held on to the pocket pistol and now he centered it on Judson's face, pulled back the hammer and squeezed the trigger.

There was a click. He tried again with the same result.

"Damn your hide." Judson was breathing in loud gasps and about to insert the cartridge.

Ash made it to the bank. He tried to climb out but slipped back.

Spreading scarlet spots stained Judson's shirt. Blood trickled from a corner of his mouth. Yet he reloaded and rose onto an elbow, his features twisted in pain and determination. "I'll show you."

Ash was out of the water. He kept slipping when he sought to stand. He spied his revolver a few yards away and threw himself toward it, only to fall.

"Scum," Judson was raving. "Scum, scum, scum." He pointed the Sharps. "This is where I send you to hell."

Fear galvanized Ash into a desperate dive. He grabbed the revolver and cocked it as he rolled. He came up ready to shoot, but didn't. The mountain man had gone limp.

His cheek was on the grass, his eyes open but unseeing. Scarlet seeped from his mouth, painting his chin red. The Sharps lay beside him.

Ash kicked the rifle away. Squatting, he felt for a pulse. There was none. "Good riddance."

Shivering from his wet clothes, Ash replaced the pocket pistol and the revolver. His shoulder was throbbing. He gingerly peeled off his jacket and then his shirt to look at the wound. The slug had caught him below the clavicle. The bone had been spared, thank God, but the exit wound was as big around as an apple. It wasn't bleeding a lot, not to the extent he had to worry about bleeding to death.

Ash moved to the pool. Lying on his belly at the water's edge, he splashed water on both the entry and exit wounds. The cold helped, but the relief was temporary. He needed to apply a bandage to stave off infection. Rising onto his knees, he went to get dressed.

"How could you?"

Rohesia had the Sharps. She was pointing it at him but staring at her brother. Tears trickled down her matronly cheeks.

"You know what he was. You know what he did." Ash was mad at himself for not hearing her.

"I know he was the best man who ever lived."

"You can't mean that." Ash began to rise.

"Be still," Rohesia warned. The click of the hammer was added persuasion. "I haven't decided what I'm going to do with you yet."

Ash was used to reasoning with drunks and rowdies and hoped he could do the same with her. "You're not your brother. You're not a killer."

"I loved Marion. I loved him dearly."

"I'm sorry for you," Ash said gently.

Rohesia sniffled. "I haven't ever killed anyone, but there's always a first time."

The way she said it, so coldly and matter-of-factly, as if killing were no more difficult than sewing or cooking, worried Ash. He started to rise.

"Don't. Be real still and quiet while I sort this out."

"Act your age." Ash clutched at a straw. "This isn't you. It's your grief. You're upset but it will pass."

Rohesia smiled an odd sort of smile. She came toward him, the rifle steady as could be, and stopped when the muzzle was almost brushing his nose. "Thank you."

"For what?"

"For telling me to act my age. It reminded me of how few years I have left. I doubt they will hang me. They don't hang women often. I might be sentenced to life behind bars, but I doubt I'll live five."

"What are you saying?"

"That I am more than upset. I don't know if I can describe it except to say that my blood is boiling like an unwatched pot and about to bubble over." With that Rohesia swung the rifle.

Ash tried to duck. He was a shade slow and paid for it with a new explosion of pain in his temple. The world swam and he felt his forehead strike the ground. He attempted to rise, but another explosion sucked him into a black well for he knew not how long.

Sounds brought Ash around. A tinkling that reminded him for all the world of a music box. He listened, and it *was* a music box. Odors filled his nose, the scents of cooked food and tobacco and wood smoke. He opened his eyes. Above him was a log ceiling. To his left a window with the curtains drawn. He was in a cabin; he could guess whose. He had been stripped to the waist and his boots and socks removed. He was on his back in a bed, tied wrists and ankles to the bedposts.

Footsteps scraped and into the bedroom came Rohesia. She was carrying a tray. "I thought you might be awake by now."

"How . . . ," Ash began, and had to stop, his throat was so dry.

"How did I get you here? It's simple—on a horse. Or did you want to ask how long you have been out? Nearly twelve hours."

Rohesia set the tray on the bed. On it was a metal fork and a curved carving knife as well as a large butcher knife and one of those thin picks for prying walnuts from their shells.

Ash couldn't believe this was happening.

Rohesia sat beside him. "I've had a long talk with myself and come to a decision. I have never done anything like this but I can't let that stop me. I must be strong as Marion was strong."

Ash swallowed and got out, "What are you talking about? What's all that for?"

"For you, Mr. Thrall. Oh yes, I know who you are. Marion told me. He guessed right away. He was so smart." Rohesia held her hand over the tray. "Which should I start with? The knives will make quite a mess, I should imagine. Maybe I should start small." She picked up the walnut pick and held it in front of his face. "This should put your eye out quite nicely."

Ash remembered the Fraziers about to torture him and trembled. Suddenly his chest lanced with agony. The pressure was back, worse than it had ever been. He arched off the bed and gritted his teeth but couldn't help letting out a sharp cry.

"My word!" Rohesia drew back in alarm, her hand to her bosom. "What on earth is the matter with you?"

"I need morphine," Ash gasped. "It's in my saddlebags." He tugged at the ropes, wishing he could double over. His chest was pounding to where he feared his heart would explode. The pressure went on and on. He was on the verge of passing out when the pressure let up and the pain faded, leaving him spent and slick with sweat.

Rohesia regarded him intently. "It has something to do with those scars on your chest, doesn't it?"

Pausing often to catch his breath, Ash told her about being shot and the bullet lodged next to his heart. He told about his suffering. "And the hell of it is, I never know whether my next breath will be my last," he concluded.

"Well, now," Rohesia said. Her hands were in her lap. She placed the walnut pick on the tray and picked up the butcher knife instead.

"End it for me. I don't care," Ash said, and meant it.

Rohesia raised the knife, looked him in the eyes and slashed the rope binding his right wrist to the bedpost. She rose and moved to the foot of the bed and did the same for his ankle, then moved around to the other side.

"You changed your mind?"

"I'm letting you go, yes." Rohesia slashed the last rope. "I was going to do things to you, Mr. Thrall. Horrible things. I was going to make you suffer for killing Marion and then I was going to end your life. But you know what? I don't need to. You're already suffering. From what I've seen, you're suffering terribly."

Rohesia put down the butcher knife. "That's simply wonderful, Mr. Thrall."

"What?"

"Yes, you go on suffering. Endure the torment of the damned. I hope God drags it out. I hope you last for months and die in the most abominable agony." Rohesia Kanderwold smiled. "Yes, that would make me happy. Very happy indeed."

Chapter 26

Life was grand again, or at least bearable.

Ash spent each day the same. He woke up in early afternoon. The first thing he did, the very first, was to inject morphine. Then he would lie in bed and savor the pleasure. After a couple of hours he would rouse and wash and dress.

Usually by five or six o'clock he was at a restaurant. He still had an appetite. The doctors said he might lose all craving for food but it hadn't happened yet. After he ate he made the rounds of various saloons, gambling dens and brothels.

Ash never went near Finnegan's. The law hadn't paid him a visit so he figured he had gotten away with killing those two men. But why push his luck and maybe end up behind bars, even if it was in self-defense?

Ash pushed his luck in other ways. He took to gambling. Nearly every night he sat for hours playing poker or bucking the tiger or if he was feeling especially reckless he would try roulette. Some nights he won. Most nights he lost. Not a lot each time but enough that after five weeks he only had a few hundred left of the bounty he collected on Marion Judson.

Horace Smithers did a story on Judson. The *Rocky Mountain News* put it on the front page with banner headlines. All about how, as Horace described him, "courageous former marshal Asher Thrall" tracked down another notorious killer and "put an end to Marion Judson's long and blood-drenched reign of terror."

Horace was enormously pleased with the account and brought over three copies.

Ash hated it. It made him sound heroic and noble. It invested him with qualities he didn't have and painted him as someone he wasn't. Horace didn't mention the morphine, thank God.

Ash learned that the journalist went up to Estes Park to pay Rohesia a visit and get her side of things. Rohesia chased him off with a rolling pin.

"The woman nearly brained me! You wouldn't think it to look at her, but she is quite formidable."

"More formidable than you think," Ash said, and let it go at that.

Now here Ash was, bending his footsteps toward the *News*. The hour was late and most of the workers had gone home. Not Smithers. He'd mentioned to Ash once that he did some of his best writing when he had peace and quiet so he often stayed late.

"To what do I owe this honor?

Ash sat in a chair and stretched out his long legs. "I need another one. Someone with a lot of money on their heads."

Horace stopped writing. "You've run out already?"

"I'm getting there," Ash confessed. And here he'd

thought he had enough to last several months if not longer.

"Living high on the hog, are you?" Horace joked, then frowned. "Sorry. That was thoughtless of me. You're entitled to live any damn way you please. You've earned the right."

"I've earned nothing but an early grave." Ash might not have much, but he still had a shred of dignity.

"That's not how the governor feels. There has been talk of a special ceremony."

"You better be joking."

"Not at all." Horace sat up. "Don't you realize the tremendous service you've done? You've rid the territory of some of its worst elements. You deserve the recognition. A banquet, say, with the governor and other leading politicians in attendance, and you receive an award. It will make the front page, I can guarantee."

Ash was slow sometimes but this was so obvious that it leaped out at him.

"This is your doing, isn't it? You contacted the governor, or someone else here did. Just so you can sell more newspapers."

"Selling papers keeps the clothes on our backs and food on our tables. Yes, my editor has been in touch with Governor Routt. At my instigation. I thought you would appreciate the gesture."

"You thought wrong."

"All right. All right. There's no need to get hot under the collar."

"Like hell there isn't." Ash swore an angry streak, then said, "Look at me, damn you. *Really* look at me. Do you think I want to get up in front of a group of people looking as I do?"

"What do—" Horace stopped and blinked and cleared his throat.

"Oh. I see what you mean. I'm used to you as a scarecrow." He apologetically added, "Honestly, Ash, I hadn't considered that aspect. I beg your pardon. You're right. There would be talk. All sorts of wild speculation you can do without."

"I'm glad you agree." Ash was embarrassed enough looking in the mirror. The hollows under his eyes, his sunken cheeks, his pasty complexion. That old Ute had been right; he was a walking dead man and it showed.

"I'll talk to my editor. He won't like it, but he'll understand." Horace slid the sheet of paper he was writing on aside and opened a drawer. "Now, then. You need to replenish your coffers. I have some notes here that might interest you." He sorted through a sheaf of papers until he found several he wanted and set them on the desk. "Ever hear of a man by the name of Skelman?"

"Can't say as I have. Should I?"

"Not particularly. He's wanted down to Arizona Territory. Seems he shot a Pinkerton, a top man in the company. The Pinkertons don't take kindly to that sort of thing so they've put five thousand dollars on his head, dead or alive but preferably dead."

Ash whistled. "That's a lot of money but Arizona is a long way to go to claim it."

Horace grinned. "You don't have to. That's why I've brought him to your attention. Skelman is in Colorado. He's been reported in the Durango area. The Pinkertons don't know yet. If you can get to him first, all that money is yours."

"How is it they don't and you do?" Ash was familiar with the detective agency's reputation.

"I was down there a few months ago covering a mine collapse that killed five miners. I happened to strike up a conversation with the marshal and he let it slip that Skelman was staying with some friends."

"Let it slip?" Ash suspiciously asked.

"I'd asked him if anything else newsworthy had taken place and he brought Skelman up. The marshal can't arrest him because Skelman isn't wanted in Colorado. He doesn't want word to get out because then he'll have money-hungry bounty men pouring in from all over. And he won't try to claim the money himself because he doesn't care to go up against Skelman."

"The marshal is yellow?"

"Not at all. He's one of the bravest men I've ever met. His record speaks for itself. But he says that going up against Skelman is the same as suicide and it's not worth it over a Pinkerton."

Ash crossed his legs and placed his hands on his knee. "There's something you're not telling me."

"Yes, there is." Horace drummed his fingers on the desk. "How do I put this so you'll appreciate what you're up against this time?" He drummed a little more. "Ever hear of Wild Bill Hickok?"

"Who hasn't?"

"The prince of the pistoleers. The fastest and deadliest revolver shot who ever lived. *Harper's* made him famous and there have been all kinds of stories since then. Many are outright fabrications—"

"Journalists do that?" Ash interrupted with a smirk.

"—but the point I'm trying to make is that for all the exaggerated tales, few could match him bullet for bullet. 'Deadly' is the word I'm looking for, I guess. Yes, that's it. Deadly." Horace leaned forward. "Skelman is deadly. They say he's about the deadliest son of a bitch who ever drew breath. He is fast and he is accurate with those two guns of his—"

"Wait," Ash interrupted again. "Two guns?"

"He wears two revolvers, yes. Colts with mother-of-pearl handles. He had them custom made, I understand."

Ash was impressed. Two-gun men were rare. Two-gun men who could shoot equally well with both hands were even rarer. "So what you're saying is that he is really good."

"No. I'm saying he is beyond good. Supposedly he has fourteen kills to his credit, but there could be more. He's not an outlaw. He doesn't rob banks or steal from people that I know of. He's someone who is lightning with his hands and that lightning has gotten him into trouble."

"Why did he shoot the Pinkerton?" Ash thought to ask.

"The Pinkerton's name was Barnes. He was after a train robber from Missouri. The man fled to Arizona and was playing cards at a table with Skelman and some others when he saw the Pinkerton trying to sneak up on him and lead started to fly. Either the Pinkerton panicked or he couldn't shoot straight and one of his shots nicked Skelman, who promptly shot him dead."

"Did Skelman know Barnes was a Pinkerton?"

"From what I can gather, no. But that hasn't stopped them from putting a price on his head. It's rare for them to do that but apparently they feel they need to make an example of him."

Ash's sympathies were with the man the bounty was on. Still, "Five thousand dollars is a lot of money."

"I hesitated to mention Skelman before because,

frankly, I like you, and if you go after him you are dead."

"Thanks for the confidence."

Horace sighed and spread his hands on the desk. "I knew I wasn't making myself clear. If you try to bring him in alive, he will kill you. Your only hope is to shoot him in the back and turn the remains over to the Pinkertons."

Ash flared with resentment. "What in hell do you take me for?"

"Someone who is desperate to stave off the dark," Horace said with surprising affection. "You're a fighter, Ash, and I admire that. I don't know if I have the courage to do what you're doing. I'd probably end it with a bullet to the brain by my own hand."

Ash said nothing.

"That's part of the reason I've helped you. It isn't only about the front page. You can pooh-pooh me if you want but I regard you as a noble man valiantly clinging to life while death slowly eats you away."

"I'm an animal pissing in the wind," Ash said bluntly.

"Is that all you are? Is that all any of us are?"

Ash uncrossed his legs and frowned. "I didn't expect that from you. A parson, maybe."

"You've lost all faith, then?"

The words were hard for Ash to say. He avoided looking out the window at the sky as he answered quietly, "Wouldn't you?" Suddenly standing, he adjusted his hat. "Thanks for the information on Skelman. I'll give it some thought."

"You do that. Think long and hard on this one. Because I was serious. I have a bad feeling about him. Go after him and he might be your last."

"Would that be so bad?" Ash turned and took a couple of steps, but the journalist said his name.

"So, that's what you're up to? It's not just money for the morphine or about doing something worthwhile before your time is up. You're secretly hoping that one of them does you in and ends the misery."

Ash wouldn't look at Horace either. "That courage you just mentioned? If I truly had any I'd do the job myself." He needed to get out of there, but Horace had a few parting words.

"Most of us are never in your shoes. We're not put to the test you are. We live and we die, but most of the time it's of old age and we pass on peacefully in our beds."

"There's nothing peaceful about dying."

The night air was refreshing. Ash gratefully breathed deep, and shuddered. He hurried through the streets to Madam Maxine's. Maxine herself admitted him. She was plump and jovial and always smelled of a perfume imported from France.

Smiling, she gave him a huge hug.

"Ash, darling! What a treat to have you visit us again!"

Ash saw the truth in her eyes but he played the game and smiled back. "I want Grace. I want her now and I want her for the entire night." He fished out the money and then some. "Be quick about it."

"But she's with . . ." Maxine stopped and stared at him. "The need is on you, isn't it? Most of the time it is a hunger, but sometimes it's a need that can't be denied."

"Quit standing there jawing and fetch her."

Maxine pulled her lacy robe about her and departed, her body jiggling like pudding.

Ash leaned his forehead against the wall and closed his eyes. "I hate you. I hate you for this. There is nothing you can do to make up for it. The hereafter can be all peace and joy and it still wouldn't."

The patter of feet brought Ash around. Maxine had Grace in tow. Grace, who was the youngest woman there and had eyes of pure innocence. Deceptive eyes, for she was anything but. Tonight Ash would grasp at the illusion as a drowning man grasped at a log.

"Here she is. Usually I wouldn't take one of my girls from a customer to give to another, but you're one of my favorites, Ash. Have I ever told you that?"

Ash took Grace's hand. "Which room?"

"Up the stairs. The first door on the left. I'll have a bottle of your usual brought up. Food too if you want."

"I want to be left alone for two hours. Anyone opens the door, I'll shoot them."

Grace giggled. "You wouldn't do that. You can't go around killing people for no reason."

"God does it all the time."

Grace thought that was terribly funny.

Ash took the stairs two at a time. The room smelled of flowers. All of Maxine's rooms did. She had fresh bouquets brought in daily. A ploy of hers, she once told him, to lure her customers back again and again. "When it smells good they like it more" was how she put it.

Ash opened the window and took the bouquet and threw it out.

Grace giggled again. "What did you that for? Those were roses. They cost Maxine money."

"You're costing me money. Get on the bed and spread your legs."

"Whatever you want, sugar." Grace shed her silken

negligee. "But if you don't mind my saying, something is eating at you tonight. Mind telling me what it is?"

Ash gave it to her straight. "I want you to help me forget."

"Forget what?"

Ash gazed out the window at the street lights and the people and the twinkling stars. "Everything."

Chapter 27

Ash had a lot to consider. It was a long ride from Denver to Durango. Over three hundred miles. He would have to cross half a dozen mountain ranges and the Continental Divide. The ride would take weeks and tax his weakened constitution. All to kill a man he had no quarrel with for the money he needed for the morphine that was keeping him from blowing his brains out.

"Hell," Ash gloomily summed up his feelings late on a cloudy afternoon. He was walking the Street of a Thousand Sinners. He had nowhere to go. He was just restless. He couldn't sleep much anymore. The pressure in his chest was unrelenting. The pain came and went. Worse, he had begun to show some of the symptoms Doc Peters had warned him about, symptoms that meant the end was nigh. *His* end.

"Eventually you'll get so sick you can't stand it," the physician had warned. "You'll be laid up in bed. The morphine will help ease the discomfort, but at the same time using it will kill you little by little until you lapse into a coma. Death will come soon after."

"How will I know when I've reached that point?" Ash had asked.

"You'll have stomach spasms, pain so bad it will bend you in half. You won't be able to keep food down. You'll have a weak pulse and be drowsy a lot of the time, and toward the very end you'll have bouts where you can't catch your breath."

"God," Ash had said.

"I'm sorry for you. Truly sorry. It's not the sort of death I would wish on anyone. At the very last your heart will give out or your lungs will quit working or maybe your whole body will just shut down."

Ash remembered each and every symptom. He was having a lot of pain in his gut. He was having severe bouts of drowsiness. He didn't need to feel his pulse to know it was weak. Twice now he'd experienced short spells where he had to suck in air to breathe. He might not even make it to Durango.

The next morning Ash bought a packhorse instead of renting one as he had before. He bought supplies. He bought ammunition. He bought more morphine, a lot more. He paid his landlady for two months in advance and told her that if he wasn't back by the end of that time she could rent his room to someone else.

That night Ash didn't go out. He cleaned and reloaded the Remington revolver and the Remington pocket pistol and his Winchester. He gathered up all that he owned in the world: an extra shirt and extra pants, his shaving kit, which he hadn't used in days, spare socks, his blankets.

Sunrise found Ash in the saddle, leading the packhorses down the dusty dung-dotted street. A dog yipped at him. A hog rooted in the dirt. A milkman smiled and nodded and Ash nodded back.

To the west reared the ramparts men called the Rockies. Peak after imposing peak, several crowned ivory with snow. That was something else Ash had to think about: the snow. It was autumn. The trees had started to turn and the mornings were brisk. He was taking a risk trying to reach Durango before the heavy snows fell. But what did he have to lose except his life? And he had already lost that.

The serpentine windings of the rutted road meandered over hill and through dale. Meadows rich with grass and wildflowers were hemmed by slopes rich with timber. Always the road led higher until he was out of the foothills and in the high country proper. Here the valleys were few and far between. Forest reigned, evergreens in all their variety, along with stands of colorful aspens, their leaves shimmering in the wind.

It was his eighth day out when Ash drew rein at noon. Climbing down, he stretched and gazed out over the country he had put behind him. Wooded slopes spread out as far as the eye could see. Bathed in sunlight, they presented a picturesque beauty impossible to deny.

"You can do this," Ash said with a nod at the natural wonderland, and then he touched his chest. "And yet you do this?"

Ash tried to stay alert as he rode but the drowsiness made it hard. He had a lot to watch out for. The Utes, for starters. This had been their land before it became white land and they resented the white intrusion. Then there were grizzlies. Most of the big bears had been wiped out lower down but up here many still roamed. Wolves and cougars and other meat eaters were abundant. So were rattlesnakes.

Fate favored Ash. He made it over the front range without mishap. At Salida he had a decision to make.

He could swing west to Monarch Pass and press on through the mountains to Durango or he could go south over Poncha Pass into the San Luis Valley and follow the valley to Del Norte and then head west. The valley would be easier. The valley would take less time. The valley had a lot more people too.

Ash went west to Monarch Pass and on into the mountains. Usually he had the road to himself. He liked it that way. He avoided travelers other than to acknowledge a few friendly waves or greetings. He never stopped to talk. He didn't want to get to know any of them. To know them might be to like them and leaving the world would be hard enough.

The nights were bad. He tossed and turned and sweated and hurt. The stomach cramps came and went. The pain in his chest was always there.

To try to get to sleep he started using more morphine. All that did was make him drowsier during the day. So drowsy he couldn't keep his eyes open. Yet at night when he closed them he couldn't drift off.

"It makes no damn sense," he fumed at the heavens.

Two days later he came on a grizzly. He was winding along a creek and around a bend and there it was, as gigantic as anything, its muzzle wet from drinking. It grunted and rose onto its hind legs. Eleven feet, Ash reckoned. He put his hand on his revolver but he didn't draw. It would be like spitting wads of paper.

The bear would rip him to ribbons.

The grizzly sniffed and took a lumbering step nearer.

The packhorse whinnied and pulled on the lead rope and would have galloped off if Ash hadn't tightened his hold. It distracted him for a few seconds.

When he looked back at the grizzly it was climbing the opposite bank.

A last stare and another grunt and it was gone.

"Thank you," Ash said.

Later that day he struck Indian sign. Half a dozen unshod horses had crossed the trail the day before. A Ute hunting party, he figured. Or maybe a war party. For the next several days he rode with his Winchester across his saddle.

Then came a cool evening high on a sawtooth spine. A campfire glowed in a clearing ahead. It might be the only spot to stop for miles. The horses and Ash were tuckered out, so with reluctance he reined off the trail into the clearing and stopped.

The people ringing the fire looked up. A family of five. Father, mother, two girls and a boy. Past them sat a covered wagon, not a Conestoga but its smaller cousin. The team of mules was tied for the night.

"How do you do, stranger?" the father said. He had a rifle propped against his leg, a Spencer. He had a beard too, only his was trimmed short. "You're welcome to share our fire if you'd like."

Ash dismounted. He was so tired and weak he could barely stand. He shuffled over, squatted and held his hands to the flames for the warmth. "I'm obliged."

The smallest girl—she had to be eight or nine—clutched her mother's wrist and said in fright, "Ma! His face!"

"Hush, child. The man is sick is all."

"What ails you, stranger?" the father asked. "It's not anything my family will catch, is it?"

"No," Ash answered.

"You're sure? They mean the world to me."

"It's morphine sickness."

"Oh," the father said, and then again, "Oh. I won't pry into why. It's none of my business."

"No, it's not."

The smallest girl still appeared to be terrified. "What's morphine, Pa? Why does it make him look like that?"

Ash turned to her. "Like what? How do I look to you?"

"Easy, now," the father said. "She's too young to understand. Don't take it as an insult."

"That's right." The mother clasped the small one to her. "Sally doesn't know any better."

Ash hadn't taken his eyes off the girl. "I'd really like to know, little miss. What do you see when you look at me? Be honest."

Sally glanced at her mother and then at her father and the father nodded. "I see a dead man, Mister. You can talk and walk but you look as if you should be dead."

"Sally Jane!" the mother exclaimed.

"He asked me, Ma. He wanted to know."

"That I did," Ash confirmed. An awkward silence fell. The family was on edge and apprehensive. He sought to soothe them by saying, "If you'll excuse me, I have horses to strip and my bedroll to spread out."

The father motioned at a coffeepot. "Where are my manners? You're welcome to sit with us if you'd like. My Martha makes about the best coffee anywhere."

"Oh, pshaw," Martha said.

"Maybe later." Ash had no intention of joining them. Not after scaring the little girl to death. He made his own camp across the clearing and got a small fire going and picketed his animals. He got out his own coffeepot and his water skin and was about to fill the pot when the father called out to him.

"Stranger, I meant what I said about you joining us. We'd be grateful for the company."

Ash hesitated. He couldn't decide if they were being kind out of sympathy or whether they were kind at heart.

"Please," Martha prompted. "We feel bad about how Sally acted. Show us there are no hard feelings."

Certain he was making a mistake, Ash went back over. He accepted a tin cup brimming with coffee. Holding it in both hands he sipped and waited for one of them to say something.

"I'm Tom Minter, by the way. We're from Pittsburgh. We're on our way to Durango to find work."

"That's a far piece to travel for a job."

"The coal mine I was working at in Pennsylvania closed. The coal vein petered out." Tom paused. "I read they are always looking for men to work the mines in Durango. I read they pay good money and don't make a man work more than twelve hours a day."

"I wouldn't know about that."

"It was in the newspaper so it must be true."

Ash laughed and they regarded him as if he were peculiar. "You can't take things you read as gospel," he said, and saw worry blossom on Tom Minter's face. "But yes, I've heard there's plenty of work to be had for those who don't mind calluses on their hands."

"That would be me. I do a good day's work for a good day's wage."

"That he does," Martha confirmed. "I married a good provider and I'm not shy about saying so."

"That works both ways," Tom responded. "You're the best wife and mother any man could want."

Ash had to turn away. It tore at his insides to look at them. They were so much in love and so very proud of one another. At that moment he envied Minter more than he ever envied anyone.

"I was about to put stew on," Martha said. "Would you care to join us? We have plenty to spare."

Ash wasn't hungry, but he said he would be glad to.

Martha went to the wagon and returned with a pot. She filled it with water and chopped up a handful of carrots and two potatoes. To that she added half a cup of flour and stirred.

"We don't have any meat," Tom apologized. "I shot at a buck today but I am not much of a hunter."

Ash excused himself. He went through his supplies and brought back more flour and sugar and six cans. "I should contribute my fair share," he said, and set it all next to the pot.

"We couldn't," Martha declared, although her stomach was growling.

"Not that much, no," Tom said.

"It would just go to waste," Ash told them. "Please. Feel free to help yourselves."

They looked at one another and at him and at the bounty of food, and Tom said, "I reckon we will, then."

Martha fetched pans and the children hovered like half-starved wolves while she prepared the meal. She hummed as she worked, smiling happily, and her mood was contagious. Before long the whole family was grinning and talking and eager to eat. And eat they did. The stew, the beans, the peaches—they ate until they were fit to burst.

The looks they gave Ash made him uncomfortable. He plucked a blade of grass and stuck it between his teeth and tried not to inhale the aroma of the food so he wouldn't vomit.

"We can't thank you enough, Mister," Tom Minter said.

"It's nothing."

"Oh, it's more than that," Martha disagreed. "We've always told our children that the milk of human kindness never runs dry and you have proven our point."

"I can't eat anyway."

"Yes, sir," Tom said. "Here we were, about out of food. We were praying for help and the good Lord sent you."

Ash opened his mouth to tell him how wrong he was, but didn't.

Little Sally had gotten over her fear and was bubbling with glee. "Thank you, Mister. Thank you a whole lot. My folks say that God rewards us when we're good so I bet he rewards you."

"It would be a nice change," Ash said.

Chapter 28

Mining towns had a reputation for being no place for the weak or timid. Durango was no exception. It bustled with life, vigor and violence.

Hemmed by the majestic San Juan Mountains, Durango was the beating heart of the Animas River Valley. It sat at the junction of the Spanish Trail, which came up from the south out of Mexico, and important trails that led west to California and to the northeast toward Denver. The River of Lost Souls, as it was called, ran through the middle of town.

Not that long ago gold had been discovered in the San Juans. Since the area was at the heart of Ute territory and the Utes were not thrilled at the prospect of having a horde of whites swarm into the region after the precious ore, the government saw fit to round them up and put them on a reservation so it was safe for the gold seekers.

And swarm in they did. Gold strikes always lured the adventurous and the greedy and those who preyed on them. Shootings and knifings were as common as teeth, to where no one paid much attention to them unless they involved someone of note.

Miners were a lusty bunch. Durango boasted almost as many saloons and brothels as Denver. It could only boast one church, though.

Ash arrived on a rainy afternoon with the wind whipping out of the northwest. It had taken longer than he thought it would, but he made it over the passes before the first heavy snows. It took him longer because he traveled for part of the way with the Minters. Tom Minter had expressed worry about running into renegade Utes so Ash offered to ride with them until they were down out of the high country and safe.

Ash didn't mind the delay. He liked the Minters. He liked that once they were over their initial shock at how he looked they treated him as they would treat anyone else. He liked that the kids enjoyed his company. He liked being with them so much that when it came time to part company, he felt terribly lonely.

The rain pattering on his hat and shoulders, Ash drew rein at a hitch rail and stiffly dismounted. His symptoms had grown worse. He had also picked up a cough and would have coughing fits that left him weak and breathless. His morphine use had tripled. He had reached the point Doc Peters had warned about, the point where the morphine didn't actually help. All it did was keep him alive while it was killing him at the same time.

Ash craned his neck to the cloudy sky and let the rain wet his face. He liked being alive. He liked it more than anything. He wanted so desperately to go on living.

The sight of the church spire made Ash frown. He tied off the roan and the packhorse and clomped into a saloon. He didn't bother to read the name. It was early yet and only a few customers were drinking or playing cards. He went to the bar and asked for a bottle.

The bartender gave him a glance and then a closer scrutiny. "I hope you won't mind me saying this, Mister, but you look like hell."

"No fooling." Ash took a long swig. Once it would have given him considerable pleasure but now the whiskey tasted flat and didn't warm him as it should.

"Maybe you should see a doctor. We have a good one down the street. Doctor Adams can patch up just about anything."

"Not me he can't." Ash tried another swallow with the same result. "Hell," he said.

The bartender misunderstood. "Don't get mad. I was just saying."

"Where would I find the marshal?"

"You go up two blocks and turn left and you can't miss it. His office is right on the river."

"What kind of man is he?"

"Lucas Olander? He's honest enough and fair enough that most folks think he makes a fine lawman. Why do you ask?"

"Curious." Ash tried a third swallow and gave up. "I reckon I'll go have a talk with him."

"The marshal won't be there. A mine payroll was held up yesterday. He's off with a posse looking for the outlaws."

"Damn." Ash started to turn. He needed to find lodgings for him and his animals.

"Word is that they know who is to blame. A hard case by the name of Sharkey."

"What did you say?"

"You were standing right there. Didn't you hear me?"

Ash had to restrain himself from reaching across and

grabbing the bartender by the shirt. "Did you say Sharkey?"

"Ben Sharkey. Or so they tell me. He and his gang showed up not long ago and have been giving Marshal Olander fits. They've killed two people and stolen pretty near fifty thousand dollars. Don't ask me what they do with the money. If I had that much I'd stop stealing and go off somewhere to live out the rest of my days quiet."

A flush of fury coursed through Ash. No wonder he couldn't find a trace of Sharkey in Denver. The bastard had run out of spending money and was back to his old ways.

"Mister, are you all right?"

"Never better," Ash lied, and left. He stepped out from under the overhang to untie the horses and again raised his face to the rain. It felt wonderfully good.

So did the fact that he had been given another chance. His last chance, because he wouldn't live long enough to have another. He must settle accounts with Sharkey once and for all.

"Thank you," Ash said to the clouds, and went in search of a livery.

On the other side of the street was a hotel called the Lost Soul. The clerk was polite enough not to comment on how he looked. He went up to his room, shrugged out of his slicker, took off his boots and sank onto the bed on his back fully dressed. He was too tired to take off his clothes. He was too tired to even inject morphine. He closed his eyes and almost instantly was asleep.

Pain woke him up. Pain in his gut so bad that Ash sat up and then doubled over and groaned. He had been a fool not to inject. He swung his legs off the bed and went to stand but the pain brought him to his hands and knees. For a few moments he thought this was it. He was dying. But after a minute the pain subsided enough that he made it to his feet and to the morphine.

Caked with sweat, Ash lay back down. A coughing fit left him weaker still. He took his handkerchief out and mopped his forehead and pressed it to his mouth and when he drew it away there was blood on it.

Ash closed his eyes. He was in the final stages. Somehow he must find Sharkey quickly or he wouldn't find him at all.

The lassitude that came over him wasn't as potent as it normally would be. He wasn't awash in pleasure. He wasn't hurting as much either, and that was what counted.

Ash drifted off. When next he awoke the window was dark and he was clammy and shivering. Tugging on his boots, he went down to the lobby. "I'd like a hot bath."

"We have a washtub in the back. The boy will fill it for you. It will cost you extra, though."

"I don't care. I really need one."

"I couldn't agree more, sir," the clerk said.

A shave and a change of clothes and Ash almost felt like a new man. The mirror, though, didn't lie. He was a walking cadaver. His face, especially, was awful; a thin-lipped skull with burning eyes, like some creature straight out of hell.

Ash made the rounds of a few saloons but his heart wasn't in it. He visited the marshal's office where a deputy told him the marshal wasn't expected back until late the next morning.

"You wouldn't happen to have any idea where I could find Ben Sharkey, would you?" Ash asked.

"Mister, if the marshal knew that, he'd find him his own self."

Ash had a good night, for once. He injected and slept the sleep of the dead, awaking more refreshed than he had felt since he could remember. He dressed and went to a place called Ma's where he stuffed himself on scrambled eggs and a slice of ham and toast and coffee. He paid and walked out and hadn't taken six steps when his stomach revolted. Ducking around the corner of the building, he was so sick it left him too weak to stand. Gasping for breath, every part of him hurting, he sat on a barrel until he felt strong enough to walk.

Any hope Ash had that he might not be as near to death's door as he feared was dashed. Not being able to keep food down was another sign of the end.

He was breathing on borrowed time.

The deputy wasn't in the marshal's office. Another man was, bigger and broader with gray at the temples and the stamp of hardship in the lines of his craggy face. The badge on his shirt told who he was.

"So you're Lucas Olander," Ash said by way of greeting.

Olander looked him up and down. "And you must be the gent Carl was telling me about. The one who came in asking about me. The one who wanted to know about Ben Sharkey's doings."

"That would be me," Ash confirmed. "I'm after him. Before you ask, I'll tell you why. I aim to buck him out in gore."

Marshal Olander sniffed several times and raked Ash from head to foot appraisingly. "Don't take this wrong. Are you sure you'll live long enough? You look fit to keel over."

"If I do he's to blame." Ash chronicled his clashes

with Sharkey in Kansas and Texas and how he had come to Colorado looking for him. He left nothing out. He even told about the slug in his chest. "I don't have much time left, Marshal. I'll be grateful for any help you can lend me."

Olander had listened with his arms folded across his chest. Now he stirred and said, "You're the one I read about, aren't you? The one who put an end to the Fraziers and Judson?"

"That would be me," Ash confirmed a second time. "I went after them because I couldn't find Sharkey. Now I can, with your help. But I need to do it quick."

"I have no objection to us working together," Olander informed him. "But the 'quick' might be hard to do. I just spent four days chasing Sharkey and his men and all I caught for my effort was a handful of empty air."

Raw emotion tore at Ash. Placing his hands on the desk, he leaned toward the lawman. "You can't begin to know how much this means to me. There has to be someone somewhere who knows where they lay low. There has to be some way of bringing them to bay."

"I am open to suggestions."

Ash pondered. What did he know about Sharkey that might help? "He is powerful fond of painted ladies. Have you sent a man around to all the brothels?"

"Surely Sharkey isn't stupid enough to come into Durango, knowing that I am looking for him."

"That's exactly what he would do," Ash responded. "He is arrogant. He likes to hide right under the nose of the law."

"Then I will go myself," Marshal Olander said, "and if I learn anything I'll contact you."

Ash supposed that was the best he could do for now. He thanked the lawman and returned to his room. He crawled into bed, curled into a ball and spent the afternoon in the limbo of the afflicted.

A gunshot out in the street woke him. Ash went to the window and heard gleeful yelling and whooping. A miner or some other well-lubricated individual on a spree, he reckoned.

Ash splashed water on his face and went out to taste Durango's nightlife for himself. By Denver standards it paled. The saloons were busy enough and a steady flow of humanity paraded the streets, but there was something missing. Ash couldn't put his finger on it until a dove sashayed past wearing an expensive dress and smelling of costly perfume.

"That's what it is."

Durango and Denver were sisters in everything, but Denver dressed better. Brass and glass and carpet and chandeliers were the ribbons that made Denver more attractive. Her saloons and bawdy houses were classier.

Not that Ash found anything to complain about in Durango. Lust and vice were on plentiful display. A greasing of a palm and a man could have practically anything—or anyone—he wanted.

Ash bucked the tiger until near midnight. He had it in mind to treat himself to a lady but oddly enough he lost the urge. Yet another sign he was at the end of his rope. Doc Peters had warned that his carnal cravings would die right before he did.

Since he wasn't tired Ash walked the dusty streets from one end of Durango to the other and back again. Once, on a side street, two men came out of the shadows as if to pounce just as he stepped into the glare of a lamp. They both took one look and got out of there. He laughed for quite a while. Then his eyes moistened.

Mood swings were another sign.

It was past one a.m. when Ash bent his boots to his room. He stripped, resorted to more morphine and lay on his back waiting for sleep to claim him. It proved elusive. So did the pleasure the morphine usually gave him. He felt little different after sticking the needle into his arm than he had felt before he injected.

When slumber did finally come so did chaotic dreams. "Nightmares" was a better term. Weird images flitted and flowed. Creatures that never existed chased him to rip and rend. Along about four in the morning he snapped awake, dripping sweat and shaking. He couldn't get back to sleep so he got up, washed and dressed.

He sat in a chair, staring out the window and re-membering. People, places, joys, sorrows, all as real as when they happened.

"God, I hate this."

Dawn was breaking when a knock on his door drew Ash from the chair. He opened the door. "You're up early."

"I have a long ride ahead of me and I reckoned you would like to tag along," Marshal Lucas Olander in-formed him.

"Don't tell me," Ash said, tingling with expectancy.

"How would you like another chance at Ben Shar-key?"

Chapter 29

Once, it had been a gold camp.

Gold had been panned from a stream in a gulch in the San Juan Mountains. Those who first found it tried to keep it secret but as always happened word got out and others eager to be rich poured in to file claims of their own. The camp seemed to sprout overnight. Made up mostly of tents and a few hastily built buildings, Gold Gulch, as it was optimistically named, lasted all of six months. By then it was apparent that the gold already taken from the stream was all the gold that would ever be taken from the stream. Off buzzed the swarm in search of more-golden pastures. They took their tents with them but left the buildings.

Only one of the structures was made of logs and sturdy enough that it survived through the next winter. The others had thin planks for walls and plank ceilings and were about as sturdy as dry twigs. A chinook blew all of them down save for the cabin.

Gold Gulch became another ghost camp. No one went there. It was too far from the main trails and had nothing to offer but cold water and the ghosts of those who had been slain during the camp's short existence.

Since no one went there, when a prospector happened to pass the gulch on his perpetual hunt for yellow ore, he thought it strange that the cabin windows were aglow with light and there were horses in the corral. Curious, he tied his mule in the pines and went for a look-see. The prospector thought it must be fellow ore hounds but when he took the precaution of sneaking up to a window and peeking in, the men he saw weren't prospectors. Each was an armory and all were gathered around a table where one of their number was counting out money from a bag stamped THE LOST SOUL'S MINE.

The prospector got out of there. He knew cutthroats when he saw them and he was partial to his neck.

A couple of weeks went by and he went down to Durango. He decided to treat himself to a night at a bawdy house. He happened to be in the parlor with a delightfully plump bundle of lips and breasts on his lap when in came the marshal. He overheard the marshal talking to the madam about a gang of outlaws and that made him think of the men in the cabin in Gold Gulch. He told the marshal about them.

"That's as much as I know," Lucas Olander ended his account as they were making for the livery. "Deputy Weaver and me are ready to head out as soon as you are."

They were under way by nine. Ash brought his packhorse.

Deputy Weaver wasn't used to a lot of riding. He was a softy, fleshy man who always seemed to roll out of his blankets on the wrong side. Nothing suited him. By the second day he complained of blisters on his backside and of stiffness in his lower back.

Ash was annoyed by Weaver's constant complaining but Marshal Olander took it in stride and told his deputy to quit being a weak sister.

"Wait until we find this Sharkey," Weaver replied. "Then you'll see how puny I am."

"If you're not, stop your griping," Olander said. "Besides, those blisters won't hurt half as much once they pop."

Weaver had another trait Ash didn't like. He showed the trait that evening when they were sitting around the campfire and he looked across at Ash and declared, "You look like hell."

"Hush," Marshal Olander said.

"But he does," Weaver insisted, with a jab of his thumb. "He should be in a hospital. And he stinks. When I'm near him I can't hardly stand to breathe."

Ash was sipping coffee. He put down his tin cup and placed his hand on the Remington revolver. "I can still draw a six-shooter."

"None of that," Olander quickly said. "We're on the same side."

"Bluster all you want," Weaver told Ash. "Your skin is like white paint and you sweat and smell and your arms have more needle marks in them than a sieve has holes."

Olander was losing his temper. "Damn it. You know about the lead in his chest."

"I was only saying."

From then on Ash talked to Weaver as little as possible. He suggested to the marshal that they could do without the deputy but Olander reminded him that Sharkey's pack consisted of five or six curly wolves and they would need Weaver when the time came.

The San Juans were gorgeous. Ash would ride for hours at a time admiring the scenery. He had never paid much attention to landscape before he was shot; he must have missed an awful lot in his travels.

On the morning of the fifth day Ash was trailing the others, his packhorse in tow, when Marshal Olander slowed so he could catch up and then matched the roan pace for pace.

"We'll be there by noon tomorrow."

"I figured from what you'd told me."

Olander gave Ash a strange look. "Are you up to this? Before you say anything, I'm not my lunkhead of a deputy. I'm only asking because I saw you struggling to lift your saddle this morning."

"I will do what I have to."

"I figured," Olander said with a grin. "Only thing is, the odds are on their side. We have to work together or we'll become worm food together. So I ask you again. Are you up to this?"

"Nothing this side of the grave will stay me from my vengeance," Ash vowed. "I have waited too long. I have come too far."

"About that," Olander said. "It could be you don't get the chance. It could be that Weaver or me has a clear shot or Sharkey surrenders. It might be you don't get to squeeze the trigger on him."

"God couldn't be that cruel." But Ash knew better. He hadn't prayed in so long, he had forgotten how. But that night after the other two were asleep he shifted onto his knees, clasped his hands and raised his head to the heavens. "I've learned not to ask for much but I have to ask for this. I want it to be me. I *need* it to be me.

Do this for me and I won't hold the other against you."
Ash caught himself. "No, that's not true. I hate you for
letting this happen. I didn't deserve it. Not this I didn't."

A gust of wind fanned Ash's sunken cheeks.

"It's some life you give us. We're born so we can die.
Along the way a wrong step or bad luck and we die
that much sooner." Ash's voice broke. He coughed and
swore. His eyes were damp. They were damp a lot of
late. Another thing he hated. "It's all I ask. Sharkey and
me. Do this one thing and I can go to my grave holding
my head high."

The wind gusted and the stars sparkled.

Ash got off his knees. He checked on the horses. He
walked a circle around the camp. He sat with coffee in
hand and waited for his three hours to be over so he
could wake Olander and get some sleep. He thought of
Gold Gulch and the coldhearted vermin he must con-
front, and a chill ran down his back. He was ready and
yet he wasn't ready.

"I wish I may be shot if I don't show grit."

A wolf howled, a long, lonesome cry that keened
down off the mountain and echoed into nothingness, a
cry that mirrored Ash's feelings to where he threw back
his own head and almost joined in. A snore reminded
him he wasn't alone.

"It's too bad I can't take my Remington with me
when I die," Ash addressed the stars. "If I could the
first thing I would do in the hereafter is shoot you dead.
Right in the chest where you had me shot. And do you
know what I'd do next? I'd stand there and laugh." He
felt silly saying it but said it anyway.

Later, as Ash sat drinking coffee, another shooting
star cleaved the night with fiery brilliance. Some people

saw them as omens. Those same people saw nearly everything in life as a sign of heavenly guidance. To Ash, the shooting star was just a shooting star and life was as empty as the tin cup he drained with a final swallow.

"Damn, I'm depressing even to me," Ash said. He woke Olander and went to his blankets to turn in.

"I've never heard anyone say they would shoot God before," the lawman remarked with a grin.

Ash frowned. "You heard?"

"Afraid so. I wish there was something I could do for you but there's not, so the best I can offer is my sympathy."

Ash used two blankets now where he had always used one. He considered using the hypodermic but decided to wait. "I used to be like you. Not anymore. A good man. A decent man."

Olander regarded him thoughtfully. "What have you done that isn't good or decent that I don't know of? The Fraziers and Judson needed to be put an end to."

"A good man would do it because they were evil. I did it for the money," Ash confessed. "Money is why I came to Durango."

"Money is keeping you alive."

"Some life." Ash shut up before he said worse. He rolled onto his side and tried to fight off a wave of self-pity. "You know," he said, his back to the marshal, "nothing is ever as we think it is. I've had to learn that the hard way. When we get to the gulch you and the deputy hang back and let me go in alone."

"I can't do that."

"I'm asking for a favor. Leave the law out of it. This is man to man. Will you at least think about it?"

"I'll think about it."

Then next day broke bright and clear. Ash was in good spirits as he saddled up. He didn't use morphine even though every particle of his being craved it.

Through force of will he blocked the need from his mind.

Deputy Weaver had his rifle out and couldn't stop fidgeting in his saddle. "We're awful close. We could run into them any time now."

"Let's hope we surprise them," Marshal Olander said. "We need an edge and that's all we have."

A last steep slope brought them to the mouth of the gulch. A bend fifty yards off hid whatever lay beyond.

Pockmarks in the dirt showed where riders had been coming and going.

"Must be them," Deputy Weaver said.

Ash turned to Olander. "Well?"

"It goes against my grain."

"But you'll let me?"

"Let him what?" Deputy Weaver asked.

"You will likely be shot," Marshal Olander said.

"A man can only take so much of dying slow," Ash told him, and smiled. "No one need know but us."

"Need know what?" Weaver asked.

Marshal Olander nodded. "All right. Go on ahead. When we hear shots we're coming in."

Ash held out his hand. "Thank you."

"Thank him for what?" Weaver said as they shook.

The gulch was narrow to the bend. A peek past it showed the gulch bed widened to three to four hundred feet. Bisected by the gurgling stream, the ground was sparse of vegetation and littered with rocks. A few plank husks marked all that was left of the booming camp.

On a low rise on the east side of the stream sat the

cabin. Deep in the shadow of the high gulch wall, it was long and low and had a crude stone chimney.

Smoke curled into the air, and muffled voices carried to the bend.

Ash debated. He had a lot of open space to cover. The window was covered with burlap but if anyone looked out they'd spot him. Or hear him. The roan was bound to make a racket crossing the rocks. Sliding down, he shucked the Winchester from the scabbard, levered a round into the chamber, and went around the bend on foot. Staying low, he crossed the stream to the east wall and moved along it toward the cabin, staying in deep shadow.

Ash thought of the look that would be on Ben Sharkey's face when Sharkey saw him, and smiled. "You're mine at last, you son of a bitch."

At the side of the cabin was a corral. Horses were dozing or milling. A claybank raised its head, its ears pricked, and gazed in Ash's direction. He hoped it wouldn't whinny.

Ash had forty yards to go and then twenty and then ten. He was watching where he stepped and he was watching the horses. He took another step and his chest exploded with pain. Pain so potent it brought him to his knees. He clutched at himself and dropped the Winchester. His senses swam.

"No," Ash bleated. Not when he was so close. Not when he could practically taste his revenge.

The pain became a pounding hammer that beat at his mind and his body. He collapsed onto his side and smothered a scream. He thought this must be it. The slug had at last penetrated his heart and any instant he would pitch into a black abyss.

Hammer, hammer, pain, pain. It went on and on until Ash groaned and gnashed his teeth and wished for the end. He had tried and he had failed. He had given it his best, though.

Ash was dimly aware of being nudged. He looked up into a bearded face with a bulbous nose and thick lips, and the muzzle of a revolver. The man was saying something, but Ash couldn't hear him for the hammering. The muzzle gouged him in the neck and then the man stepped back, studying him. Ash tried to speak but couldn't. He closed his eyes and waited for the end. It wouldn't be long. He was sure.

As abruptly as it brought him down, the pain went away. The pressure eased. Soaked with sweat, Ash tried to swallow, but his mouth was bone dry. He didn't open his eyes when he was poked, or even when someone rolled him onto his back. But Ash did when someone laughed and declared, "Well, what do we have here?"

It was Ben Sharkey.

Chapter 30

There were seven men in the cabin and not a shred of sympathy on a single face.

There certainly wasn't any sympathy on the face of Ben Sharkey. There was only glee. He walked back and forth in front of Ash, who lay doubled over on the floor where they had dumped him, and chortled. "If this don't beat all. If this surely don't beat all." He stopped pacing and bent down. "I didn't recognize you at first. I doubt your own pa would, as pitiful as you look."

Ash had been stripped of his revolver and the pocket pistol. He was unarmed and weaker than a sick kitten and completely at the mercy of men who did not know the meaning of the word.

"Can't talk?" Sharkey said. Laughing, he kicked Ash in the side, then turned to the others. "Some of you might recollect me talking about my old friend Marshal Asher Thrall."

"The tin star you shot down in Texas?" a sour-faced man asked.

"That's the one and this is him." Sharkey touched Ash with the toe of his boot. "I hate the bastard, but I have to admire his grit. He came all this way to find me, as bad off as he is."

"He must want you dead really bad," another said.

Sharkey stopped grinning and rubbed the stubble on his chin. "The questions is, boys, how did he find us? He can't have tracked us. We've been too careful. He had to know we were here." Sharkey glanced at the burlap covering the window. "In fact, I doubt he came alone, not in his condition. Buck, Tyree and Kline, I want you three to go down the gulch and see if he brought friends."

"If he did?" a lump of flab responded.

"Bring them back alive if you can. If you can't, bring back their bodies and their horses. Go out the back door in case they're watching and crawl until you think it's safe."

The three outlaws moved toward the rear of the cabin.

Ash struggled to sit up but couldn't. He prayed that Olander was on his guard and wouldn't be taken by surprise.

"Now, then," Sharkey said, and hunkered. "It will take them a while, so suppose you and me have us a nice talk." He jabbed Ash with his finger. "You listening, Thrall?"

Ash took a few breaths and licked his lips. "My ears still work."

"Ah. He speaks at last." Cackling, Sharkey pushed his hat back and bent lower. "I thought I killed you that day in Mobeetie."

"You almost did."

Sharkey sniffed and crinkled his nose. "You look like hell and you smell like hell. What's the matter with you? Did you come down with consumption?"

"You," Ash said.

"Me what?"

Ash dearly wished he was strong enough to make a fist and smash it against Sharkey's smug face. "You are the matter with it. It's not consumption. It's your bullet."

"What the hell are you talking about?"

Ash told him.

Sharkey listened without comment, and when Ash was done he straightened and burst into peals of mirth, laughs that shook his whole body. He laughed until he was holding his sides. "Did you hear that, boys? He's been suffering all this time on account of me. I am so happy I could bust."

"What do we do with him?" asked a tall man rolling a cigarette.

Sharkey bent back down. "What *do* I do with you, Thrall? I could shoot you but that would only put you out of your misery. Or I could carve on you with my knife, but I doubt I'd make you suffer any worse than you already are." He chuckled and shook his head. "No. I think the smart thing is to leave you be. It will amuse me to sit here and watch you die."

"You miserable bastard."

Sharkey laughed and stood. "This will be fun. We can bet on how long we think he'll last. I say in ten hours he'll be a goner."

"That long?" a man said. "From the way he looks I don't reckon he'll last one hour."

Ash was inclined to agree. He had never been this weak for this long before. He couldn't lift his hand more than a few inches. The pain and the pressure were easing, though.

Two of the outlaws sat at a table to resume playing

the card game he had interrupted. The tall one went over to the stove to light his cigarette. Sharkey limped to the window and peered out.

"Any sign of them?" asked the man at the stove.

"No. But Buck knows what to do. Whoever is out there is as good as caught or as good as dead."

"I came alone," Ash said.

"Sure you did." Sharkey snorted. "I haven't lasted as long as I have by being stupid."

Ash glanced at the front door. If only he could make it to his feet and somehow get outside, he could yell to warn Marshal Olander and Deputy Weaver.

Sharkey leaned against the wall. "Tell me something, Thrall. Was Horton right?"

"Who?"

The outlaw who had said that Ash must really want Sharkey dead looked up from his poker hand. "That would be me."

"He's right, isn't he?" Sharkey asked again. "The reason you came all this way was to kill me. It has nothing to do with the law, nothing to do with you once toting a badge. This was personal."

"This was personal."

"I'll be damned." Sharkey went to the table, took hold of a chair and dragged it over next to Ash. Straddling it, he laced his fingers under his chin.

"Do you know what I think?" Sharkey didn't wait for Ash to reply. "I think me and you are more alike than you'll admit."

"Like hell we are."

Sharkey cocked his head as if listening and then went on. "All those years you wore the tin, you walked the straight and narrow. You were like a hawk sitting high up in a tree and looking down your beak at everyone, waiting for them to break the law so you could swoop down. You thought you were better than the rest of us."

"Like hell," Ash said again.

Sharkey seemed not to hear him. "You did love to swoop too. In Salina the folks used to joke that all it took was for a man to miss the spittoon and you would haul them to jail."

"That's not true."

"Remember that night when you shot me in the leg? You didn't have to do that. You could have knocked me down with your pistol. Or fired a shot into the ceiling to warn me to drop my knife. But no. You drew your smoke wagon and shot me."

"I didn't shoot to kill," Ash justified the act. "I wasn't trying to cripple you either."

"I believe you. I believe you are stupid enough to think that blowing a hole in my leg was an act of kindness."

Anger flared, and Ash rose onto an elbow. "How dare you, you son of a bitch. You sit there and put the blame on me when you were the one who was drunk. You were the one who drew his knife and was about to stab the marshal in the back. I was his deputy. I had to protect him."

"You didn't have to shoot me," Sharkey insisted.

Ash's anger brought newfound vitality. A burst of energy shot through him and he was about to push to his feet when he realized he shouldn't. Instead, he slumped to the floor in shammed weakness. "Blame me if you want to but I was only doing my job."

Sharkey shifted toward the card players. "Do you hear him, boys? He crippled me and acts as if he did me a favor."

"Lawmen," Horton said in disgust.

"They always act so high and mighty," said the other one.

Sharkey stood and limped to the burlap. "What's taking them so long? We should have heard something by now."

Ash moved so both his hands were in front of him, at his waist. Now came the crucial part. Could he make Sharkey mad enough? he wondered. "It's my turn to ask a question."

"Only if we let you," Sharkey responded, and the others laughed. "But go ahead. Amuse us. What do you want to know?"

"Where are your parents?"

Sharkey glanced sharply around. "What the hell kind of question is that? What do you care where they are?"

"Do they know what their son has become? Do they know what you've made of your life?"

"Be careful," Sharkey said.

"I bet they do. I bet they don't want anything to do with you. Not with a son who turned out to be scum."

"I have killed men for less."

"I'm already dead so your threats don't scare me." Ash slowly sat up. He put on a show of barely being strong enough, then swayed a little as an added touch.

"Answer me. Do your folks know how worthless you are?"

Sharkey was red in the face, his expression carved from stone. Turning, he lowered his hands, his right brushing his Colt. "Keep it up and I'll change my mind. You won't get to die slow."

"It's just like you to shoot an unarmed man," Ash said sarcastically. "Want me to roll over so you can shoot me in the back? That's how you killed that stage driver near Bixby, as I recollect. Come to think of it, there's three or four you've gunned down from behind."

His jaw muscles twitching, Sharkey took a step. "I think it's time I put it to the test."

"Put what?" Ash asked, hoping he would come closer.

"A while back I got the idea to stake a man out someday and beat on him with a rock and see how long he lasts. That day has come. I'll start with your fingers and your toes, then work my way up from yours wrists and the ankles. You'll scream and squirm and beg me to stop, but I won't."

Horton piped up with, "That would be a sight to see. I'll stake him out. Just say when."

Ash needed Sharkey closer. "Do they shoot men in the back for you too?"

Horton went to stand, but Sharkey gestured. "Stay put. He's asking for it and he's going to get it. I'll do him myself."

Ash was ready. He tensed as Sharkey started toward him. The next moment shots boomed from down the gulch followed by shouts and more shooting and the squeal of a horse in pain.

Sharkey spun and dashed to the front door. Flinging it open, he palmed his Colt. "Something must have gone wrong. Horton, Nickels, you two come with me. Slim, you stay and watch our guest. Not that he's in any shape to go anywhere."

The tall outlaw over by the stove patted a Smith & Wesson revolver on his left hip. "Don't you worry. He'll be here when you get back."

All Ash could do was watch Sharkey and the other

two hurry off. He had lost his chance—or had he? "Any objection to me having something to drink? Water will do but red-eye would be better."

"A last drink for the dead man?" Slim said. "Why not? I had a cousin who was hung once and they gave him steak and pie for his last request." Puffing on the cigarette, Slim reached into a cabinet and flourished a bottle of whiskey. "There's not much left, but you're welcome to a swallow."

Ash held out his hand. "I'm obliged."

"Don't tell Ben. He tends to fly into a rage at the drop of a hat, and he drops the hat."

"At least one of you has some kindness in him," Ash said. "I didn't figure you could all be like Sharkey."

Slim stopped a few feet away. "We are none of us saints, Mister. I'll like watching him beat you to death, the same as the others." He held out the whiskey. "It'll be the most fun we've had in a coon's age."

Ash accepted the bottle. He wiped his sleeve across the top and swirled the coffin varnish. Five or six swallows were left. He chugged and coughed and smiled. "It's been a while."

"Go easy. I want a swallow when you're done."

"Whatever you say."

More shouts drew Slim to the door. He stood with his back to Ash and said, "What are they yelling about? Can you tell?"

"No." Ash gripped the bottle by the neck and stood. He took a step and drew up short. In the center of the table were his Remingtons. Horton and the other man must have been using them as poker stakes, playing to see who would get them. Keeping one eye on Slim, he sidled over to them.

Slim cupped a hand to his mouth. "Ben! Ben! Is everything all right over there?"

There was no answer.

Ash grinned in fierce delight. Another couple of feet and he could fight for his life. He held the bottle out to set it on top of the table but misjudged and clunked it against the edge. The clunk wasn't loud, but it was loud enough.

Slim glanced over his shoulder. "What the hell?" he exclaimed, and came around with his Smith & Wesson sweeping clear.

Ash dived and grabbed his revolver. He also grabbed at the pocket pistol, but his shoulder caught the table and it and him crashed to the floor with the table between him and the door. Cocking the revolver, he pumped to his knee. He thought he was quick but Slim was already there, towering over the table and bringing the Smith & Wesson to bear.

"You sneaky bastard."

Twin blasts rocked the cabin.

Chapter 31

Slim missed. His shot buzzed past Ash's ear and thudded into the floor.

Ash didn't miss. His shot cored the tall outlaw between the eyes, snapping Slim's head back. Slim tottered, then crashed down across the table, the Smith & Wesson falling from nerveless fingers.

Quickly Ash scrambled up. The pain in his chest had mostly gone away and the pressure had eased. Turning, he ran to the back door. He worked the latch and plunged outside. He considered taking a horse, but the outlaws had the end of the gulch blocked and would likely as not blast him off if he sought to break through them.

To go right was to go down the gulch to where the outlaws and the lawmen had their gun battle. It was quiet now so the battle was over.

Ash went up the gulch. He moved as swiftly as his racked body would let him, seeking a spot to make a stand. As surely as the sun rose and set, Sharkey would come after him and be out for blood.

Ash stayed in the shadows. He had gone some sixty

feet when he was reminded of his infirmity by a stab-
bing pain in his chest that shot clear down to his feet.
Gasping, he bent with his hands on his knees, praying
the attack would pass.

It did and Ash moved on. He had the Remington, so
he had a fighting chance. He should have grabbed the
other one but he had forgotten it when he had run out.
He'd like to have the Winchester for the extra range but
there had been no sign of it in the cabin.

At the next bend the gulch narrowed and was littered with boulders. The stream meandered among them,
now closer to the west wall and then closer to the east.

Ash was desperately thirsty. He stopped and cupped
both hands and drank greedily. The cold mountain water revitalized him. On he ran, thankful for the stamina
but worried about the next attack and anxious about
his morphine should the outlaws get their hands on his
saddlebags.

First things first, Ash thought. He must stay alive.
He smiled at that, at the irony of a man who was dying
struggling so hard to go on breathing.

Another bend and the gulch narrowed even more.
It was here Ash decided to wage his fight. Two huge
boulders left a gap of some twenty feet, a third of which
was taken up by the stream. He crouched behind the
boulder on the right and leaned against it.

"This is where I die," he declared.

Ash was under no illusions about the outcome. There
were six of them and one of him. This wasn't a dime
novel. He wasn't the vaunted Wild Bill, who could supposedly hit coins thrown into the air and outshoot most
any man alive. He was a good shot, but he didn't always
hit what he aimed at and his aim wasn't what it once
was thanks to his wasting away. He would give the best

account of himself that he could. The important thing
was that no matter what, he must get Sharkey.

The quiet was unnerving.

Ash listened for shouts and the pounding of boots
but there were none.

A raven flew overhead, squawking. A rattlesnake
slithered from under a flat rock and crossed the stream.

"Where are you?" Ash wondered aloud.

The sun climbed. He was growing tired. He sat with
his back to the boulder and yearned to lie down and
sleep. His eyelids became leaden. They would droop
and he would snap them open. Again and again it happened until finally he drifted to sleep.

A laugh startled Ash awake. He rose into a crouch
and shook his head to clear it.

It was a cold laugh. A vicious laugh. A laugh devoid
of the qualities that made a laugh a laugh.

From around the bend came a shout.

"I know where you are, Thrall. I know you're waiting for us to show ourselves."

Ash didn't reply.

"Cat got your tongue?" Ben Sharkey taunted. "I'm
mad as hell about Slim. How did you do it? How did
you get the better of him?"

Ash ran a sleeve across his forehead. He was sweating again, never a good sign.

"You must be curious about your friends," Sharkey
yelled. "So I'll tell you. One of them is dead. A deputy
by his badge. Buck put a bullet through his head before
he could get off a shot. Slow as molasses, that one."

Ash felt no regrets for Deputy Weaver. The man had
been a constant irritation.

"The other one, though. Was that the marshal? He
put up a good fight. He got Tyree in the arm and Kline

in the leg and then held the rest of us off for as long as he could. We were closing in and thought we had him, but he got on a horse and got out of there. I think I winged him."

Ash was glad Marshal Olander got away. Olander wouldn't let it rest, not with Weaver dead. He'd come back with a large posse and hunt Sharkey to the ends of the mountains.

"Come on, Thrall. Talk to me. What can it hurt? Or is it that you can't? That you've collapsed again?"

Ash knew better but he answered anyway. "I want you dead so much I can taste it."

"Well, now," Sharkey called out, and laughed.

"You are pure scum. You should have been stillborn and saved the world the misery."

"A little upset, are you?" Sharkey rejoined.

Ash had an idea. An insane idea, but it appealed to him. "What do you say we end this? Just you and me, man to man?"

"Does that morphine do things to the brain?"

"I'm serious. I'll hold my fire. You come around the bend with your six-shooter in its holster. I'll come out into the open with mine the same. Whenever you want you can go for your hardware and I'll go for mine." Ash had no intention of doing that; the moment Sharkey appeared he would shoot him.

"I told you before, I haven't lasted as long as I have by being stupid."

"Why not? You want to kill me as much as I want to kill you. Let's finish it."

"Oh, I'll finish it, all right, without giving you the chance to take me with you. I can wait out here until you starve or your own body does you in."

"I thought so. You're all talk."

"It won't work, Thrall. I'm not ten years old. Making me mad won't make me careless."

Ash put his forehead to the boulder and closed his eyes. He was feeling weak again. The pressure was worse too.

"You still with us, Thrall? When you go quiet I wonder."

Nausea filled Ash and he groaned.

"Want to hear a secret, Thrall? It will amuse you. It sure amuses me. That night you shot me? I was supposed to get hitched the next day and I was out celebrating. I bet you didn't know that. There was this gal I was fond of. She thought I was wild and reckless, but she'd agreed to be mine. Then you went and put lead in me and she decided she didn't want a man who goes around getting himself shot."

Ash roused. "Maybe she didn't want a man who tried to stab a marshal in the back."

Sharkey was quiet for a bit. When he called out again, he was almost solemn.

"You changed my whole life. If I'd married her I might have changed my ways. I might have become a rancher or opened up a livery or been anything but what I am."

"You never give up trying to make me feel guilty."

A hot stream of cuss words blistered the gulch, ending with "Everything isn't about *you*, damn it. When you die the world will go on just fine without you. *I'll* go on just fine, and every life I take, every bank I rob, will be on your shoulders."

"Go to hell."

"No doubt I will. But first I am fixing to have some fun with you." Sharkey paused. "You there yet, Horton? You've had plenty of time."

From behind Ash came the reply.

"I'm here."

Ash whirled, or tried to. The Remington was swatted from his hand, a pistol muzzle was shoved in his face and an iron hand roughly grabbed him and shook him as a cat shakes a mouse.

"Didn't know there was another way into the gulch, did you?" Horton gloated.

Beyond him, revolver leveled, stood the man called Buck.

"You got him?" Sharkey hollered.

"We got him."

Ash was flung to the dirt and kicked.

"That was for Slim. He was my pard."

The rest came around the bend: Sharkey, wearing an ear-splitting grin. Tyree, with his left sleeve rolled up, his arm crudely bandaged. Kline, limping like Sharkey. Then the last outlaw, Nickels.

Sharkey put his hands on his hips. "The trouble you've given me, I should blow out your brains here and now, but I won't. You have it coming and I will by God give it to you."

Ash had no need to ask what "it" was. He resisted when Horton and Buck seized him by the arms, but they were much too strong and he was much too weak.

Sharkey swaggered along beside them. "You've delayed what I had planned for you, but that's all."

"I cost you a man."

"And that will cost you in pain," Sharkey promised. "As for your lawman friend, it will take him a week or more to make it back with help and by then the buzzards will have pecked your eyes out."

The others didn't laugh. They weren't in the mood with two of them hurt and Slim dead.

"Remember what I told you about staking you out and breaking your bones one by one with a rock? I've changed my mind. There's a lamp in the cabin. From the smell it's filled with whale oil, not kerosene, but whale oil will do." Sharkey slid a box of Lucifers from his pocket. "I aim to pour that whale oil over you and set you on fire."

"Oh hell, Ben!" Horton declared, and grinned. "The brainstorms you come up. I wish I had your head."

Sharkey was watching Ash's face. "Nothing to say? Didn't you hear me? I'm going to burn you alive."

Ash was too depressed to care. He had let himself be taken unawares. Now he would never have his vengeance. It served him right for being so careless.

"They say it hurts like hell," Sharkey mentioned with sadistic delight. "I expect you'll scream like the very devil."

"That will be the day," Ash blustered.

Buck said, "I saw a man burned once. His house caught on fire. When they brought him out his skin was burnt to a cinder and all his hair was gone. He lasted half an hour, caterwauling the whole time."

"Did you hear?" Sharkey said. "That's what you have to look forward to. Still have nothing to say?"

Ash refused to give him the satisfaction. He slumped so they had to virtually carry him.

In front of the cabin was a small area clear of rocks. They threw Ash onto his back and two of them held his arms and two others his legs while Sharkey pounded stakes into the ground and tied him to the stakes.

Horton and Kline drew knives and cut Ash's jacket and shirt from his body, leaving both in shreds. Kline cut Ash a few times, on purpose, while doing it.

"Those are for the hole your friend put in me."

Sharkey reappeared with an old lamp, a model that had gone out of fashion when kerosene replaced whale oil. He swished it and grinned. "I reckon there's enough to do the job."

The stuff was slimy and stank. Sharkey poured it onto Ash's chest and then took out a well-used handkerchief to smear it over Ash's torso and neck and face. Ash nearly gagged. He turned his face away, but Sharkey gripped his chin so hard it hurt and rubbed the whale oil on his cheeks and forehead and even his hair.

"Don't you smell pretty?"

"Bastard."

"Now, now."

The rest were in a ring, watching. Tyree was retying his bandage.

Kline glowered.

Ash couldn't say what made him do what he did next. Fury? Frustration? It didn't matter. Sharkey was rubbing the whale oil over his mouth. Ash saw Sharkey's hand, saw Sharkey's little finger poke from under the handkerchief like a pink worm on a hook. He bit down and locked his jaw.

Sharkey cried out and tried to jerk back.

The salty taste of blood filled Ash's mouth. His teeth met bone and he bit harder, seeking to break it.

"Get him off me, damn it!" Sharkey pulled and tugged, swearing mightily.

The other outlaws, stunned, were slow to rush to his aid. Horton sought to pry Ash's mouth open while Buck held Ash's head, but Ash's clamped his teeth for all he was worth and wouldn't let up even when they punched him.

Sharkey was nearly beside himself. "One of you idiots do something!"

That was when Kline stepped up with a Colt in his hand. He grinned down at Ash and said, "This is for the hole your friend put in me too." And with that he brought the barrel slashing down.

Ash's world faded to black.

Chapter 32

Stars filled the vault of ink sky and a stiff wind stirred wisps of dust in the gulch.

Ash looked about him, amazed he was still alive. He had just come around and no one else was there. That they had not left anyone to guard him seemed strange, but then he wasn't going anywhere, tied as he was. He tried to move his arms; the stakes wouldn't budge.

The cabin window was lit and the door was open. From inside spilled gruff mirth and the clink of a bottle or a glass.

From the position of the Big Dipper, Ash guessed it must be pushing midnight. He had been unconscious for hours. No wonder his throat was bone dry.

Higher on the mountain something roared. A bear, Ash reckoned. If it caught a whiff of him it might become curious.

Someone filled the doorway. Silhouetted against the light, the figure upended a bottle, then came out. Walking unsteadily, he chuckled. "I am three sheets to the wind."

"And a bastard besides."

"Don't start. I am feeling too fine to burn you, but I will if you make me mad." Sharkey sat next to Ash and took a long swig. "How are you holding up?"

"What do you care?"

"I don't want you dying on me before I burn you. That would spoil my fun."

Ash hurt all over. He needed morphine, needed an injection as he had never needed anything. "Do me a favor."

"This should be good."

"I need morphine. A hypodermic is in my saddle-bags. It's easy to use. I can tell you how to do it."

Sharkey drank, and snickered. "This is comical. You're asking me to keep you alive long enough for me to burn you dead. I tell you, there are days when I think if there is a God, the Almighty is as crazy as we are."

Ash didn't hide his surprise. "I've had the same thought of late. Then you'll do it?"

Shaking his head, Sharkey belched. "I'll do no such thing. You can lie there and suffer. Tough hombre like you, I doubt you really need it."

"Go away."

"You're in no position to make demands." Sharkey went to take another swallow and chortled. "Get it? No position? I am downright hysterical when I am drunk."

"You aim to let me lie out here all night, don't you?"

"How did you guess? I plan to burn you at dawn. We can set you on fire and then cook our breakfast over your burning body. I've done a lot of things but never that. It will be a first."

Emotions tore at Ash. Anger. Resentment. Sorrow. Self-pity. The last brought him near to tears and he looked away so Sharkey wouldn't notice.

"Well, I just wanted to check on you." Sharkey started to rise and had to catch himself to keep from pitching onto his face. "Damn. Everything is spinning. I reckon I should have waited until after I burn you to celebrate." He made it to the cabin and went in, leaving the door open.

Ash lay quiet. He was worn out. His craving ate at him like acid to where he had to stop himself from pulling at the stakes like a madman. His chest hammered and the pressure climbed. He thought that maybe this was it, that at long last the end had come. He was wrong. The night dragged on anchors of torment. Every muscle ached. He sweated. He shivered with cold and then he was hot and shivered with cold again.

"Kill me," Ash said to the heavens. "If you are what they say you are, kill me."

When Ash finally did succumb, he slept the sleep of total exhaustion. Only twice did he stir. Once when a wolf howled. The second time he struggled up out of a pit that was shaking as if from an earthquake. Someone was whispering his name urgently, over and over. "Who's there?" he demanded, and felt a hand pressed over his mouth.

"Not so loud! Do you want them to hear?"

Ash was too befuddled to make sense of what he was seeing. "How did you get back so fast?"

"I never went anywhere," Marshal Olander said. He bent and steel flashed. The ropes binding Ash's wrists fell away. Swiftly, the lawman did the same with the ropes securing his ankles.

It took all of Ash's strength to sit up. "They said that you rode off, that you were wounded."

"I rode off but I came right back. Can you walk?"

"No."

Olander looped an arm around Ash and lifted him to his feet. "I was nicked in the side, but that's all."

They moved down the gulch. Olander kept glancing back. "I've been spying on them and waiting my chance."

"What time is it?"

"About four. I needed to be sure they were asleep. We'll be long gone before they're up and find you missing."

"We could take them," Ash said.

"Not with you in the shape you're in," Olander disagreed. "It's better we get you to safety."

"I'm dying anyway, remember?" Ash reminded him. "We'll never have a better chance. They've all passed out from too much red-eye."

"You know for a fact they were all drinking?"

"No, but . . ."

"I've already lost my deputy and that's one too many. I'm getting you out of here," Olander insisted.

One again Ash was denied his vengeance. He submitted to being hauled to the lawman's mount and boosted onto the saddle. "We have to ride double?"

"Unless you can sprout wings and fly."

Ash clung on as Olander climbed up.

"Hang on."

Ash didn't remember a lot of that ride. He faded in and out. The movement of the horse under him provoked the pressure in his chest to return. Pressure, but little pain. He clung to the marshal's shoulders, his forehead against a shoulder blade. That he didn't fall off was a miracle.

Then strong hands were helping him down and Olander was saying, "We need to rest. My horse is about done in."

Ash blinked, and was astounded to find the sun high in the sky. It had to be ten o'clock, maybe later. He wearily nodded. They were in a clearing in the forest.

The sorrel was lathered with sweat, its head hung in exhaustion. Ash moved to a log and sat with his back to it, his head hung the same way.

"How are you holding up?" Olander had squatted in front of him and was cradling a Winchester.

"I've never been better," Ash said, and could barely hear himself.

"I'm no sawbones, but if I had to say, I'd say you're not long for this world. Is there anything I can do for you? I have water in a canteen. I have food in my saddlebags."

"The water would be nice," Ash said. The thought of food churned his stomach.

"Be right back."

"I'm not going anywhere," Ash joked. A feeling came over him, a conviction that indeed he wasn't long for the world, that he wouldn't need to find the gun shark called Skelman and have Skelman end it for him. The lead lodged against his heart was about to finally do what it had been threatening to do for months. It could happen any minute.

Olander returned. "Here you go."

Ash was strong enough to hold the canteen, which was something. He gratefully drank the wonderfully delicious water. Simple water. He gazed at the blue of the sky and the green and brown of the forest, and never in his life had the sky and the forest seemed so beautiful, so . . . enchanting. A silly notion, but there it was.

Olander brought him back to reality with, "They're after us. I've seen their dust about a mile back."

"Sharkey won't rest until he's caught me," Ash predicted. "You'd be smart to leave me and light a shuck."

The marshal tapped the tin on his shirt. "You know I can't do that. You wouldn't have either once, would you?"

"No," Ash admitted. He had always tried to be the best lawman he could be. Maybe it wasn't much as ambitions went but he could look back with pride and say he had done something right in his life or as right as any life ever got. He looked down at himself, at his stick arms and his stick legs, and shriveled inside. "Oh God."

"What? Is it the pain?"

"Give me the rifle and go. I don't want you to lose your life on account of me."

"I've already told you I can't." Olander rose. "If we can keep our lead until dark falls we can shake them. They can't track at night."

"They can use torches."

Olander nodded. "But it's slow work. No, we'll keep going and pray for the best."

Tears trickled down Ash's sunken cheeks and he didn't care. "For what it is worth, I'm obliged."

The marshal regarded him a moment, then said, "I want you to know something, Thrall. I've hardly ever said to any man what I'm about to say to you." He paused. "I admire the hell out of you."

"What?"

"I admire you. I can't say it any plainer. I hope to God when my time comes I face it with half the courage you have."

"Courage?" Ash repeated.

"You're a walking dead man, as you called yourself, yet you keep trying. You've never once given up. You made it your work to track down the worst killers there are knowing you were the one person who could do it without having to worry about the outcome. Hell, yes, you have courage to spare."

Ash's chin touched his chest. He wanted to say, "I did it for the morphine," but he didn't.

"You are a credit to the badge you wore and I'll be damned if I'll let those murdering coyotes get their hands on you."

"Please."

"No, and that's final. So drop it."

Ash stifled a sob.

The marshal wasn't finished. "Thank you for showing me what a life can be worth."

Ash thought of the wife he lost and the children he never had and the home he never had, and only now, on the threshold of never, did he realize what he had missed. All those bawdy houses, those henhouses with their perfumed chickens, were a poor substitute for something a man could hold in his heart when his end came. "The emptiness of it all."

"What was that?" Olander had moved over by the edge of the clearing and was peering through the trees.

"I wish," Ash said, but he did not say what he wished. He passed out, only to be shaken awake he knew not how long after.

"We have to go. I can't spare any more time or they'll catch us."

Once again Ash was boosted up. Once again he clung to Olander in order not to fall. The pressure, though, eased. He felt stronger. Not a lot, but enough that when they stopped on a bench that overlooked a winding valley, he made bold to say, "We should make our stand here."

Olander shook his head. "It'll be dark in a few hours. We keep going and we shake them and we're safe."

"I don't want safe. Give me a gun and ammunition and I'll hold them while you get away."

"No."

"They won't be expecting it."

"The answer is still no."

Ash gripped Olander's arm. "Listen to me. I feel all right at the moment. But I don't know how long it will last. I have to do it now, while I'm able."

The marshal looked at him.

"Think of all the people Sharkey has bucked out in gore. Do you want more to lose their lives because you wouldn't let me stop him?" Ash gripped harder. "I can do it. I give you my word that if I only get one of them, it'll be him."

"Hell," Olander said.

Ash had it worked out in his head. He pointed at the thickly wooded slope above the bench. "They'll come down out of the trees like we did. They'll be moving fast because they'll want to overtake us before nightfall. Since we've been running all day they won't be expecting me to make a stand. I'll have them right where I want them."

"We. We're in this together."

"Get away while you can, Lucas. You have a life. Mine is about over. I'm the one with nothing to lose."

"You keep forgetting this," Olander said, and tapped his badge again.

Ash argued, but it did no good. He moved to an outcropping of boulders that bordered the west end of the bench while Olander rode partway down the slope below and circled around. That way it would appear they had kept going.

Olander concealed his horse, then joined Ash.

"I only have the Winchester and my Colt. Which do you want?"

Ash was about the same with either but he had practiced more with his own revolver so he said, "The six-gun if you don't mind."

Olander held it out. "I'm better with a rifle anyway." He unbuckled his gun belt. "You'll need this too."

After that they waited, the quiet occasionally broken by the chatter of a squirrel or the squawk of a jay. The sun dipped on its downward arc until it hung above the boulders. Ash grinned. It was exactly as he'd hoped; Sharkey and his men would be staring into it.

Then, with a crash and crackle of vegetation, the outlaws burst onto the bench and drew rein.

Chapter 33

They were all there: Ben Sharkey, Horton, Kline, Tyree Buck and Nickels.

None had their rifles shucked or revolvers in their hands. They weren't expecting trouble.

Sharkey rose in the stirrups and stared down the mountain. "I don't see them yet. Damn."

"We'll get them," Horton said. "With them riding double and us pushing so hard it's only a matter of time."

Ash smiled grimly as he extended the Colt. To his dismay, his arm shook a little, enough to throw off his aim. He gripped the Colt in both hands and lined up Ben Sharkey for the kill.

Tyree pressed a hand to the bandage on his arm. "I don't see why we're going to all this bother. So what if they get away? You can kill Thrall another time."

"My feud with him has gone on long enough," Sharkey declared. "One way or the other this ends before the day is done."

Ash thumbed back the hammer. He breathed deep

held himself rock steady and was ready. He didn't shoot, though; he savored the moment. He had wanted this for so long he owed himself that much.

"What are you waiting for?" Marshal Olander whispered.

Ash went to squeeze the trigger.

"Look out!" the man called Nickels shouted. "There in the boulders! It's an ambush!"

Ash fired. Just as he did, Tyree, lashing his mount to get out of there, came between Ash and Sharkey. The slug intended for Sharkey caught Tyree in the chest.

A split instant later Olander cut loose with the Winchester.

Bedlam ensued. Some of the outlaws broke for cover. Others returned fire. Nickels was trying to control his plunging mount.

Ash fired as fast as he could work the hammer and the trigger. Olander was doing the same. Tyree took lead. A horse crashed down, whinnying.

The Colt went empty and Ash crouched to reload. He pried a cartridge from the gun belt, his fingers not responding as they should. He was slow, much too slow.

Olander was still firing.

Lead screamed off the boulders and a sliver of stone sliced Ash's cheek. Ignoring the pain, he inserted another cartridge. Four more to go.

Hooves drummed. Buck was charging the boulders, shooting as he came, and he was a good shot too. Ash had to duck when he dared a quick look; a slug nearly took the top of his head off. He slid another cartridge into the cylinder, saying to himself, "Hurry, damn you!" A glance showed Olander swiftly reloading.

The hoofbeats were thunderous. Buck had reached them. His revolver banged and Olander said, "Oh!" and staggered back.

Ash reared up. He only had five cartridges in the cylinder. It had to do. He fired at Buck's face and Buck's nose dissolved. Shifting, Ash saw that Tyree was down and wasn't moving. Kline's horse was down too and Kline was firing from behind it. Of Sharkey, Horton and Nickels there was no sign.

Hunkering, Ash scanned the forest. "How are you holding up?" he asked without looking over his shoulder, and didn't get an answer. "Lucas?"

Olander was propped against a boulder, the Winchester across his legs, his mouth opening and closing. No words came out but blood did, an awful lot of blood.

"No." Ash scrambled over. A bullet hole high in the chest explained the blood. "Damn it. Why didn't you listen?"

"Sorry," Olander said, more a wheeze than a word.

"For what?" Ash was the one who should apologize. Olander was dying because he came to Durango.

"Leaving you to fight them alone." Olander suffered a coughing spasm. "Take the rifle. Get as many as you can." His eyes widened, "You never figure. . . ." That was as far as he got; his next breath was his last.

Ash slid the Colt into the holster. Grabbing the Winchester, he flattened and crawled to a different boulder. The outlaws had stopped shooting. The forest had gone quiet. Kline's hat, or the top of it, was visible above the dead horse. Ash was tempted to shoot but he would have to expose part of himself to do it and be a fine target for the outlaws in the trees.

"Can you hear me, Thrall?"

Ash had no reason not to answer. "I hear you."

"You and that tin star have shot my boys to pieces," Sharkey shouted. "I don't take that kindly."

What a stupid thing to say, Ash thought.

"How about your friend the marshal? Is he still with us?" When Ash didn't reply Sharkey gave voice to that cackle of his. "I reckon he isn't. Serves him right for coming after me. He didn't have cause like you do."

Ash was reminded of Gold Gulch. He remembered how Sharkey had kept him talking while two others circled around to come on him from behind. It was said that only a greenhorn tried the same trick twice. But Sharkey might reckon it had worked once, so why not? Shifting so his back was to the boulder, Ash scoured the vegetation. He wouldn't have much warning.

"It's just you and us now," Sharkey gabbed on. "Five against one. Not the best of odds."

Ash didn't take his eyes off the woods. The odds be damned. He had something else in his favor. He wanted Sharkey dead more than Sharkey wanted him dead.

"Make it easy on yourself. Drop your artillery, throw your hands in the air and come out in the open. I give you my word we won't shoot."

"Your word isn't worth a cup of dog piss."

"Why do you think I always find men to ride with me? They know I will back their play when they need backing."

Ash let him jabber. He was as tense as tight wire, waiting for Horton or Nickels or both to show themselves.

"The devil of it is that now they'll blame that marshal on me," Sharkey blathered on. "I didn't pull the trigger. It was Buck. But that's always been how it works. I've been blamed for all sorts of things I never did. One time in Nebraska a man riding with me shot a gambler and the lead went all the way through him and through a wall and hit some woman walking down the street. I had nothing to do with it. That didn't stop the newspapers from saying it was somehow all my fault."

Ash squinted against the sun and focused on a particular shadow. Was it his imagination or had that shadow not been there a minute ago? He centered the Winchester on it.

"I know what you're thinking. That I gripe too damn much. But if you saw what I have to go through you would gripe too."

Ash fired. He'd half anticipated he was wrong and the shadow would turn out to be nothing, but the shadow leaped up with an oath and hurtled toward him, working the lever of a Winchester. It was Horton. Leaden death buzzed past Ash's ear. Another slug tried to part his hair. Ash dropped onto his side and Horton kept coming, thinking he had been shot. He shot Horton in the chest.

Quiet fell.

"How about it, Thrall? I'm sure I saw you take a bullet."

Ash lay on his side. He drew the Colt. He would have one chance. He must make it good. It worried him there was still no sign of Nickels. Kline was still out by the dead horse, so far as he knew.

"If you are finally dead I'll dance on your grave," Sharkey gleefully boasted, "and when I'm done dancing I will use your grave for an outhouse." Ash was sure Sharkey couldn't see him because of the boulders. Sharkey would have to come close to confirm the kill, which was exactly what he wanted.

He stared in the direction Sharkey would come from, every nerve tingling. "Please," he said softly.

There was no response.

Ash prayed he wouldn't have another attack. He prayed he wouldn't pass out. He prayed Sharkey would fall for his trick. When he realized what he was doing he went on praying anyway.

A shadow moved across a nearby boulder.

Ash locked his eyes wide as they would be were he dead. The shadow grew bigger. Ben Sharkey's face and shoulders appeared above the boulder. Sharkey saw Ash and started to raise a revolver; then he stopped, his mouth curling in a vicious smile of triumph.

"At last."

Ash prayed Sharkey would come around the boulder to check that he was in fact dead.

Sharkey did, smiling and chuckling and saying, "You were harder to rub out than anyone I've ever known." He bent down. "It's too bad I didn't get to carve on you some, but dead is dead."

Ash moved in a blur. He jammed the Colt's muzzle against Sharkey's forehead and in the instant that Sharkey was frozen in astonishment he said, "Yes, it is." Then he squeezed the trigger.

Blood and bone and hair splattered Ash and the body thudded next to him. He stared at it but didn't feel the joy he expected. All he felt was a strange sort of emptiness inside.

Ash rose and warily entered the woods. He circled around and discovered Nickels, dead. Olander's doing, since Ash hadn't fired at Nickels. The shot had taken Nickels in the ribs and exploded out the other side and somehow Nickels lived long enough to make it to cover.

Kline was still breathing, if barely. He was on his back, propped against his horse, a rifle on one side of him and his revolver on the other. He had been shot in the lungs. He tried to grip his six-gun when Ash walked up, but he was too weak.

"Damn."

"Life," Ash said.

"The·rest?"

"Dead."

Kline wheezed and growled, "You can go to hell."

"You first," Ash replied, and shot him in the head.

It took all he had in him, but Ash made it to Durango with Olander's body. The sensation he created, the buzz of talk when he passed in the street, another newspaper story, meant nothing. All that mattered was what a local doctor told him; he was close, but it could still be weeks yet.

The morphine didn't help anymore. All it did was waste him away but much too slow.

So it was that one evening Ash stood in front of the mirror in his hotel room. He didn't look human. His face was a haggard skull. His fingers were reeds. Still, he had a trace of vanity left, and he'd bought a new suit and new hat and boots. He had paid his bill in full and made arrangements with a lawyer for disposing of his belongings and his horse. He only had one thing left to do.

Ash stepped to the bed and picked up his gun belt. He strapped it on and hitched at it so it was comfortable on his hip. He took the Remington revolver and unloaded it and placed the cartridges in his pocket.

Then he shoved the Remington into the holster and went out.

The sun hung on the brink of night. The air was filled with scents and sounds and Ash did not miss one. He was surprised at how keenly alive he felt.

The saloon was called Soledad's. A pretty senorita in a billowy blouse and a long skirt served drinks. At a corner table sat a handsome man in a sombrero, playing a guitar. At the bar was another man who always came to Soledad's in the evenings. This man wore a black slicker and a black shirt and pants. His hat was black, his boots were black, his gun belt was black. His slicker had been swept back and on each hip was a black-handled Colt. His eyebrows quirked when Ash stopped a few yards away.

"You're Skelman."

The man nodded. He had a glass in his hand. "What's wrong with you? You look like hell."

The question threw Ash off his mental balance. He'd worked it all out, imagined how it would be, and this wasn't beginning right. "I've heard tell you are the quickest there is with those Colts of yours."

"People like to talk."

Ash moved his jacket aside so his hand was next to the Remington. "Whenever you are ready."

Skelman showed no alarm or fear. He sipped his whiskey and looked Ash up and down. "You're not a Pinkerton. You're not the law. Bounty man?" He shook his head. "Who are you and what is this about?"

The bartender said something in Spanish. Skelman listened and frowned.

"He says you're the gringo who goes around killing badmen. He says he has seen you around town and heard the stories."

"Whenever you are ready," Ash said again. He was afraid he would lose his nerve.

"Go away."

The saloon had fallen quiet and everyone was staring.

"I'll count to three," Ash said. "Then I will draw and shoot you." He took a deep breath. "One."

Skelman set down the glass. His hands dropped to his sides and he let out a long sigh. "I have no quarrel with you."

Ash glimpsed his reflection in the mirror on the bar and sadness gushed through him in a flood. His legs grew weak and he swayed. With a toss of his head he shook it off. "No," he said.

"Are you talking to me?" Skelman asked.

Setting himself, Ash stared at Skelman's hands and only at Skelman's hands. They were thin hands, almost as thin as his, but bronzed by the sun. "Two," he said loudly.

"Mister, whatever you are up to, it's not worth it."

Ash looked Skelman in the eyes. "I need it done. I'm sorry it's you but there is no one else."

"What are you talking about?"

"I will shoot you unless you shoot me. I mean it."

"Don't, damn you."

"Three," Ash said, and drew, and it was true what they said: it was true that Skelman was living lightning. Those bronzed hands flashed and there were twin peals of thunder.